A Woman Loved

Also by Andreï Makine

A Woman Loved

✦✦✦ *A Novel*

Andreï Makine

Translated from the French by Geoffrey Strachan

With an introduction by Francine Prose

GRAYWOLF PRESS

This publication is made possible, in part, by the voters of Minnesota through a Minnesota State Arts Board Operating Support grant, thanks to a legislative appropriation from the arts and cultural heritage fund, and through a grant from the Wells Fargo Foundation Minnesota. Significant support has also been provided by Target, the McKnight Foundation, Amazon.com, and other generous contributions from foundations, corporations, and individuals. To these organizations and individuals we offer our heartfelt thanks.

This work, published as part of a program providing publication assistance, received financial support from the French Ministry of Foreign Affairs, the Cultural Services of the French Embassy in the United States, and FACE (French American Cultural Exchange).

Published by Graywolf Press
250 Third Avenue North, Suite 600
Minneapolis, Minnesota 55401

www.graywolfpress.org

Published in the United States of America

ISBN 978-1-55597-711-5

2 4 6 8 9 7 5 3 1
First Graywolf Printing, 2015

Library of Congress Control Number: 2014960050

Cover design: Kyle G. Hunter

Cover images: Getty Images

French Voices logo designed by Serge Bloch

for GD

Introduction

Beginning Andreï Makine's novel *A Woman Loved*, we might briefly imagine that we have been plunged into the midst of a racy historical drama, a bodice ripper about the Empress Catherine of Russia, and her many lovers. A mirror keeps rising and lowering to show us her boudoir: a theatrical device, we may think, until we realize that it actually *is* a theatrical device.

The amours of the Russian empress are not only a matter of history but also the stuff of fantasy, specifically a fantasy that a screenwriter named Oleg Erdmann is trying to turn into a script for a film that is worth filming and that *can* be filmed—given the cultural climate in which he lives. This is the pre-glasnost Soviet Union, where the censors decide about art, and where the artists who run afoul of them can be in serious danger.

As Oleg wrestles with the complexities of the empress's long and, as they say, colorful career, he also tries to figure out what sort of person she was and how to structure what he wants to say—and what can be said, on film. Meanwhile the world around him could hardly be less like the world he is describing, unless we include the often nonsensical and capricious dictates of government, of political and personal power, the inequities and abuses that persist from era to era. The empress lived in lavish style, while Oleg is sharing a Leningrad communal apartment with an increasingly disaffected girlfriend and several other unfortunate citizens. To pay the rent for this paradise he has a job moving carcasses of meat in a slaughterhouse.

Andreï Makine was born and raised in Russia, but lives in France and writes in French. So it could be said that he brings a Franco-Russian perspective to a universal subject: a soul in torment. Predictably, nothing goes quite right for Oleg as he attempts to bring his vision to the screen. Less predictably, the society in which he lives changes dramatically, and things began to go very right—or are they merely going wrong in a different direction?

Deftly translated from the French by Geoffrey Strachan, Makine's novel moves so rapidly, and so amusingly, that only gradually do we realize how many complex and weighty themes Makine has chosen to address. Among the most interesting of these is the question of why artists are attracted to the subjects that engage them, why a writer (a screenwriter, in this case) is drawn to a particular character and that character's life—out of the endless number of subjects and lives that could have been chosen. As the novel progresses, we come to understand that Oleg's interest in the Empress Catherine goes deeper and is more complicated than we—and even he—have realized: that his fascination with the Russian ruler reflects his own most profound feelings about his origins, his heritage, his childhood.

Makine is also very good on the ways in which life informs art, and vice versa; how the victories and failures of Oleg's professional and romantic career change his views on the empress's reign and her love affairs. "Once more he is struck to notice how easily life and performance blend into one another, creating an intermediary world in which everyone is acting out the role of themselves, while at the same time cribbing from his fellow human beings."

In the latter sections of the novel, Communism has fallen; the dictator and the Politburo have been replaced by the oligarch and the gangster.

"Political parties proliferated, the economy was privatized, frontiers were opened." Figures from Oleg's former existence reappear with new jobs and in new guises. Once more Oleg is given a chance to bring Catherine's life to the screen—this time to the small screen, in the form of a sensational and exploitative television series—and the new set of difficulties and challenges he faces mirror the problems besetting the larger society. The dilemmas that Oleg has been confronting all along, among them the question of what constitutes historical truth, take on a wholly new and unexpected dimension. And his new understanding of the nature of love answers at least some of the mysteries that have confounded him all along.

What's remarkable is how much depth, how much complication—and how much history—Makine has packed into a novel about a man who wants only to make a film about a famous and notorious woman who claimed for herself the freedoms that so puzzle, intrigue—and elude—her smart, sympathetic, beleaguered cinematic biographer. And what stays with us is the intelligence and the depth of feeling with which Makine has portrayed the victories and compromises that sustain the unlikely and inspiring union of art, life, and love.

Francine Prose

Translator's Note

Andreï Makine was born and brought up in Russia, but *A Woman Loved*, like his other novels, was written in French. The book is set mainly in Russia (but also in Germany, Switzerland, and Italy). The author employs some Russian words in the French text, which I have retained in this English translation. These include *shapka* (a fur hat or cap, often with earflaps), *izba* (a traditional wooden house built of logs), *kolkhoznik* (a worker on a collective farm in the former Soviet Union), *Politburo* (the principal policy-making committee of the Soviet Communist Party), *gulag* (the system of Soviet corrective labor camps, of which the Kolyma complex was the most notorious), *apparatchik* (a member of the Soviet Communist Party administration, or *apparat*), and *dacha* (a country house or cottage, typically used as a second or vacation home).

The historical references in the text include the famous Nevsky Prospekt, one of the main streets in St. Petersburg (formerly Leningrad), which lies on the river Neva; Peterhof, the palace and park, with commanding views of the Baltic, built by Peter the Great in 1723 on the outskirts of St. Petersburg; and "Potemkin villages," sham villages reputedly built for Catherine the Great's tour of the Crimea in 1787 on the orders of her chief minister, Prince Grigory Potemkin.

I am indebted to many people, and to the author in particular, for advice, assistance, and encouragement during the preparation of this translation. To all of them my thanks are due, notably to Jennifer Anderson, Thompson Bradley, Edward Braun, Mary Byers, June Elks, Scott Grant, Martyn Haxworth, Wayne Holloway, Barbara Hughes, Russell Ingham, Ann Mansbridge, Damian Nussbaum, Geoffrey Pogson, Pierre Sciama, Simon Strachan, Susan Strachan, and John Weeks, and my editor at Graywolf Press, Katie Dublinski.

GS

A Woman Loved

I

The great mirror falls like a sash window. The woman who has just pressed the lever smiles: always a tense moment. What if the frame hit the floor with a crash and the glass shattered? But there is padding at the point of contact, and now the world is cut in two. On this side a white-and-gold salon. On the other, hidden by the mirror, a vaulted recess, a candle, a naked man breathing heavily . . .

A chamberlain sidles into the salon. "Majesty, the chancellor is here." The woman is already seated at a desk, pen in hand. Beneath her long dress, her body is sated with love. "Ask him to come in!"

She gets up to greet an elderly man with watery eyes, whose frame is too massive for those slender calves in their white stockings.

"Prince, I hope you've come to report that order has been restored in the governance of Kazan . . ."

The audience ended she rushes over to the lever. The mirror rises to reveal the alcove . . . The man whose embrace she had interrupted had a powerful, scarred body. The new secret guest is svelte; his mouth forms a sweetly petulant line . . . He is uttering a cry of pleasure at the moment when the chamberlain coughs outside the door before announcing another visitor. The woman breaks free, adjusts her dress, arranges her hair. The mirror falls, hiding the curve of the recess . . .

"His Excellency, the English ambassador, Sir Robert Gunning."

She crosses to an armchair where a cat lies sleeping, drives it away with a swift caress.

"Come and sit by the fire, Your Excellency. You will not be used to our Russian hoarfrosts . . ."

The Englishman leaves. The mirror rises again. The lover now has tight curls, blond like an albino, with thick lips. At the court he is known as "the White Negro." The woman gives herself to him with expert deftness . . . The man is on the brink of orgasm when there is a discreet cough in the antechamber.

"Majesty, Field Marshal Suvorov."

"Dear Alexander Vassilievich! They tell me the sultan is in retreat from our victorious armies. So, when shall we lay siege to Constantinople?"

The alcove opens up. An almost timid lover. It feels to the woman as if she were possessing him, and at the same time teaching him how to possess her . . .

"His Excellency, the French ambassador, Monsieur de Breteuil!"

She remains seated with an indifferent air and, as she allows the man to approach her, fiddles with a pinch of snuff.

"So, Monsieur le Baron, it seems your court persists in thinking my hatred does you more honor than my friendship?"

The mirror rises: a very young lover weeps, stammering out griev-ances, then calms down, like a comforted child.

"Majesty, His Majesty, the King of Sweden!"

As she talks with the king the salt from her lover's tears is still on the woman's lips . . .

"Majesty, Monsieur Diderot!"

"Dear friend! You philosophers merely work on paper, which is long-suffering. While I, poor empress, work on human skin, which is a good deal more irritable and ticklish . . ."

Diderot gets carried away, gesticulates, makes prophetic pronounce-ments, departs.

The woman makes the mirror rise once more. Her lover is laugh-ing. "Did he beat you black and blue again, that lout of a Frenchman?"

She presses against him, smothers his laughter with a kiss. "No. I take refuge behind a little table now . . ."

"The Right Honorable, the Count of Cagliostro!"

"Great Tsarina! I have had this alloy smelted deep within the fire-vomiting bowels of Vesuvius. It possesses rejuvenating virtues . . ."

The mirror rises, descends, rises again . . . The president of the Academy, Princess Dashkova. Lever pressed. Giacomo Casanova, agent of the Inquisition. Lever pressed. Prince Paul, her unloved son. Lever pressed. Count Bobrinsky, her illegitimate son. Lever pressed. The marquis d'Ormesson. Lever pressed. The comte de Saint-Germain. Lever pressed.

Oleg Erdmann turns a pocket mirror over and over in his hand. The back is made of black leather: the dark alcove. The glass: the salon where the empress receives visitors.

The reflection cuts into segments the cramped room where he lives: a sofa, an old wardrobe, shelves groaning under the weight of books. On the worktable a typewriter's metallic grin. Three leaves of paper, with sheets of carbon paper between them—the text of his . . .

"Of my utter madness," he says to himself, anticipating the judgments that will be passed on his screenplay. The worst would be simple contempt. "So, young man, you've been browsing through a few pamplets about the life of Catherine the Second, have you?"

"Well, more than any of you ever have!" Oleg whispers defiantly, challenging the scorn of an imaginary jury. He has read and made notes on everything. He knows the empress's life better than . . . better than he knows his own! The notion astounds him. But it's true, he no longer knows what he was doing on, say, March 22, 1980. Nor on the day before, nor the day after. These dates, still so recent, have been completely erased. It's easier to reconstruct the empress's life at two centuries' distance.

So, what is she doing, already in the early scenes? Well, of course! Taking snuff. With her left hand, the other is reserved for people to kiss . . . And then there's that occasional table she puts between herself and Diderot. When he gets excited the philosopher starts thumping her on the knees. "I'm covered in bruises," she complains with a laugh . . . Breteuil? Catherine has little time for him, as for most of the French diplomats. In 1762 she asks him to finance the coup d'état that is being prepared. Versailles refuses. London foots the bill. Result: a quarrel with France, juicy contracts for England . . . One of the visitors to the alcove is "Scarface"—Aleksey Orlov, as reckless as his brother, Grigory, the current lover. One night, taking advantage of his resemblance to Grigory, Aleksey manages to slip into the young tsarina's bed. The darkness facilitates the fraud. At the height of their transports, Catherine comes across the scars on the man's face . . . And Cagliostro? He dupes the simple souls of St. Petersburg, converses with spirits, offers elixirs of youth . . . Catherine banishes him, she has no love of charlatans or Freemasons. Or maybe she is jealous of his wife, the ravishing Seraphina? The Italian departs in the style of a true magician: at midnight twelve carriages ride out through each of the city's twelve gates. Each of them contains one Cagliostro and one Seraphina. And in the travelers' register, at every one of the barriers, the sorcerer's signature . . . Who else? Count Bobrinsky, the son of Catherine and Grigory Orlov. The child is born just before the coup d'état. He must be hidden from the tsar. Wrapped in a beaver fur (*bobr* is the Russian for "beaver"), he is spirited away to safety . . . The comte de Saint-Germain, the adventurer, arrives in Russia in the spring of 1762. To take part in the plot? The marquis d'Ormesson is one of the rare Frenchmen to find favor in the empress's eyes, is he not the cousin of Louis-François d'Ormesson, who opposed the opening of the Estates General in France in 1789, predicting catastrophe? When Giacomo Casanova comes to Russia he buys himself a female serf, nicknames her "Zaire," and, wonder of wonders! he falls for her. While at the same time cheating on her with a handsome army officer, Lunin, much to Catherine's amusement. She prefers Giacomo's brother, Francesco, the painter whose brush immortalizes Potemkin's victories . . . And then there is her unloved son, Paul! A sickly child who changes the cards on

the place mats before dinner so he can be seated next to his mother . . .
A mother who signs peace treaties, receives Diderot, corresponds with
Voltaire, defeats the Turks (which delights the author of *Candide*). And
who, at intervals, walks over to the great mirror and presses a lever . . .

"That's going to make it like a Brazilian soap opera," one of his fellow
students teased him one day. "A TV series in three hundred and a half
episodes." Confused, Oleg faltered: "Why 'and a half'?" The other burst
out laughing. "Well, you'll need half an hour at least just to list all of
Katie's lovers!"

Mockery did nothing to alter his resolve. Oleg wanted to know
everything about Catherine: how she spent her time (she worked fifteen
hours a day), how she dressed—very simply—her restrained tastes in
food, her fads (the snuff she took, her intensely strong coffee). He knew
her political views, what she read, the personalities of the people she
corresponded with, her carnal cravings (the "uterine rage" derided by so
many biographers), her custom of rubbing her face with ice every morning, her passion for the theater, her preference for riding astride a horse
rather than sidesaddle . . .

Yes, everything about Catherine. Except that often this "everything" seemed strangely incomplete.

Perhaps the key to the enigma could be found in the naive observation that this ultracerebral woman from time to time let slip: "The real
problem in my life is that my heart cannot survive for a single moment
without love . . ."

"Were you asleep or what? I rang ten times! It was your boozy neighbor who let me in . . . Aha, I see our scriptwriter's been writing about his flighty Katie. May I read your masterpiece? Come on, wake up, Erdmann! Give me a kiss! Make me a coffee, you mummified zombie . . . !"

Oleg smiles through a fog of images: a white-and-gold salon, a mirror going up, a vaulted alcove . . . Lessya's lips are freezing cold. He comes back to the present: a bedroom in a communal apartment, fifteen occupants housed in seven rooms, a shared kitchen, a single bathroom. A daily hell, yet one where you can be happy (in his parents' time they used to say: "If you're in hell, enjoy the fire . . ."). He's happy to feel the snow on his girlfriend's coat as she hands it to him, the warmth of the body that briefly squeezes against him. Happy to see Lessya settling down amid the disorder and, by her presence, creating harmony within it. Happy to make his way along the endless corridor where the exhalations of lives crammed together hang in the air, and to find himself in the kitchen—bliss, he is alone! And to slide his coffeepot onto the stove that is laden with heavy saucepans full of family soups. A transom is open—the chill air sharpens the scent of roasted beans. He's giddy with happiness: waiting for him at the other end of the communal labyrinth is a woman he loves . . .

Still in the corridor he peers into his room: Lessya is reading, stretched out on the sofa. With a girlish pout she puffs away a lock of hair tickling her cheek . . . He has recently taken to noticing details he would never have remarked on but for his obsessive scrutiny of Catherine the Great's life. The woman historians call "the Russian Messalina" but who, for Oleg, is gradually turning back into a child of long ago—a little German princess watching the snow as it falls on the Baltic . . .

He longs to tell Lessya how picturing that forgotten child makes it possible to imagine another way of living. And loving . . .

"Erdmann, undo your bootlaces. You're going to need a rope!"

Lessya is being melodramatic: this comes with the territory in their world of young filmmakers. But he gasps as if he had been hit in the solar plexus.

"No, it's the truth. You'd better go hang yourself! Your screenplay's clinically insane. And it's not even funny! Look at me: am I laughing? No. I'm frankly confused. This mirror, this alcove, what's all that about? Can you picture the audience's faces? They're not going to be laughing either . . ."

Oleg hands Lessya a cup and tries to remain calm.

"Look, it's not a script that's meant to be played for laughs . . ."

"Excuse me? You're not going to tell me this grotesque vaudeville is meant to be taken seriously?"

"Yes, I am. This is just the way I see history . . ."

Still clowning, Lessya chokes on her coffee. Oleg feels too weak to fight back . . .

"How many pages have you read, Lessya? Eleven? You'll see. Later on, it all falls into place. Chronologically, biographically . . . Catherine's childhood in Germany, her arrival in Russia, where she's going to marry the future Peter the Third. She'll take lovers and when her husband comes to the throne, her lovers'll kill him. Then she'll reign, introduce reforms, defeat the sultan, seduce French philosophers . . . Don't worry. All the historical details will be accurate, down to the width of the crinolines . . . Now, wait a minute. You're not going, are you?"

His voice lurches into a plea and he realizes that to hold on to

Lessya he would even be prepared to write a platitudinous biopic: child-hood, youth, illustrious reign . . .

"Yes, I am. There's going to be a party at Zyamtsev's. He's just been given the green light to make his film. And as he's not your best buddy . . . Besides, you've got work to do. You've got a good story line! First of all young Catherine in her dreary little principality back in small-time Germany and then, hey!, we see her at the head of an empire! It'll be a great rags-to-riches movie. But there's just one thing. Promise me you'll scrap the first eleven pages . . ."

Lessya grabs the little pocket mirror lying beside the typewriter, and starts putting on lipstick.

He goes with her to the entrance hall. In the kitchen a woman is sitting on a stool, her gaze lost amid the swirl of snowflakes outside the dark window. "The boozer," whispers Lessya, with a wink at Oleg.

The door bangs shut, he goes back past the kitchen, greets the woman: "Hi there, Zoya. Thank you for opening the door to my friend just now . . ." The woman nods, lost in a dream. She has a fine face, aged by weariness and, doubtless, by drink . . . He has never seen anyone come to call on her. From time to time Zoya's ancient kettle appears on the stove, a utensil probably dating back to the time of the Second World War.

Once more in his room Oleg gathers up the scattered sheets, the pages Lessya advises him to scrap: the mirror going up, the alcove re-vealed, the mirror coming down . . . The shadowy figures come and go, every one of them, for Catherine, epitomizing the impossibility of being loved.

That night insomnia pays him a visit, a familiar caller. Lessya had referred to his screenplay as "a grotesque vaudeville." But is life truly anything else?

A year before he had submitted the idea for this film to his teacher—his master—Lev Bassov. The old man listened to him with a sympathetic expression, then began addressing him like a convalescent who needs gentle handling. "Look, it's a tough subject . . . For a lot of reasons: both practical, because it would cost a fortune (costumes, battle scenes . . .) and political, well, I don't need to spell those out. What's more, there's enough material here for several full-length films. There's the coup d'état in 1762, Catherine's untimely pregnancy, the murder of the tsar. And what about Potemkin? A character like that's going to act everyone else off the screen. And Pugachev and the peasant uprising? It's true Pushkin wrote a pretty brief short story about it, well a narrative writer can just say—'Pugachev ordered the attack and the city fell.' But you try filming it with four hundred extras! And the trickiest thing, by the way, is not the need to compress time. No, it's the human mystery. Her son Paul: who is he really? An idiot who loves all things German and whom his mother detests? Or a tragic individual destroyed by this hatred? No, if you do a complete A to Z of Catherine you'll get just another costume picture. Or maybe a cartoon film. You're not thinking of going into animation, are you?"

The idea had made them both laugh and Oleg promised not to follow in Disney's footsteps. He began reading, piling up the mountains of books that were taking over his living space. Catherine insinuated herself into every corner of his thoughts and, at night, into his dreams. The air was impregnated with the aroma of "the Catherine century," as the Russians call it, the fragrant and bitter scent of old leather bindings . . . His research became painful to him, his most private moments were invaded by hundreds of historical figures, tormented, extreme beings, characters with larger-than-life destinies. And all these had to be moved deftly from one scene to the next, in a film of an hour and forty minutes.

He lived through periods of despair, time and again he decided to abandon the whole thing. Then one day the thought struck him: it really did need to be filmed like an animated cartoon.

The great mirror rises, the alcove is empty, the young lover, Mamonov, has just told Catherine he loves another woman. The empress weeps, grows bitter, meditates on revenge . . . The mirror falls. Behind it now the tsarina, who is over sixty, is in the arms of a new favorite, aged twenty-two. The mirror rises. The war against Turkey. The mirror falls. July 1789. The faithless Mamonov is cruelly punished. Mirror. In Paris the wretched French rabble are taunting the king— Ormesson was right! Mirror. Catherine rereads Montesquieu's *Persian Letters.* Mirror. The favorite is called Zubov ("tooth" in Russian). "I'd like to get my teeth into him," grumbles Potemkin, who divides his time between fighting the Turks and the delights of his own harem, which includes five of his nieces. Mirror. Louis XVI's guards are decapitated, their heads, hoisted aloft on pikes, follow the king's carriage . . . Mirror. Catherine gets up at five o'clock as usual, rubs her face with a lump of ice, makes herself coffee. From Paris her ambassador informs her that the people have amused themselves by curling the hair of the heads mounted on their pikes . . .

History: a gory animated cartoon, in black and red. Catherine comes to loathe the French philosophers' delightful doctrines.

The insomnia continues. "Your script's crazy," that's what Lessya said . . . Oleg gets up and, without switching on the light, makes his way between the piles of books, climbs onto a chair, leans on the wardrobe. There is a greenish glow from the lamppost out in the street, just enough to locate that glass cylinder. It looks like a lamp held in a bronze ring. But in fact it is an old magic lantern. He grips it carefully, sets it on the table. The mechanism is broken, once upon a time, activated by a spring, figures cut out of black cardboard would slowly rotate: ladies in crinolines, gentlemen in wigs . . . Oleg makes the cylinder turn by hand, the glow from the lamppost projects a procession of phantoms across the door of his room.

He tries to hold back his tears, bites his lip, quickly gathers up the silhouettes, puts the lantern away before going back to bed. This broken relic belonged to his mother . . .

The room where Dr. Rogerson carries out his duties. It is not at all like a doctor's office. Ponderous decor, classic eighteenth-century French furniture, crimson hangings. The light from a candelabrum picks out the silent presence of a naked young man. He submits to being palpated, tensing while the doctor's hand explores his genitalia. The patient's languid acquiescence gives the scene the appearance of a surreptitious sexual transaction . . . But soon the Englishman utters a satisfied grunt and invites the patient to get dressed. The latter does so—blue uniform, thigh boots, cocked hat: a handsome officer in the horse guards. He leaves the room with spurs jangling.

He proceeds through a dark gallery, where statues loom as if in the storeroom of a museum: classical profiles—muscular marble . . . He passes through a winter garden, inhales its muggy atmosphere, and once through a low door in oriental style, he finds himself in a steam room— the pavilion of the Moorish baths. A woman helps him to undress. She is clad only in a shift, which she removes once they have gone into the bathhouse. A candle flame reveals a robust little body with firm breasts. Her nakedness makes her tied-back hairstyle highly provocative. Kissing the guest, she murmurs fond words. Encouraged by her free manner, he clasps her forcibly, and tries to drag her over to a covered bench. Nimble as a lizard, she slips away, skips round the room and, from the bench, beckons to him to come to her. He rushes over clumsily, excited by her giving him the slip. She escapes again, laughing and arousing the man. He catches her again, grasping her fugitive body and toppling her over onto her back, then comes to his senses. He is not there to satisfy his carnal appetite but simply to give proof of its vigor. He feels a hand squeezing his penis, the woman is checking that the passage of time has not weakened the tension in this young suitor's muscle . . .

The wick of a candle is drowning in wax. The snap of tinder can be heard and the fire leaps up. But this is an utterly different place: a bedchamber, with a bed beneath a brocade canopy. The man who struck the light tries to reassure his young wife who has been woken by a noise . . . They have no time to return to their bed—several soldiers stampede into the room and bind the man. His wife is raped in front of his eyes . . .

Soldiers making their escape along a gallery paved with marble. An adolescent girl lost in a vast palace. Terrified by the clatter of their footfalls. Will they see her and kill her to be rid of the witness to their crime? Now she hides in a room that looks like a naturalist's laboratory. Glass-fronted shelves, jars with strange reptiles preserved in fluid . . . And suddenly these two jars! Two human heads with wide-open, cloudy eyes. A man and a woman.

Outside the door the boots thunder by.

"I must have the courage to look these severed heads in the eye. Only then will I be able to tame this insane country!"

She stares at the two faces entombed in liquid. She is afraid of nothing now. When she emerges from this cabinet of horrors, soldiers see her and stand to attention. Their officer salutes her. There is an element of theater about this encounter—the only way of not seeing the world through the glazed eyes of the severed heads . . . Now for more theater. A confession. The adolescent girl, who has grown into a beautiful, voluptuous woman, makes an admission. An army officer accuses her of having known fifteen lovers. "No, only five," she assures him. The man absolves her and goes off to dine with his mistresses. For dessert there is an unusual dish—a vessel crammed with diamonds. The women help themselves freely . . . The woman who made that confession is not present at the meal. Meanwhile her footman comes and sets down a great gilded armchair before her: the throne of a vanished country. Thinking what she will do with this relic, she laughs until tears come to her eyes.

Oleg is fast asleep, but checking off names and dates . . . The effort of memory wakes him up. For those visions were not fantasy! The episode at the Moorish baths? True. Before qualifying for admission to Catherine's alcove, her favorites undergo this double examination: Dr. Rogerson attests to their physical health, Countess Bruce makes sure of their sexual vigor. The rape of the young bride? The tsarina's favorite, Mamonov, abandons her for a lady-in-waiting. Vengeance strikes the lovers during their honeymoon . . . The heads in alcohol? Back in her youth Catherine had come upon them in Peter the Great's cabinet of curiosities: Marie Hamilton, a mistress unfaithful to the tsar, and Wilhelm Mons, the tsarina's lover . . . A helping of diamonds for dessert at Potemkin's table? The date of that dinner is on record. Catherine's admission of her love affairs? The text of her confession exists . . . A ceremonial chair brought to her as a trophy? The throne comes from Poland after that country has ceased to exist. The tsarina will later turn it into a commode!

He closes his eyes, takes refuge in sleep. One more detail comes to mind: the monarch whose throne is to be pierced is Poniatowski, one of Catherine's first lovers. A myopic dandy who had begged her not to make him the king of Poland.

The hubbub of an argument. The long galleries of the palace merge into the corridor of a communal apartment. Oleg's neighbors are bickering as they wait in line for the bathroom—the habitual verbal warm-up that will give them the courage to go down to a street still in darkness, and hurl themselves into the assault on a bus.

He draws the blanket around himself, conscious of being one of the lucky ones who do not have to get up at six o'clock in the morning.

And here's another piece of luck: in his screenplay there'll be no need for him to describe the characters' emotions. On the film set the actors will find the right tones of voice, the necessary gestures. Whereas, if he were a novelist . . . Well, would he write that Countess Bruce slipped away from the candidate's embraces as nimbly as a lizard? No one ever gave a female lizard the job of testing the prowess of one of her species.

The idea makes him smile. At last he can sleep a dreamless sleep.

At the moment of waking the ghosts are gone. Sunlight, hoarfrost crystals on the windowpanes, the rapid jolting of a streetcar down below. On the wall above his bed hang long charts with texts in red felt-tip pen.

The first is based on the schedule Catherine II drew up in 1781, listing the achievements of the first twenty years of her reign:

Provincial governments organized according to the new form	29
Towns built . . .	144
Treaties concluded . . .	30
Victories won . . .	78
Memorable decrees . . .	88
Decrees for the benefit of the people . . .	123
Total	*492*

Despite the extravagant boastfulness of this detailed account, historians uphold it: at her death Catherine leaves behind a modernized country, a powerful army, a good public education system. The Russian Academy is presided over by a woman, the press is encouraged, censorship has been whittled down to "the observations of an illiterate woman"—the way Catherine describes the criticisms she addresses to authors from time to time . . .

The second chart summarizes the chronology of her reign:

1729: Birth in Stettin (Pomerania) of the Princess Sophia Augusta Fredericka of Anhalt-Zerbst.

1744: The Empress Elizabeth summons her to Russia where, converted to orthodox Christianity and rebaptized, the princess is to marry the future Peter III.

1745–53: Her husband shows little inclination to consummate the marriage. Catherine takes this opportunity to educate herself and study the machinery of power . . . And to embark on her first love affairs. Peter is operated on for his genital malformation.

1754: Birth of a son, the future Paul I.

1761: Death of the Empress Elizabeth. Brief reign of Peter III.

1762: Coup d'état. Peter III is overthrown, then killed, by men loyal to Catherine. She ascends the throne.

1763: The start of her reforms. Pilgrimages to the key centers of orthodox spirituality. Her aim: to innovate, like Peter the Great, while demonstrating her faithfulness to Russian traditions.

1764: A journey to the Baltic provinces.

1766: The Great Commission sets out the legislative bases for the State; even the peasants have their representatives.

1767: Publication of the *Great Instruction*, Catherine's political credo.

1768–74: First Russo-Turkish war.

1772: First partition of Poland.

1773–75: Uprising led by Pugachev, who passes himself off as Peter III, miraculously preserved.

1775: Land reform in Russia.

1779: Freedom for entrepreneurs in Russia.

1784: The Crimea annexed to the Russian Empire.

1787–91: Second Russo-Turkish war.

1793: Second partition of Poland.

1795: Poland no longer an independent state (third partition).

1796: Death of Catherine II (November 6).

For Oleg this framework evokes intimate memories. Lessya's body molded closely to his own, in shapely abandon, on spring mornings during the previous year. The dawning sun would light up this chart and, as they embraced, they would amuse themselves by giving each other history exams. "What was the date of Catherine's coronation?" Lessya would ask with a frown. And Oleg, acting the dunce, would say: "Search me. Maybe it was around 1812 . . ." She would pull his ears and their fight would turn into an embrace . . .

The screenplay he envisaged in those days was to have a gaily light-hearted, erotically piquant flavor to it. A setting in the style of Fragonard, the last years of a century that cultivated the art of taking nothing seriously, apart from trifles and trivia. A frivolous, modish world, somewhat rococo, with a touch of "The Rape of the Lock," a dash of *"après nous, le déluge!"* A deliciously theatrical existence.

"Now here's a chance to redeem yourself. How many plays did Catherine write?"

(The answer is half a dozen at least, her favorites acted in them, Diderot applauded them . . .)

At first Oleg had pictured his film as a sequence of romantic adventures, alternating with melodramatic conspiracies.

The third chart sets out this politico-erotic trajectory. The list of her lovers and the duration of their remaining "in favor":

Saltykov (1752–54)
Poniatowski (1756–58)
The Orlov brothers, Grigory and Aleksey (1761–72)
Vassilchikov (1772–74)
Potemkin (1774–76)
Zavadovsky (1776–77)
Zorich (1777–78)
Korsakov (1777–79)
Lanskoy (1780–84)
Yermolov (1785–86)

Mamonov (1786–89)
The Zubov brothers, Platon and Valerian (1789–96)

At the foot of the list there is a note of some less durable liaisons: Vyssotsky, Bezborodko, Khvostov, Kazarinov . . .

Lessya is amazed: "You say she admitted to five lovers? And back in 1774 Potemkin accused her of having had fifteen. He must have been clairvoyant. All those men she would end up loving!"

This remark introduced the first jarring note into the airy mood of his screenplay. Oleg gave an ironic whistle to dispel any feeling of seriousness. "No, no! She didn't love them! She just needed a man in her bed, that's all. And, by the way, her favorites were under no illusions. 'I was just a kept woman.' That's what Vassilchikov, lover number four, said. The tsarina's pleasures cost the State a fortune! Just look at the figures . . ."

The fourth chart shows the sums paid in rewards. Lessya's eyes open wide: "Vassilchikov got six hundred thousand rubles and Mamonov, the one who left Catherine for a young mistress? Nine hundred thousand! The Orlov brothers seventeen million . . . Didn't you put one zero too many? Potemkin, fifty million!"

"In those days," explained Oleg, "you could live for a month on a few rubles . . . Catherine was buying herself pleasure. She didn't worry too much about questions of morality. The truth is they were less hidebound than we are and not afraid to live life to the full. Hold on, I'll read you the epitaph she wrote:

"*'Here lies Catherine II, born at Stettin on 21 April 1729. She came to Russia in 1744 to marry Peter III. At the age of fourteen she made a threefold vow—to please her husband, the Empress Elizabeth, and the people. She neglected nothing to achieve this. Eighteen years of solitude left her little choice but to read widely. When she came to the throne, she sought the good of her subjects and strove to give them happiness, freedom, and wealth. She forgave easily and hated nobody. She was compassionate, sociable, good-humored, with a republican soul and a kind heart—and not lacking in friends. Work never tired her, she loved company and the arts.'*"

"A lot of women could identify with that portrait," Lessya had remarked softly. "I guess even I could . . ."

Now he walks through the apartment, remembering those carefree "history exams" and their routine for making "an assault on the front line," as they called it: these were times when Lessya needed to go to the bathroom. She was nervous of running into a boorish neighbor, or of mistaking the door and disturbing someone who was asleep. He would go with her to spare her from embarrassing encounters. On other occasions they went on a mission to "disable an atomic reactor," surreptitiously removing a saucepan from the stove where a stew was bubbling away and slipping their coffeepot in its place. If the saucepan's owner appeared in the corridor they had to put it back hastily on the heat and pretend to be innocently waiting until they could make themselves coffee . . .

Oleg does the same thing now, thrusting aside a mighty kettle. And for the thousandth time he seeks to fathom how the airy frivolity of his original concept could have given birth to this palace swarming with murdered tsars, bloodthirsty court favorites, madmen, traitors, sadistic women . . . True, he has read a great deal since those days and a whole network of subtext has tunneled its way underneath the chronology shown by those charts. "Peter III is overthrown, then killed, by men loyal to Catherine . . . ," the red felt-tip pen noted. A tsar loathed by the people, a puppet more German than Russian, gets bumped off by officers smitten with Catherine. A scene halfway between farce and pathos: one sword thrust and the puppet collapses like a bundle of rags . . .

But it did not happen like that. Peter has enough time to realize he is going to be killed. Invited to a dinner among the men who will murder him, the tsar still clings to a little hope. Then one of the officers insults him, slaps his face. Peter does not respond, aware they are looking for a pretext . . . He is defenseless, confronted by these hefty men, all fired up with wine. A moment of confusion, briefly the killers hesitate . . . And then they begin baying for his blood: the tsar is knocked down, they hit him, they squeeze his throat. He still has enough strength to crawl toward the door on all fours. This only sharpens the brutes' appetites. They finish him off, beating his face to a pulp . . . Before the funeral, this tattered mask is restored by a painter. The very artist who had painted a portrait of the young couple: Catherine and Peter, tenderly holding hands . . .

"Oh, I'm sorry. I'm afraid I took your place!" Oleg removes his coffeepot and puts the kettle back on the heat. Zoya protests gently: "No, no. I'm not in a hurry . . ." She sits down facing the window, goes into a dream, seems to be hoping for someone to appear outside. But outside there is just a tiny yard surrounded by high walls, a bare tree, white with hoarfrost . . .

A mad notion occurs to him: why not talk to Zoya about Catherine II! Yes, come right out and say to her: "This must have happened to you at some time: a person interests you, you dig deep into their past . . . And all of a sudden you realize that the truth about them doesn't lie inside their life . . . but far away from it . . ."

He walks back to his room mentally repeating these words. Confess his woes to poor Zoya? He must be losing his marbles. Lessya was right, he ought to concoct a straightforward historical movie: an insipid Peter III, whose wife is a nymphomaniac regicide, who makes humanistic speeches to please Voltaire. And then, hey presto, a peasants' revolt, a forest of gallows, and instead of an enlightened young tsarina—a fat German woman on the Russian throne, choosing handsome athletes for her pleasure.

Oleg drinks his coffee with his eyes fixed on the charts. Poniatowski, Orlov, Potemkin . . . The mirror rises and falls. The alcove attracts young bodies, consumes them, tosses them aside.

He knows there is something missing from these texts in red felt-tip pen. A reference to be added there, as a footnote, in among those alcoves, wars, murders, and fortunes . . . a word or two about the thousands of Germans Catherine II brought into Russia's endless spaces. Not princes and magnates but ordinary people, artisans, soldiers, farmers. Hans Erdmann, one of Oleg's ancestors, was among them. A stonecutter who came from Magdeburg. And on his mother's side the settlers came from Kassel. One of his ancestors made musical boxes, telescopes, lorgnettes. And magic lanterns . . .

Instead of carrying the load on his shoulder, Oleg has adopted a different grip: he takes the full weight on his back and walks along, bent double, to avoid the dead flesh pressing against his cheek.

For six months at the Leningrad slaughterhouse he has felt as if he were carrying corpses rather than animal carcasses. Now it is all routine: the air thick with blood, the flaccid feel of the meat, the equanimity of the workers as they slaughter, eviscerate, cut up . . . Working there one night out of three earns him enough to live on and time for writing.

The job is exhausting and filthy, but at a certain level of tiredness his muscles perform automatically, leaving his mind clear to reflect calmly. By day he is forever repeating: "Lessya's changed," analyzing in detail everything that is no longer the same about their relationship. During his nights at the slaughterhouse, all this analysis makes him smile.

His first short film had been released a year earlier . . . The criticisms were disproportionately violent, given that it was a modest thirty-five-minute film. "A false and glamorized view of the Great Patriotic War," "an ideologically dubious standpoint" . . . Bassov, the teacher who had overseen his work, was nearly expelled from the Party. Oleg was bracing himself for the grim plight of a director banned from filming. Then events took a sudden turnaround: his film, he was told, had just been viewed in Moscow, at the Ministry of Defense, the minister himself liked it, and, what's more, other members of the Politburo were of the same opinion!

The film was called *Return in a Dream.* In 1941 a young architect goes off to the war and for five years sees nothing but devastated cities, flattened by bombing. In Russia, in Poland, in Germany. The sites whose architecture he had once studied now present a vision of broken pillars, shattered domes . . . On his return he finds his native town on the Volga completely wiped out. Beneath the rubble of his own house—there is a portfolio filled with drawings: airy arcades, galleries open to the sky . . .

What must have moved Oleg's "defenders" at the Ministry of Defense was the sight in that film of a young soldier lost amid the ruins . . . As they themselves had been forty years before . . .

The reaction of these elderly leaders, while it saved Oleg, also brought home to him the extent to which the government of the country belonged to another era.

Thus, against all expectation, he acquired this singular status: after a spell among artists on the blacklist, he found himself basking in the protection of the Kremlin! Bassov, his teacher, was exultant. "Your film woke up the drowsy old men in the Politburo! Some of your laurels belong on my bald head. But this is where it gets serious. For your next film, don't pick the wrong story . . ."

Bassov used the word *story* in the sense of "subject," "scenario." But Oleg already had in mind the story of a little German princess who one day became the empress of Russia.

He had met Lessya during those mad days of anguish and triumph. In his little world of young filmmakers, she occupied a special place: her father worked at the Soviet Embassy in Sweden, and she had made a name for herself working on a film magazine. Their love affair was no doubt colored by the unexpected success of Oleg's film, but also by the light of an early spring and, a few months later, the celebrations for the Moscow Olympic Games . . .

This image stuck in his memory: July 1980, dazed by sunlight and love, they lay there in his room, vaguely listening to snatches from a neighbor's television as it gave the results of the sporting events. A warm wind, the sounds and smells of a big city at night. Above the bed the chart setting out the story of Catherine II's life. "You're going to make a great film!" Lessya had whispered and he felt like an athlete being cheered on by a woman he loves.

"Go and get the last three, Erdmann. There's still room in the truck."

The foreman's voice rouses him from his daydream, propelling him toward the blocks where the carcasses are stacked up. Under pressure the flesh has the elasticity of a body recently alive.

The ease with which a living creature is destroyed never ceases to surprise him. At one moment a young animal stood there breathing in the fresh air, then its skull was smashed by a blow from a poleax and now here is this meat, which will feed the voracious appetite of a big city. Oleg stoops, picks up the carcass, carries it, sets it down. Pick up, carry, unload. Gradually the torpid state arrives where his thoughts settle down, in a simple, bare, stark world . . .

His short film has given him a choice between two enviable identities: either that of rebellious filmmaker or, following his unhoped-for success, artist protected by the regime. Some were of the opinion that, like a fool, he had failed to cash in on this stroke of luck. This was because he was a spineless provincial hick, said Zyamtsev, the ringleader of a little group of friends Lessya spent time with. And so a consensus was formed: Erdmann was a Siberian peasant, gullible enough to think he was going to get a second helping of luck. The Oleg Erdmann Lessya loved was one who was empowered by that double destiny of his. If he reneged on it, he would become a different person.

"Hey, Erdmann, another for number two!"

Absentmindedly he nods, grasps a carcass, carries it to exit number 2. There he flexes his knees like a weight lifter and with an abrupt straightening of his whole body, heaves the burden onto a pile of flesh.

This place is a long way from the hall where the living tissue becomes dead meat. Over the top of the perimeter wall nocturnal facades can be seen. People are asleep, or talking late into the night, or else making love. With no thought of the death that fills these trucks . . .

Oleg always tries to prolong this moment of relief at exit 2. Here he feels liberated from all identity: he is no longer the carrier of carcasses, nor the filmmaker inspired by a crazy project . . . And, above all, not that Russo-German mutant, a "German from the Volga region," according to the official records.

It is this ill-defined status that must have displeased Lessya. By dint of writing about Catherine, Oleg was increasingly identifying with ghosts two centuries old. With a childish prince, the future Peter III, who lined up his little soldiers on the floor of a salon in the palace. One night, these little figures, carved from starch, attracted a gluttonous rat. One of the corporals was devoured. Peter summoned a court-martial, built a little gallows, and the rat was judged and hanged.

In the early days Oleg could only laugh at this childish behavior. Later he came to believe he could detect a logic in it less absurd than it at first appeared. And that was when a quarrel came to mar his happy life with Lessya.

"Are you going to spend your life doing postmortems on rats?" she exclaimed. "So now it's a great philosophical debate: why did Peter the Third send a rat to the gallows? In your original synopsis everything was clear, remember? Catherine marries an idiot, for want of anything better, and gets rid of him at the first opportunity. OK, this fellow loved his little soldiers, brought his dogs into the marriage bed, got drunk with his servants and taught them to do the goose step, Prussian style. And what else? Oh yes! He couldn't have sex on account of his foreskin! So are you going to unveil a treatise on circumcision now? Is that it?"

Oleg remembers vainly attempting to justify himself: Peter III was far from being the idiot described by the historians. It was more that he was maladjusted, weak, a dreamer. And the world always punishes weak dreamers.

Lessya hooted with laughter. "So he was a little Hamlet, your softy? OK! You stick with your craziness! But do you know what? This stuff about rats and foreskins, I've had enough of it!"

And she walked out, leaving him distraught, amid his pages of draft text . . .

They were to meet again the following evening. It was the same group of young artists, a lot of laughter and drink, dancing, some of it sensual, some of it unbridled. And around him the mocking whispers: "the Siberian peasant" . . . An arm brushed against his face in the throng and knocked off his glasses. He crouched down, began feeling for them on the floor amid the prancing feet. With his hazy vision, he caught sight of Lessya from below. A man was thrusting her away, then pulling her toward him, to the crazy rhythm of the music, they were laughing . . . They would soon be sure to notice him, there on all fours, with his blurred vision, feverishly fumbling around on the floor. Suddenly he thought of Peter: the tsar has fallen, the killers' heavy boots are clattering around before they strike, as he crawls there, surrounded by yelling and stinking breath . . .

His glasses, minus one lens, had ended up under an armchair. He put them on and made his way to the door, braving the looks that followed him. He glimpsed Lessya's face with a mixture of myopic haziness and sharp clarity.

"Hey, Erdmann, you savage! No eating raw pig! You're not in the wilds of Siberia now . . ."

It takes Oleg a moment to snap back to reality. It is Ivan Zhurbin, the young actor, calling out to him. The one who had said: "You're going to make a TV series in three hundred and a half episodes!" Yes, the indomitable Zhurbin . . . What they have in common is their status as provincials. As well as the fact of being hard up. Ivan showed him how to repair his shoes with leather from an old suitcase and it was thanks to him that Oleg secured this job at the slaughterhouse.

The sky is still dark, it's seven o'clock in the morning and after a sleepless night the notion seems bizarre: here is his redheaded friend with his somewhat boyish grin about to take over the same job of carrying dead meat . . . The foreman's summons can already be heard. "Hey! Zhurbin, you goddamned shirker, come and load up! Otherwise I'll take two hours off you . . ."

Oleg moves away. An icy sidewalk, a streetcar stop, and, despite his drowsiness, this hallucinatory clarity: rocked by the swaying of the streetcar, he reviews Catherine's life with the intimacy of a memory of his own. Yes, those spectacles he dropped, his fumblings amid the dancers' feet—the confusion that reminded him of how Peter III crawls around as Catherine's officers prepare to kill him . . .

The passing of the streetcar causes some snow to fall from a branch. He has time to see a brief, iridescent flurry. And he conjures up what is seen by the little German princess, aged ten, as she holds the hand of a young prince, barely older than herself. The children are watching great snowflakes falling over the sea at Kiel, where they meet for the first time in 1739. Twenty-three years later this boy, now the Russian emperor, is beaten to death by the lovers of his wife, that same little girl who once held his hand beneath a slow swirl of snow.

The murder of Peter III is Catherine's reign in a nutshell. Violence, trickery, the power of sex, the desire to dominate, cynicism! And, above all, drama! Mounted on horseback, dressed up as guards officers, Catherine and her young friend, Princess Dashkova, go prancing along at the head of the troop who are to be seduced—pure cloak-and-dagger stuff!

Could this coup d'état have turned out differently? With Peter rallying his faithful Holstein regiments, reminding them he is Peter the Great's grandson and crushing the conspirators . . . No chance! He runs away, abdicates, begs the tsarina for mercy, and in the end gets himself murdered by her lovers.

In the first draft of his screenplay, Oleg had already noted this recurring theme of dominance and carnal appetite. In 1762 Peter III assassinated. In 1775 Pugachev, the fake Peter III, executed. In 1772 and 1793 Poland violated and in 1795 wiped out . . . Each time the same modus operandi: Catherine feeds the ardor of her men with a cocktail of sex and violence.

This outline had the advantage of being clear. On the other hand, his detailed research into the labyrinths of History was making Catherine's life seem impenetrable, ambiguous.

"You're trying to make too good a job of it," Lessya would sigh, and, in one sense, she was right. One day Oleg recollected the German saying his father used to quote: *"Zu gut—schlecht."* That was it, too good is bad. He continued to hope that from the murky confusion of the archives a shining light would burst forth—some thrilling truth that went beyond History itself!

In the meantime, the mystery grew deeper. Did Catherine order the murder? Or did her favorites deduce her secret wish? And who is to be believed? The historians who claim she was grief-stricken at the news of the murder or those who portray her as overjoyed? And how is one to judge the tone of the bulletin she issued? *"On the seventh day of our accession to the throne we were advised that the former Tsar, Peter III, suffered another of his hemorrhoidal attacks . . . Aware of our Christian duty, we issued orders for him to be given the necessary medical attention. But, to our great sorrow, we learned that God's will had put an end to his life . . ."* Did she need the posthumous mockery of the obscene parallel between a "hemorrhoidal attack" and the bloodlust of the men falling upon the half-naked Peter?

In the crushing of the peasants' revolt in 1774, there is this same mixture of physical violence and grotesque farce. The false tsar, Pugachev, is taken prisoner by his own staff officers: a body stripped naked, a bloodstained piece of goods, delivered to the tsarina to spare themselves from the gallows.

And Poniatowski? The lover who betrayed Catherine . . . She punishes him like an empress: the tsarina makes him king of Poland, then abolishes his kingdom. Symbolically she violates the proud Pole! They meet again only once in thirty years—in the Crimea. A brief interview, just to show him how happy she is to be at the head of a victorious army, in the arms of a young favorite. The Pole resumes his place in the battalion of the defeated: the cast-off lovers, the decapitated rebels, and the sultan of the Crimea, who is now an impotent vassal. Catherine plans new predatory expeditions! Constantinople, Persia, and, why not?, India.

At what moment do these political and carnal machinations grind to a halt? In July 1789? Catherine is accustomed to giving her favorites their notice. Handsome Mamonov breaks it off first. The tsarina is sixty, her rival is twenty, and even the great magician Potemkin can do nothing about it. The latter is to die in 1791 and in him Catherine will lose her alter ego, her damned soul, the incarnation of the Russia she loves and fears. "I am more than an emperor," he says. "I am Potemkin!" He was the one who chose fresh lovers for her. All except the last of them, Zubov, a pretentious gigolo whose insignificance will show how her reign is in decline. The delicate mechanism that allied sex and the throne has a few last feeble maneuvers to go through.

"It's all brilliantly clear!" Lessya would say. "A tsarina who holds a man's prick in her fist, instead of a scepter. That's the way the Polish cartoonists drew her, isn't it? But take care. Don't get bogged down in subtleties!"

As a film critic, she sensed the danger: too much detail ends up fragmenting the image of the main characters. Excellent advice. But Oleg, for his part, was experiencing the fever of a painter eager to add yet one more touch to a portrait that is already complete. And this was it: Peter III plays the violin. According to the historians, he was childish and coarse, yet he was a fine musician whose talent was sacrificed to the hullabaloo of military parades. Was he a violent drunkard, as Catherine told it in her *Memoirs*? Once deposed, Peter looks more like a lost teenager. On board a pathetic sloop among the ladies-in-waiting from his scattered court, he attempts to land at the fortress at Kronstadt. Turned away by the garrison, he takes to the sea again—in the panic the anchor chain is cut (a neat detail for the film!). And he withdraws from the game of politics "like a child who has been packed off to bed," as one general will observe. All around him the grown-ups are playing the game. They bribe the Imperial Guard, occupy the Winter Palace, install the tsarina on the throne. And one more detail: just before this violent coup takes place, Catherine gives birth to a son. The future Count Bobrinsky. The fact of her being in labor must be concealed from Peter. Knowing that the tsar adores watching conflagrations, one of Catherine's valets sets fire to his own izba, thus attracting Peter and his courtiers to watch the spectacle . . .

"Stop adding in all these walk-on parts," Lessya had advised him, already a little concerned. "The plot will get lost under them all!" But amid History's intoxicating mass of detail every fragment seemed important. A man gallops to warn the tsar about the coup d'état: a certain Bressan, a subject of Monaco, the only one to remain faithful to him . . .

"What on earth's the point of bringing him in?" Lessya asked in amazement. Oleg was quick to justify this gallant soul's inclusion. And also that of this martyr: Ivan VI, who, as a young child, had come to the throne in 1740, before being imprisoned by the Empress Elizabeth. Twenty-two years later Catherine inherits the throne from this captive. In 1764, while she is on her journey through the Baltic provinces, an officer attempts to set him free. As the first shot is fired, the jailers cut Ivan's throat. On the tsarina's orders . . .

Lessya was still smiling as she listened to him: "Your pal Zhurbin was right. You're going to end up writing a TV series . . ."

These warnings were becoming useless. Oleg was getting more and more lost in the twists and turns of a past whose secrets were now actually weaving the fabric of his own life. The game of power and sex? And when a favorite is dismissed, what fresh game is embarked on? Banished, Grigory Orlov plans his revenge: he is the one who stirs up the Pugachev revolt. At that time in Italy a certain Princess Tarakanova proclaims herself to be the daughter of the late Empress Elizabeth and therefore the true heir to the throne. Catherine fights on two fronts: with her armies against the rebels, through her spies against this pretender. Pugachev is executed in Moscow. Tarakanova is lured onto a Russian ship at Livorno. Aleksey Orlov, Grigory's brother, deceives the lovers, promises her the Russian throne. Taken prisoner, she dies in St. Petersburg . . .

In his enthusiasm, Oleg really did feel capable of writing a series in three hundred episodes.

For example, at the height of the coup d'état Catherine encounters a young officer: they are both on horseback, the tsarina has lost her sword knot and this stranger—it is Potemkin—offers her his own . . . And this is better still! Peter III loves ice cream, and it is by promising him this dessert that his murderers lure him into the trap! And while the coup d'état is being hatched in St. Petersburg—Jean-Jacques Rousseau's *Émile* is being burned in Paris. In 1775 Pugachev is due to be quartered, then beheaded. Catherine gives orders for the procedure to be reversed, out of charity, people think. In fact, she wants to show herself to be more humane than Louis XV of France: Robert-François Damiens, who had stabbed the French king, had been savagely dismembered . . . And there is also this concurrence of events: July 1789, at the very moment when the Bastille falls, the tsarina is in tears, for her lover Mamonov has jilted her.

"You'd better go shoot your film in India!" Lessya exclaimed. "I guess they'll put up with this *Mahabharata* epic of yours over there . . ." She no longer held back from making fun of him.

Oleg's screenplay now featured Voltaire, Diderot, Rousseau, d'Alembert (who corresponded with Catherine and her courtiers), Frederick the Great, Maria Theresa and Joseph II of Austria (military allies of the tsarina), Louis XV and Madame de Pompadour (Catherine loathed them), Louis XVI and Marie Antoinette (she found them adorable), the sultan and his harem (an agent of Catherine's managed to get inside it), the Casanova brothers, Cagliostro and the comte de Saint-Germain, Olivier Ormesson and Count Louis-Philippe de Ségur . . .

One day Oleg sensed condescension in Lessya's comments, as if he were a child.

"You see, what I can't figure out is how your screenplay is going to be in any way different from all those endless tomes you've been reading about Catherine . . ."

He protested vaguely, then fell silent. His script did, in fact, reiterate all the clichés: a tsarina both enlightened and despotic, a feminist in advance of her time and a nymphomaniac, a friend of the philosophers but hostile to the revolutionary fruits of their ideas . . .

"At best, you'll just be filming what's been told and retold over and over again. In a thousand historical novels," Lessya added, with a yawn.

For some time now their relationship had become altered. "Ah, that summer of love," Oleg said to himself. "That ray of light from the

setting sun fading on the faces of the statues at the Winter Palace . . ."
(and even this image came from a novel about Catherine II!). He puzzled
over the reason for this waning: his work at the slaughterhouse, the job of
section head Lessya now held at her magazine . . . Yes, they had less free
time than before. But, above all, Lessya had hoped to see him acting out
one of those two glamorous roles—either that of a dissident filmmaker
or else a director who was one of the regime's blue-eyed boys. While he
just wanted to remain himself.

They had loved one another but made no promises, "a modern
love affair," he thought bitterly. During nights at the slaughterhouse he
pictured his girlfriend dancing in someone else's arms. Or sleeping in
someone else's arms?

One particular director's name, that of Valentin Zyamtsev, often
came up when Lessya was talking. A way for her to prepare Oleg for a
breakup. Zyamtsev had the self-assurance of those tall, dark men who
graciously allow women to fall in love with them. He was the one who
had come out with that epithet: "Siberian peasant . . ."

Oleg had carried hundreds of carcasses while thinking about this
new situation: himself and Lessya, the banal injustice of physical prefer-
ences, one face finding favor more than another, Zyamtsev and himself,
a winner and a loser . . .

One mild, misty November evening Lessya came to see him, as in the old
days. A belated echo of the affection they had once known . . . He went
to make the coffee. While waiting for the water to boil he looked in at
his friend, who was reading on the sofa, in the little room at the end of
the corridor. They spent the night making love, talked for a long time.
The charts on the wall still displayed the chronology of the reign, the
list of favorites . . . They recalled their "history exams" with a smile, but
did not dare repeat the game.

"What it would be interesting to film," murmured Lessya, "is what
Catherine was not . . ."

He was struck by this turn of phrase.

"You mean, imagine what her life might have been, if . . ."

"No. What her life really was like. An evening like this, the mist, the last mild weather before winter sets in . . . There must have been times in her life that allowed her to be herself. She wasn't just a machine for signing decrees, writing to Voltaire, and devouring her lovers . . ."

Oleg made no reply. They had just hinted at the truth about a human being, this Catherine, of whom, for months now, he had only succeeded in capturing the gestures and actions. It even occurred to him that if they could only have found words with which to express this truth just touched upon, then their own lives—this love affair now ending— might have been reborn, wonderfully different.

Those words were not found, life resumed its course. Lessya came rarely, did not stay, and the comments she made about the screenplay served only to cover up the emptiness in their conversations . . . There is nothing more remote than a woman who is becoming involved in a new love affair. An extraterrestrial, a gentle, distracted monster, whose face, close up and already unrecognizable, is more attractive than ever, tormentingly and hopelessly so.

The rough work at the slaughterhouse put things in perspective: Lessya's friend, Zyamtsev, had more to offer than a penniless provincial without living quarters worthy of the name, and to make matters worse, one struggling with a crazy project.

So it was that one day, choking back his shame, Oleg had got himself an invitation from the people who made up Lessya's little artistic world. The celebration for a screenplay that had just been approved by the SCCA—the dictatorial State Committee for Cinematic Art . . . Oleg drank, forced himself to relax, tried to dance. In the crowd, animated by the music, an arm caught against his glasses . . . The next day his friend Zhurbin brought him the missing lens, which had been retrieved from under a table. On opening the door Oleg was confronted by a grotesque face: Zhurbin had managed to screw the lens into his left eye, like a monocle. He burst into song: *"La donna è mobile . . ."* His intention was praiseworthy, to tease his friend, to make him see the funny side of the situation. His voice broke off, so palpable was the anguish that crumpled Oleg's face. As a born actor, Zhurbin found the right tone. "Aha! I hereby predict that you will make a great film. You've got the fury for it now!"

Prophetic voice, flashing eyes. Oleg smiled: little, red-haired, grimacing Zhurbin was like one of those court jesters—tsars' fools—much prized at the St. Petersburg court.

"Fury" only served to sharpen his perception a little more: History is governed by an appetite for domination and sex.

There was no shortage of examples in Catherine's life. There she goes, passing between two lines of handsome officers with a faint smile and a piercing gaze. An hour later one of these stallions is sent to her by Potemkin on some kind of apparent commission. The chosen one submits to examination by Dr. Rogerson (state of health) and Countess Bruce (sexual performance). Following which, he is installed in the palace and showered with titles, military ranks, and wealth.

Favoritism as an institution, sex as a form of government, orgasm as a factor in political life. Yes, the alcove that allows Catherine to conduct the business of the State without interrupting her amorous adventures.

The story in a nutshell, but historically accurate. In her early youth Catherine experiences surges of sensuality that she will speak of in her *Memoirs:* with a cushion squeezed between her thighs the little princess tosses and turns frenziedly, her face flushed, her eyes rolled upward. At the age of thirteen love at first sight throws her into the arms of an uncle, and it is only the desire to marry Peter, so as to ascend to the Russian throne, that puts an end to this passion.

There was also a scene that would have a powerful impact in the film, Oleg was sure of it. Peter and Catherine are living with the Empress

Elizabeth in St. Petersburg. Sometimes a bigot, sometimes dissolute, Elizabeth indulges in orgies of unbridled debauchery. One evening, Peter, armed with a gimlet, makes holes in several partition walls between rooms in the palace. With one eye glued to these peepholes he comments on what he can see. Here the guards are having dinner. Next door the dressmakers are at work. And there . . . He splutters with excitement: "She's so fat!" Catherine takes a look through the hole and freezes. Candlelight, the white bulk of a body—a woman being crushed by a man. It looks like a battle, a murder! Elizabeth, with her hair in disorder, is panting, uttering oaths . . . The man breaks free from her, exhausted. Another man hurls himself at the empress, embraces her brutally . . . Peter pushes Catherine aside ("Let me, it's my turn!"), and she begins walking blindly away with only one thought in her head: "Better far to die . . ."

Thirty years later, in the twilight of her reign, an obese old woman can be seen being serviced by two young men, the Zubov brothers. This woman is Catherine herself . . .

Between these two episodes—the whole of her life. Men who provide the interlude of desire, men who kill, men who die. Potemkin becomes infatuated with a serving maid, Catherine insists on her chief enforcer punishing the foolish girl. The zeal is excessive: the girl is immured alive. Catherine does not like her son Paul's wife, the princess is too free-spirited. And in poor health—just one potion brings about her death. Poison? Now that's an ugly word! And then there's Mamonov, the betrayer, condemned to witness soldiers raping his young wife.

The film he now had in mind was targeted at an audience of just two: Lessya and Zyamtsev. Like all artists, Oleg was talking about himself. Catherine II or Julius Caesar, what difference does it make, if, through History, he could declare his love, portray the arrogance of the strong, the rarity of true affection?

It was easy for him to paint Catherine black, there was no shortage in her life of stinking tar that would stick: murders, rapes, debauchery, treachery . . . And he would have continued with this exercise in blackening her if, one day, a few steps away from the Winter Palace, he had not chanced upon Lessya and Zyamtsev, in a lovers' embrace . . . He turned toward a shop window, pretending to be an anonymous passerby . . .

Back home he threw himself into his screenplay. Thrones, wars, tortures, soldiers impaled on bayonets, horses ripped open by a hail of bullets and those young males from among whom a woman chose herself a favorite . . .

He knew no blinding inspiration. Simply from the jumble of pages there suddenly emerged a clear grasp of what he must write. He recalled the words of his teacher, Bassov: "You're not going to treat us to an animated cartoon?"

On the contrary, precisely that! To compress the farce of History, to extract from it a series of sketches, of masquerades. A great mirror rises up, there on a bed a breathless lover can be seen, the mirror descends and the tsarina, all flushed with love, signs treaties, receives Casanova, Diderot, Potemkin . . .

Within a fortnight the screenplay was completed. And, as if she had guessed as much, Lessya came to see him in his little room in the communal apartment. The echo of their evenings together in the old days was poignant: the woman he loved sitting there on a sofa piled high with books, the smell of coffee . . .

"Erdmann, you'd better go hang yourself. It's crazy!"

That was her verdict, but Lessya attached scant importance to it, her life was by now so far removed from this little room.

The next night at the slaughterhouse was tough: carcasses of horses, bloody burdens, and the sight of a tub into which the workmen hurled viscera. A dark, glistening magma that looked as if it were moving. "Men fight to dominate their fellow men," he thought, "to grow rich, to win the most beautiful women. Death comes and what remains of all they desired or hated, all they have been, is this pulp . . . The idea's not a new one, but I now have this tub here in front of my eyes. And Lessya so alive within me . . ."

And the memory returned of his girlfriend's words in November, on that last evening of their love: "You should film what Catherine was not . . . A misty night, the frail mildness that comes before winter . . ."

He made a sudden decision: when he left the slaughterhouse that morning he went to Zyamtsev's place. A sleepless night is a bad counselor, it caused him to picture an encounter happening as easily as in a dream: as Lessya emerges from the apartment building, he speaks to her, she understands him . . .

She came down with Zyamtsev and they were heading straight for Oleg, as if they wanted to call out to him, pursue him. The courtyards between Leningrad apartment buildings are famously labyrinthine. Keeping his head down, he beat a retreat, restraining himself from running, turning this way and that. The two lovers were following him relentlessly, seeking to corner him and make fun of the childish way he had waited under their window . . . Out of breath, he finally came to a halt, realized that nobody was hounding him, found himself in front of a little unofficial garbage dump stacked up against a brick wall. To one side stood a chair with a battered seat. He sat down without thinking, realized his knees were shaking. A cat walked by, stared at him, incredulous. Oleg broke into a laugh, on the brink of tears . . . "Just look at me sitting here on the Polish throne Catherine had installed in her privy. And on November 4, 1796, they'll find her on the floor beside this desecrated relic. Dying. She's had a dizzy spell just as she was relieving herself. Two days later she'll be in her death throes. Death, decomposition. That tub of viscera. That's all there is in life, my dear Lessya. Violence, the absurdity of desire, the drama of love affairs. And the tub . . ."

He got up, seeing a woman walking over to the wall, a bucket of garbage in her hand.

Back at home he found a letter from Bassov, his teacher. "I've read your screenplay. We need to talk about it . . ." As a postscript, the acronym Bassov had invented—"datdot": "don't attempt to discuss on telephone." Oleg reflected on the censorship, the telephone tapping, and all the prohibitions Lessya's friends used to rail against. He now perceived that the impossibility of expressing oneself was not just about this. What was even harder to talk about was a misty night, an avenue of bare trees at the approach of winter, the silence of a woman who felt herself to be someone quite other than the famous tsarina whose name she bore.

Going to see Bassov is quite an expedition: subway, suburban train, a rickety bus jolting along amid wooded hills. Finally this housing development of dachas belonging to "representatives of the creative intelligentsia," the official term that makes Oleg smile. (What about the uncreative intellectuals?) For these "representatives" it is simply a vacation resort for the summer. Bassov, on the other hand, stays there all the year round, having nowhere to live in Leningrad.

Three years before he had married a young actress, a student of his. It was the euphoria of love alone that helped this sixty-year-old remain blind. Once she became the joint owner of the square feet allocated to him in Leningrad the lady demanded a divorce and brought in her boyfriend. Bassov, a director of films in which rugged heroes grappled with evil, found himself destitute in real life. He made appeals to moral conscience, to honesty! And then grasped that for this girl such an apartment was the chance of a lifetime. "Oh well, I guess she could have poisoned me," he said, tickled by his own brittle wit. He made a gallant last stand—delivered a homily on the glory of art and the squalor of mercenary calculations—and then went off to live in his dacha.

Those who gained from this were his students. He devoted more time to them, motivated by the passionate altruism of bruised souls. His selflessness extended to his support for an ideologically suspect short film, *Return in a Dream*, by a certain Oleg Erdmann . . .

This time the teacher receives him ceremoniously. A long handshake, his eyes screwed up as a sign of complicity. This is how you greet your fellow gladiator before he enters the lists.

"What a cat among the pigeons of Russian history!" He gestures at the manuscript lying on his desk. "She's a bombshell, your Catherine the Great . . . Hold on, I'll make some tea. Take this chair. They'll soon be strapping you into an electric chair, you'll see."

An anxious wait for his verdict and, outside the window, a February day, a snowy somnolence, nature's mild indifference toward all the frenzy of human plans.

The previous year, when talking to Bassov about Catherine, Oleg received this advice: "Drive her from her throne!" When he looked puzzled the teacher explained: "Show the woman in her. She took off her crown when she made love, didn't she? Search the streets for a look, a face, gestures that might be hers. Find a woman who might be Catherine in any period. An ice cream seller, a gym instructor . . . Try to fall in love with a present-day Catherine the Second." Keeping his eyes peeled, his ears cocked, Oleg would walk through the city, comparing passing women with the stereotyped portrait of Catherine. And in addition, the more he studied the empress's life, the more the young, frivolous figure took on serious, tragic features. Beyond the princess disporting herself beside the Neva there appeared a mature woman, at the same time more powerful and more vulnerable. There were perceptible similarities between her and women he came across—the fluttering of tired eyelids in a railroad station ticket office, a tourist speaking in husky tones close by the Hermitage, a voluptuous and supple gait . . . All this, made flesh, and disturbingly real, was Catherine. Bassov had been right: Oleg fell in love with her, set about defending her. Her sexual appetite? Just picture a young woman hungry for love who has been married off to that poor Peter, incapable of the least carnal act! Regicide? It was a duel rather than

a murder: Peter was planning to get rid of her and to give the crown to
his mistress, Vorontsova . . .

Bassov brings some tea, a pot of jam, bread. He moves slowly, only
embarking on conversation after he has poured tea for Oleg and drunk
a long draft.

"What concentrated fire, your screenplay, phew!" he mutters, with
a snort. Then, staring straight at him, he blurts out: "This submachine
gun style of writing is very effective!"

He snorts again and continues in somewhat grumpy tones: "I
wouldn't have staked a ruble on that technique! You promised me you'd
not do a Walt Disney. And, goddamnit, it works! Like that vignette
based on a Polish caricature: Catherine drinking blood—that of the
Warsaw insurgents, I guess—and gobbling male genitalia, those of her
favorites . . . Oh yes and that alcove! The mirror comes down. The lover's
hidden. And there's the empress, cool as a cucumber, receiving Casanova
or Diderot . . . The whole masquerade of History in a few shots. So,
Poniatowski, whose father was a footman, becomes a prince, then king of
Poland, and, at the very end, the king of the commode! And Potemkin? A
fabulously rich potentate who dies on a bare steppe under the open sky.
A soldier closes his eyes with copper coins . . . And Voltaire? What a base
flatterer! You don't mention Catherine's hatred of the French Revolution.
We just see a footman carrying off the bust of Voltaire, to hide it in the
attic at the Winter Palace . . ."

Ensconced in his armchair, Bassov first acts out Potemkin, lying
there in the middle of the steppe, then the footman, carrying the bust of
the philosopher hugged to his stomach.

"The high point, of course, is Catherine's love life. A hundred lovers! Take a minute for each of her favorites and you'd have no time left
to film anything else. Happily your animated cartoon cuts to the chase:
power and sex. And Catherine is the one who dominates all these males.
She's the one who fucks them!"

Bassov waves a clenched fist in what is intended as a manly gesture, but, on the lips of a cuckold this paean of praise for female libertinism does not ring true. His face takes on a disillusioned look.

"Now, here's the problem . . . The technique of an animated cartoon is perfect for dealing with simple situations. Count Orlov setting out to hunt a bear single-handed, then servicing the tsarina with equal energy. And when the Tsar Peter begins to annoy them, these lovebirds bump him off. It's all clear—predators massacre a weak herbivore. But . . . I've read Catherine's letters to her correspondent in Paris, Melchior Grimm. The catch is that she idolizes her lovers. Like a starryeyed young girl, she's forever saying the same thing: this Korsakov, this Mamonov, this Yermolov, this . . . well, every one of them is a total masterpiece, a lofty soul, an unequaled intelligence . . . She believes it. Her heart is won. She's in love!"

This exalted observation, "She's in love!," arouses Oleg. Hitherto he has allowed himself to be lulled by the words of praise, sweet music after months of setbacks and mockery. At last he has been understood, appreciated, given a seal of approval by a master.

"And then, her letters to Potemkin," Bassov continues. "*My dear heart, my little sweet soul, the master of my life's breath . . .*' Simpering endearments, sugary billing and cooing, agreed. There's nothing original in this babble of words. But there are deeds. Once Potemkin falls ill Catherine watches over him as if he were her own son! And that's something your animated cartoon could never show, because . . ."

At this moment Oleg knows that, through the tsarina's life, Bassov is talking about himself: his young wife had left him instead of "watching over him like her son."

"Catherine had just as much affection for Orlov. The rejected lover grows old, loses his wits, is sunk in solitude and squalor. And it's she, the empress, who goes to his house to feed him, to care for him. To wash him! Filming a bitch who gets herself a new male every day is easy, a Disney cartoon suffices. But now try showing this German woman rolling up her sleeves and giving an old Russian madman a bath! . . ."

Outside the window a bird perches on a snow-covered sorbus tree. They both watch the bullfinch moving with drowsy slowness toward a cluster of red . . .

"Your screenplay is reinforced concrete," Bassov concludes. "But take care. The slugs on the State Committee know how to find cracks where they can slither in. Given the novelty of the project, things are bound to get hot. Especially since your protectors at the Kremlin will already have forgotten you. Comrade Alzheimer has a seat on the Politburo . . ."

He snatches up a brochure, leafs through it . . .

"Listen carefully . . . the SCCA, the State Committee for Cinematic Art, always calls in an outside expert. In your case it's bound to be a historian. I've managed to get his name: Luria. He's the one who'll be lighting the bonfire under your feet. Now there are three historians called Luria in Leningrad. Well, these days there are only two. The first, who was denounced as a Trotskyist, was shot in '37. The second Luria is an absolute bastard. At the end of the thirties he gave up history to devote himself to modern political theory, or more precisely, to singing Stalin's praises. *Stalinist Retort to the Betrayers of Socialist Culture* is his magnum opus. After Stalin's death this Luria number two went through contortions that would make a yogi's eyes water: he revealed himself to be a sworn enemy of Stalinism . . . The third Luria is much more mysterious. There's a gap in his résumé between 1948 and 1956 . . . You'll know his publications: articles on microscopic subjects. He discusses the fiduciary system of paper money in the reign of Catherine the Second: a real 'mass market' topic . . . This particular Luria sounds to me like a cast-iron pedant. He's the one you really need to be wary of. As for the jury . . . Four or five doddery old men, born about 1900, who still think Eisenstein was a dangerous formalist. A trio of apparatchiks who can smell subversion everywhere. A few castrated yes-men. And a small pack of young upstarts who will fan the flames . . ."

Oleg clears his throat to lighten his voice dulled by the tension: "And . . . the dice aren't loaded from the start?"

Bassov, like an old skeptic philosopher, heaves a sigh: "Everything's loaded from the start, my good friend. Talent is trampled underfoot. Mediocrity reigns supreme. Cowardice takes the place of judgment. But . . ."

He realizes his pupil needs practical advice, encouragement.

"But . . . You've won already! The screenplay exists and, as Bulgakov said, manuscripts don't burn. Unlike their authors, I might add . . . So, take heart! And by the way . . . Don't hold my personal digressions against me. It's hard at my age to feel like an old lover with no tsarina who wants to share his solitude . . ."

At the moment of saying good-bye Bassov murmurs petulantly: "And look, I know you cherish it like the apple of your eye, but do me a favor. Drop the horse!"

Oleg shakes his hand, walks away, slipping and sliding over the snow.

Drop the horse . . . There is a horse in the screenplay, one that is referred to in talk of Catherine's sexual extravagances. A myth, no doubt, except that in a storage room at the Hermitage, an obliging member of the staff did show a wooden confection for restraining the horse, whose genital vigor the empress, in thrall to her lewd appetites allegedly, sought to enjoy . . . In France the revolutionary tribunal accused Marie Antoinette of succumbing to depravity in the company of her very young son. In Russia, to discredit the tsars, they failed to come up with anything better than these equine cavortings. In its grotesque enormity this calumny is almost anodyne compared with the infamy that was directed against the French queen . . .

In the train Bassov's verdict seems to him spot on: his project will never be approved by the SCCA jury. With fatalistic glee, Oleg resolves to present the manuscript to the judges with "the horse" included. Yes, he'll have the chutzpah to leave it in!

The "horse" came up again a week later . . .

His friend Zhurbin had got them two small parts in a film. "You stooge around for two or three hours and end up earning what you get for five nights at the slaughterhouse. Not bad, eh?"

The scene to be filmed is short: some "revolutionary sailors," guns in hand, faces smeared with black ("I look like a chimney sweep," Oleg says to himself), are supposed to invade a palace.

The director is not happy with the way they attack. First he finds them too slow, then he bawls them out for galloping along "like a pack of monkeys in rut" . . .

To be an authentic son of the people Oleg has removed his glasses. Without his being able to identify them, his foggy gaze lights on a couple standing close to the camera. The umpteenth assault by the sailors has been judged acceptable. The actors put down their weapons, begin removing their makeup . . . As he puts his glasses back on, Oleg gives a start: at the other end of the studio the director is talking to Valentin Zyamtsev and Lessya. Having arrived in the middle of the filming they must have seen this shortsighted sailor bounding up the staircase . . .

"Hi, Erdmann. This must make a change from your work at the slaughterhouse!" Zyamtsev pats him on the shoulder. "I guess Stanislavsky never knew that to prepare for the role of a sailor you need to train with pigs' carcasses, eh?"

It was Lessya's laughter that sounded the most disdainful: "Oh, and apart from the pigs, how's your Catherine the Second screenplay coming along? Have you finished episode a hundred and fifty yet?"

The director gives Oleg a pitying look: "A screenplay about Catherine? Deadly!"

Oleg is just about to move off when Lessya calls out to him in a voice whose mocking chill freezes him: "So where's she got to with her sleeping around, your Cathy? Who's her boyfriend now? Korsakov? Or is it Lanskoy?" And in a muttered aside, she adds: "Filthy sow! She had the hots for all of them . . . !"

There are hoots of laughter; a smutty remark made by a woman generally gives rise to wild hilarity in men. Oleg feels the flush rising to his neck. He sees Zhurbin on the far side of the studio coming toward them. And just then he makes this unpremeditated reply: "No, Lessya. We've moved on from pigs. What Catherine prefers now is studs, especially tall, dark ones. And, do you know . . ."

She slaps him, hitting him more on his brow than his cheek. His glasses fly off. Zhurbin makes a dive, falls, catches them, and exclaims: "What a save!" He gets up, hands Oleg his glasses, mutters a brief "There you go again!" and accosts Zyamtsev: "As for you, Valentino, why don't you get yourself a sailor's uniform and join the assault with the rest of us, instead of writing dumb screenplays like that? . . ." And to the director: "OK, chief. When do we get our dough?"

In the street night has fallen. "It's just like coming out after a movie," remarks Zhurbin. "Except that we were in the movie . . ." His voice is a little mournful. "Don't let it upset you, Erdmann. Women, men, love . . . that's all a big movie, too. At the time you feel sad, but when it's all over, you don't even remember the actors' names . . . Well, so long then! Don't throw yourself in the Griboyedov Canal. It's too dirty. Tomorrow at the slaughterhouse we'll try to grab some calf's liver. OK?"

He goes off. Oleg does not stir. He ends the sentence Lessya interrupted. "And do you know . . . I'm toting horsemeat around too . . ." It
had been intended as a joke against himself. The impossibility of retriev-
ing it now is so complete that it brings with it a certain relief. The last
tie is cut, that of speech, which yesterday could still bring him Lessya's
voice, her breathing. From now on nothing more. So what was it Zhurbin
said? You'll end up forgetting even the actors' names . . .

His footsteps lead him away from the district where he lives and
for an hour this distancing serves as an end in itself.

The tourists' Leningrad gives up the ghost, changing into suburban streets, dreary faded walls, ground floors spattered with dirty snow
thrown up by trucks. Warehouses, factories, and dwellings whose occupants one pictures with perplexed compassion, yes, some old woman
hesitating to cross this thunderous ditch of a road.

His destination is an apartment building that looks like a lone
mountain crag. A narrow structure on three stories, which chaotic urban
planning has left behind in a running noose of lines of communication:
a cat's cradle of railroad tracks and viaducts with rusty skeletons. Against
all logic, lighted windows can be seen, potted plants behind the panes of
glass, little tulle curtains . . . People are still living there!

But then, after all, this is where Oleg spent most of his childhood.

He goes in at the main entrance, cocks an ear to the echo from
the stairwell, begins climbing. At the top landing a staircase leads up
between floors to an attic door. There is a lock whose creaks and groans
he knows how to master. He closes the door behind him, remains in the
darkness, waits for the beating of his heart to calm down.

Feeling his way along the top of some shelving he locates an electric
flashlight. He has no need to explore the premises. To the left a corner
that served both as kitchen and bathroom. A zinc bathtub is there, thrust
beneath the angle of the stairs. And this memory: his father pouring
warm water over his back, it is winter, the steam makes a rainbow around
the lightbulb . . . To the right a bed made of thick planks and a little

couch, which gives the measure of the body that used to curl up there. There are ankle boots neatly lined up against the wall. Their wrinkled leather reminds him of the pain of the great frosts: the child walks along, counting the crossties, then, having lost all feeling in his toes, remembers tales of frostbite, runs, climbs the staircase, comes in, squeezes up against the great stove on which a bucket of water is heating. Soon it will be paradise, a hot stream of water, the resinous smell of the soap, his father softly whistling a tune . . .

Oleg walks over to a drawing board: his father's "office." Huge sheets of paper, sketches of pediments, of blind arcades . . . the beam from the flashlight slips across a tiny window and suddenly conjures a confused structure out of the darkness, a towering mass of columns, galleries, spires, cupolas.

A model of a palace, at least six feet high, the summit of which touches the attic ceiling.

The chaotic nature of this construction has a hypnotic effect. The eye follows the curves of a spiral staircase, becomes lost amid flying buttresses . . . It is a mixture of all styles. Classical facades are loaded with baroque sculptures, surging ogives rest upon antique colonnades . . . A castle? A cathedral? Or perhaps a whole city compressed by a violent folding of the rocks beneath? Fragments under construction blend in with ruins cunningly re-created.

There is also this mystery: directed at a certain angle, the beam lights up a forgotten object at the heart of this labyrinth, which looks like a fragment of coral.

Oleg calls to mind the child who spent hours in front of this model. In his daydreams he thrust open the gates, made his way in beneath the vaulted ceilings. Prophetically, his father's voice used to ring out: "Here there will be a narthex with unfluted columns. And over there a hall in the form of a basilica . . . Palladio . . . Piranesi . . ." These mysterious mantras were part of the joy of being with his father, the smell of wood glue and the scent of the fire on which their evening meal was cooking . . .

"The Gallery of Mirrors at Herrenchiemsee Castle . . . The abbey at Ottobeuren." These strange syllables were lodged in his memory, notations of a happiness that would turn out to be all too transient.

It never occurred to him that what this palace betokened was a descent into madness. Granted, his father sometimes flew into a rage, smashed a part of the structure. "They said Renaissance perspective was illusionism. Idiots! Everything is illusion. Our lives, our passions . . . And even matter. Look, I'm going to break this staircase and then it will lead into nothingness!"

But the child knew he would soon start building again, a pediment would be added, a line of pillars . . . And that life would return to its simple pleasures: hot water in the bathtub, the spicy odor of the soap, his father whistling tunes to himself.

He was all the more shocked when the break came because it occurred during one of those periods of calm. One day the teacher told him he would not be going back home because his father had "health problems" . . . He did not weep. Not thanks to any particular stoicism but because he was overcome by obscure feelings of guilt: he had concealed the fact that his father was constructing this insane palace and that sometimes he used to speak in German . . .

Shame helped the child to endure the separation, the transfers from one educational establishment to another and the mockery—his schoolfellows always ended up learning the truth: "Your dad's crazy, is that it? And I guess you're nuts too! So are you a Nazi, Erdmann, like your old man?"

These insults would follow him throughout his school days, even during the months when the doctor allowed his father to return home. Increasingly the boy rebelled against such reunions, dreading the brief paradise and the inevitable subsequent banishment.

Adolescent selfishness liberated him from feelings of guilt. It was now his father who was the accused, a man incapable of finding anything better than his job as a land surveyor and this life in the attic. His son even held their German name against him—"a Nazi name!" But above all this palace, forever growing taller, collapsing, making a spectacle of incredible ruins. No longer seeing this father of his allowed him to feel like the others . . .

He must have reached the age of eighteen when, right at the center of the city, close to the Admiralty, he came across this thin little old man, his pate covered with silver threads. His father! The stab of pity Oleg felt was so sharp that the other emotions came only later: his old shame at having such a father and his current shame at having abandoned him. He lacked the courage to go up to him—the old man went on his way, muttering in a mixture of Russian and German, his gaze, now hazy, now piercing, alighting on the facades of buildings. To make up for his cowardice, Oleg went to visit him that same evening.

On this occasion there was no grand reunion. The old man seemed no longer aware of the passage of time. He spoke as if his son had just slipped out for a moment. "Look, I've constructed this colonnade but as time goes by only ruins will be left of it. Ruins are beauty liberated from time. Painters depict ruins without imagining the complete building. But we architects have to create the building and wait for it to collapse . . . Life is nothing more than waiting for that collapse. We spend our lives amid the ruins of what we have loved . . ."

Oleg began coming to see his father every day. The remarks that in the old days had seemed obscure to him now revealed their meaning: the phantasmagoria of the palace brought together projects that had been too ambitious ever to be realized. "Bernini designed the Louvre, but for lack of money his dream never saw the light of day. Fischer von Erlach, for his part, drew up plans for Schönbrunn Castle. Nobody dared to give physical form to such splendor . . ."

This architectural utopia epitomized his father's whole life. His Russian sorrows, his German dreams, that apartment building choked by railroad tracks, monumental structures dreamed of in his ancestors' fatherland. "Now, you've never seen the monastery at Wiblingen and its baroque library . . . What perfect proportions!"

On occasion he had a great desire to hug the old man, to extricate

him from his delusions: "But Papa, you've never seen it either!" Oleg did
not do so, aware that the delicate equilibrium his father now enjoyed
depended on the continuity of his illusions.

One day, with his head thrust deep into the entrails of his model,
his father murmured: "And here I'm going to install a Great Hall of the
Knights, like the one at Weikersheim Castle. Part of our family came
from there . . ."

Oleg whispered to him softly, as one addresses a sleepwalker engaged in his perilous progress: ". . . so they lived not far from that castle:
What did they do in life?"

His father must have taken these words for the echo of his own
thoughts. He continued the story and swiftly told the tale of the life clos-
est to them, the one that had led to them, him and his son, ending up in
this building like a mountain crag amid the railroad tracks.

The disappearance of the family portraits during his boyhood marked Sergei Erdmann, Oleg's father, more strongly than the great events of the period. Born in 1924, he had spent his childhood amid their solemn black-and-white faces. Russia was shaken by revolutionary challenges, by futuristic promises. Old people still called it St. Petersburg, but when Sergei was taking his first steps it was already Leningrad. Hundreds of men were arrested every night and their deaths behind barbed wire were acclaimed in the newspapers as the welcome fruit of the most humane of judicial systems. Even school textbooks did not escape punishment. Their teacher would order: "Open your books at page . . ." (he gave the number). "The photograph here shows an enemy of the people recently unmasked by the Party. Black it out with ink! Begin with his mouth which uttered calumnies against our socialist fatherland."

From one month to the next a good many pages were sullied by black rectangles. And in his parents' conversations Sergei detected hints of more discreet disappearances, neighbors on the same landing, colleagues, former acquaintances.

Only the ancestral portraits seemed calmly aloof. Their calm was disrupted in 1936. The photographs came down from their hooks and took refuge in the depths of a wardrobe. His parents' answer was evasive: "It's better to be on the safe side." Now in his teens, he did not try to discover more: the link between the hiding of these portraits and the inked-out squares in his history book was only too evident.

What crime had these ancestors committed? Doctors, engineers, merchants, booksellers, soldiers, they had always kept themselves well clear of politics. The 1917 revolution had not turned them into implacable opponents of the regime. His father, an optician, followed a profession little suited to controversy.

"It's because we're German . . . ," Sergei's mother murmured one day. German? No! The name of Erdmann had never given rise to suspicion. Not even in 1914. Several Erdmanns had fought at the front, like so many Russians of German origin. It seemed as if the revolution ought to eradicate these survivals: titles, origins, nationalities . . . And yet the more they preached about "internationalism," the more this ancient German kinship came under suspicion.

Sergei's father died of a heart attack early in 1937. During his final months he used to go to bed fully dressed, convinced that one night there would be a knock at their door. Out in the street a black car would be waiting for him, then there would be long sessions of interrogation, torture . . . The day he was buried, Sergei's mother burned their family portraits. For some time now the newspapers had taken to denouncing not only "the enemies of the people" but also "Hitler's lackeys."

All that had survived was this optical toy: a stereoscope equipped with a hundred photographs of European cities, Berlin, Vienna, Milan, Rome . . . Sergei remembered how one day his parents had talked about their trip to Italy, a few years before the revolution. Nowadays thinking of going abroad seemed more unrealistic than traveling to the moon.

The cities in the stereoscope and their buildings inspired in him a taste for architecture, a passion that forever bore the stamp of the trip he pictured his parents making, when young and in love.

For these Russians, now on the spot because of their German roots, there came a respite, which lasted from August 1939 until June 1941. The pact with Hitler had just been signed, Germany was becoming an almost friendly ally. "This is only borrowed time," his mother observed.

"War will break out and then both sides will regard us as enemies. How can we make them forget about us?"

She decided to get rid of all the optical equipment her husband used to use. "They could accuse us of who knows what military espionage on Hitler's behalf."

As for Sergei, his intention seemed even more difficult to achieve: to change nationality. In that land of total surveillance his chances of success were minimal.

He was helped by the chaos of the first days of the war. The bombing caused fires in a number of apartment buildings in their district. Sergei went out into one of the courtyards, threw his papers in the fire, allowed his clothing to become scorched in the flames. Then he rushed to a mobilization center. The military bureaucracy had few scruples. The only hazard was his name, Erdmann. "You're of German origin!" gasped the official in charge. "No, I'm Jewish . . . ," replied Sergei. This was duly noted along with more anodyne information: his age (he added an extra year), his status as an architectural student . . .

To begin with he was posted to an engineering unit that was preparing the ground for the retreat of troops in disarray. His distance from the fighting allowed him to hold on to the memory of a Germany his parents used to speak of, a fatherland of romantic poets and inspired musicians. An image that survived the sight of fields covered in frozen corpses.

The Russian counteroffensive would cure him of the Germany he had dreamed of. Enlisted in the infantry, he one day passed through a village that had been torched about seventy miles from Moscow. The spectacle of izbas burned to a cinder was not new to him. What froze him was the line of four charred bodies punctuating the snow alongside a fence. Bodies of children. Little fugitives who had been caught in the jet of a flamethrower. A German soldier must have killed them, more or less out of curiosity, testing whether his weapon would reach them . . . Behind the fence Sergei saw one who had escaped—a wild-eyed little boy, babbling incoherently.

There was an intensity about this madness that was contagious, Sergei would never free himself from it, for no words could express the horror of those little faces reduced to the state of smoldering brands.

His war was going to be a long-drawn-out replica of that burned village. Towns reduced to black shreds, bodies crushed by tanks . . . The memory of the wild-eyed child often returned, giving rise to a thought that pained him more than the wretchedness of a soldier's life: "If my ancestors had not left Germany, I should probably have come to that village armed with a flamethrower . . ." He shook his head to drive away this phantom version of himself, noting that if his family had not settled in Russia he would never have been born. His distress was numbed.

Before the war he had always felt himself to be Russian. Back from the front in 1945, he felt as if a small part of the German crimes could be laid at his door. He called himself a fool, fingered the medals that jingled on his uniform jacket, told himself that few of his comrades had gone right through the war, from Moscow to Berlin! But the closer he got to Leningrad the more he was tormented by a feeling of being a German fifth columnist.

This sense of a split personality became unbearable when he learned that from the start of the war Russians of German origin had been deported beyond the Urals. He gathered that his mother had suffered this same fate, made inquiries, and went to look for her in a small town in western Siberia. He was directed to a group of huts where several families lived, a few forlorn old men and three or four young women who had come there as children and grown up without parents. One of them, Marta, told him about how they had fetched up in this deserted spot, the hunger, the snowstorms, the despair, the guilt felt by these innocent Germans, who were being made to pay for the others, Hitler's lot. This distress killed more of them than disease. Sergei's mother had died late in the fall of the first year of the war. "She asked me to keep this lamp," said Marta.

It was not a lamp but a magic lantern, the old Erdmann family relic.

The following year they got married. Marta, legally obliged to live there, managed to leave Siberia—thanks to this purportedly Jewish husband, decorated with medals that bore the image of Stalin.

The apartment where Sergei had lived before the war was occupied. By neighbors who had benefited from the deportation of the "filthy Nazis" . . . The young married couple rented a room, tried to survive, glad, at least, to see a sky where no bombers flew. Sergei resumed his architectural studies, got through the degree course in two years, completed his qualifying project . . .

He was not uneasy when a new witch hunt was unleashed in 1948, under the name of the "struggle against cosmopolitanism in culture and the sciences." What this was about, he thought, was a reining in, aimed at those intellectuals who had been seduced after the war by the brief opening up toward the West. He talked about it to Marta, explained the secret of the false Jewish nationality noted in his passport . . . "Well, why not tell them the truth?" she asked him.

He would have done so if he had not been arrested in the middle of the following night. They tried to make him admit he had been involved in a clandestine Zionist organization. Subjected to increasingly brutal torture, he stuck by the truth: his German origins, his four years at the front. All this was very easy to check. And in the end it was checked and confirmed. The verification of his life history, undertaken with the usual administrative indolence, took two and a half years.

After his release he found Marta again, and life resumed, but what they lacked now was an essential ingredient: faith in this life of theirs. They were like twigs put into water—the leaf buds open out, they give off a scent of spring, and, where the twig was broken off, they even put forth tiny roots, but these seek solid earth in vain.

They lived like that, in suspense, had a son, Oleg, born in 1954, to whom Marta, who died three years later, managed to give what no ordinary child would have received in so short a time—the certain knowledge of having a mother who loved him as no one else would ever love him.

Oleg was six years old when his father went to live in the attic of that crag-building. Triplets had been born in the family of an old regimental comrade of his, and Sergei had handed over his own room in a communal apartment and moved into this "studio apartment" where the newborn babies would not have survived.

In his teens Oleg knew the humiliation of having to admit where he lived. Little by little he forged a status for himself that was admittedly not very flattering but less ludicrous: he claimed he had been born in a small town in Siberia and therefore could not hope for decent accommodation. All things considered, being saddled with the nickname "Siberian peasant" was less hard to bear than being addressed as "German scum."

And besides, this invention brought him closer to his mother, to the memory of her bedside table: what he always saw there as a child was a tiny pearl necklace, a porcelain cup, a well-worn book and . . . There his memory faltered over an object whose position he could recall without being able to picture it. He often told himself that if only he had been able to call its appearance to mind, his mother would have seemed much more present to him. More alive . . .

"Mica simulates stained glass very well. This will be a copy of the Liboriuskapelle, a masterpiece of High Gothic style that stands in Creuzburg . . ."

Oleg was listening to his father as he sliced off a layer of mica with a fine blade. Inside the model a lamp shone upon an object that resembled a fragment of coral. Oleg did not dare to ask the why and wherefore of its presence among the columns. His father seemed to him too frail to be brought back to reality.

Only once did Oleg dare to put the question to him that for years he had been burning to ask: "What if you'd been on the other side,

Papa, in a German regiment, and they'd ordered you to burn a village . . .
Would you have done it?" An outburst of fury, a shout of laughter, a
shrug of the shoulders . . . Oleg could have imagined any one of those
reactions. But not this shaking face that crumpled into little wrinkles of
pain and became reduced to eyes, silently weeping.

A week later his father tripped on a crosstie, fell, dislocated an arm.
That evening Oleg found him sitting beside the track, moaning softly,
oblivious of the passing trains. He took him up to the studio apartment,
heated some water, washed the little old man in the zinc bathtub . . . His
father fell asleep holding his hand and it was just as he was beginning
to drop off that, in his soft and somewhat ironic old man's voice, he
murmured: "When I think that all this has happened to us because of a
little German princess . . ." Oleg recognized the formula the Erdmanns
were given to repeating from time to time, when commenting on their
Russian destiny.

His father died at the end of the following year, while Oleg was doing
his military service.

In the years ahead, at the most taxing moments, the young man
would recall their family saying with a smile: "Well, what do you know?
This is all happening to me because of that little German girl who became Catherine the Great."

II
◆◆◆

"One of your characters steals a hundred rubles from a stocking maker. Logically these would have been copper coins, given the low prices of the goods. Well, at that time a kopeck coin weighed two-thirds of an ounce. So those hundred rubles would have weighed some two hundred and twenty pounds. The sum could have been made up of silver coins, which would have reduced the weight by, let us say, three-quarters. Running with a bag weighing fifty-five pounds on your back is possible, in principle. But with all that for ballast your hero swims across the Neva!"

Luria adjusts his glasses, peering down at a thick notebook with dog-eared pages. Oleg is surprised to find he is holding his breath, which irritates him, and he stirs on his chair to shake off this frozen posture of a prisoner in the dock.

His teacher, Bassov, had forecast correctly—the members of the State Committee for Cinematic Art, the famous SCCA, have given the floor to an "expert": this Luria, a lean man with a harsh, testy expression. "A shabby academic," thinks Oleg. "They've brought him out from an attic so he can delight in humiliating an ignoramus . . ."

His method is effective: without criticizing the screenplay from an artistic point of view, Luria attacks a particular sequence, demonstrates it is based on factual errors. The "judges" appear to be delighted. They are just as Bassov had described them: bureaucrats of the cinema with very little footage to their credit and all the more eager to denigrate the work of others. Oleg recognizes the types his teacher had described: four old dinosaurs who see the danger of formalism lurking everywhere, a trio of bleak apparatchiks and a group of young upstarts, dressed in Western style . . . Luria resumes his speech for the prosecution.

"Don't think I'm only paying attention to monetary matters. But that is the field in which your screenplay departs the furthest from historical truth. For example, the scene where Peter the Third throws rubles to the ground that are freshly minted with his image. According to you, this gesture derives from his short temper. But in reality the tsar is furious with the hairstyle the engraver saw fit to adorn him with: a wig with curls, in the French fashion. A fatal choice, for he detests Louis the Fifteenth of France. You make a similar blunder with Cagliostro. According to you, he promises Catherine that he'll transmute iron into gold. This is an unlikely conversation. She considers Cagliostro to be a charlatan and later pours scorn on him in a stage comedy, *The Deceiver.* On the other hand, one practical idea of the 'wizard's' is a roaring success in Russia. One day Potemkin learns that someone has stolen the buttons from all his soldiers' uniforms. The inquiry produces nothing. Cagliostro puts forward a chemist's explanation: these buttons are made of tin and in the coldest weather this metal disintegrates into dust. This is known as 'tin plague.' The Italian advises them to replace it with an alloy of zinc and copper—brass. From now on the Russian army buttons itself up 'Cagliostro fashion.' As you can see, a little precision would do no harm to your artistic imagination. Now let us move on to much graver concerns . . ."

Oleg forces himself to look his "judges" in the eye. Their faces are wreathed in smiles, condescending . . .

In the historian's voice a note of glee can be detected as he prepares for an imminent coup de grâce.

"Now then . . . Catherine's son, the future Paul the First. According to you when he goes to Paris and Rome, he needs interpreters. Wrong! Paul, who has been denigrated by his biographers, spoke at least eight languages. Next. Catherine, in the company of Mamonov, listens to Vivaldi. Most improbable. The tsarina doesn't like music. She really doesn't have an ear for it. Rather than virtuoso musicians, she prefers eccentrics who play the piano with their noses or their toes . . . Next: in 1796 the Swedish king Gustav the Fourth breaks off his engagement to Alexandra, Catherine's granddaughter. You rightly insist on the grief this causes the tsarina, the shock hastens her death. But the reason for the refusal is quite different. For form's sake, Gustav insists that his fiancée should convert to Protestantism. But the truth is that he is appalled by the licentiousness that prevails at the court: Catherine, at the age of almost seventy, is sharing her bed with the Zubov brothers, who are twenty-eight and twenty-four, respectively . . . Next: the 'Potemkin villages': a persistent cliché. This is a sham that never happened. Yes, as the tsarina made her tour the peasants prettified their izbas. Yes, they built landing stages where Catherine came ashore during her journey by river to the Crimea and residential staging posts where she spent the night. But all this went no further than the usual triumphal arches, red carpets, and garlands of flowers. And there's another legend you give credence to: Catherine's lesbian relationships. This rumor is due to a misunderstanding. One night at a masked ball Catherine accosts a young officer whom she'd be happy to take back to her alcove. But, as it happens, this is a young woman concealed behind the mask. However, when it comes to the homosexual relationship between Casanova and Lunin, you draw some kind of veil of silence around it. Yet that kind of physical intercourse was quite commonplace at the time . . . And then you must look to your language! 'General N. has been wounded in his privates,' says one of your heroes. In Catherine's century they'd have said: 'A sword thrust has made a eunuch of him!'"

There is a hiss of glutinous satisfaction in the sniggering of the jury.

"And finally, there are two scenes without any basis in truth. First of all, no serving maid of Catherine's was ever immured and certainly not walled up alive. A pure invention by historians for ideological purposes. And what is more, the faithless favorite Mamonov and his wife never suffered any reprisals. The raping of the young bride is an ancient piece of gossip that we owe to the antiroyalist propaganda of 1917. Quite the contrary, it is Catherine who marries off the two lovers. And, by the irony of fate, it is Mamonov, quickly disillusioned by the routine of married life, who begs the tsarina to reinstate him in her alcove . . ."

The hawk-like nose dives deeply into his notes once more, and already sotto voce exchanges between the members of the SCCA can be heard. In a moment of distraction, Oleg pictures Lessya . . . To win her back he could renounce everything! As a matter of fact, in order to please these judges, he has already cut the empress's "equine love affair" from the screenplay.

A new nuance enters the historian's tones—a certain sympathy for his victim: "The subject is a complex one. Pushkin himself put forward contradictory opinions about the tsarina. 'A Tartuffe in petticoats,' he called her. 'A debauched old woman.' And then he declaims: 'Russia, your glory died with Catherine!' The Empress Elizabeth should be mentioned, she was the one who invited this young German woman to St. Petersburg. The facts are known. Elizabeth is a capricious and tormented individual who never sleeps in the same bedroom on two consecutive nights and never wears the same gown twice, a mentally disturbed person whose whims everyone dreads. Catherine lives there as a prisoner: her letters are read. When she goes out she is closely watched. And yet Elizabeth is no monster. She's the one who abolishes the death penalty in Russia. What other monarch in Europe could boast of such a thing at the time? However, when she dies, and the victims of her reign return from Siberia, a whole crowd of mutes appears: their tongues had been cut out, a common punishment . . . And before Elizabeth? The Tsarina Anne. Condemned men blessed her when beheading with the ax replaced impaling. And Peter the Great? He loved torture, especially with the strappado. Catherine put an end to that madness. And also to the law that legitimized the torturing of children from the age of twelve upward. To push this limit up to the age of seventeen, she has to do battle with the Holy Synod, which, doubtless out of pure Christian charity, was opposed to the change. Similar laws, one might mention in passing, existed in Stalin's time . . ."

Slumped on his chair like a boxer reeling under blows, Oleg realizes that Luria's attacks are no longer aimed at his screenplay. A glance at the "judges": the faces have lost their mocking satisfaction. This Luria, brought in to demolish his screenplay, has ventured outside the role imposed on him. He dares to refer to inventions "by historians for ideological purposes," and goes so far as to compare Peter I with Stalin!

"Of course heads were rolling in other countries as well. You mention the execution of the Frenchman, Damiens, who tried to stab Louis the Fifteenth. The way in which Damiens's body was dismembered, such sophistication by far outstrips the skills of the Russian executioners. As for the Holy Synod advocating the torture of children, let us recall that in 1756 in Mainz, in Germany, two dangerous witches were burned, one aged seven and the other, five: I mention Germany, Catherine's native land. Examples from Spain could be even more illuminating . . ."

Luria puts aside his notebook, seizes a glass, drinks deeply. A clearing of the throats falters out from the jury: several members of the committee are preparing to speak. The historian gives them no time to do so.

"Thanks to Catherine, even humor changes in Russia. Elizabeth, jealous of the beauty of young women, had her own way of handing out compliments: 'Oh what a pretty little neck! How I should love to see it on a block . . .' At Catherine's court such a 'witticism' would have seemed perfectly barbaric."

Oleg guesses at Luria's tactic: to throw the "judges" off balance, in order to be able to continue. No, he's not a pedant intoxicated by his role as a worldly lecturer. He's a man staking his all, grasping the chance to speak freely. And asking himself: "If I don't do it now, faced with these custodians of authorized thought, who will do it? And when?"

"Catherine's *Great Instruction,* the manifesto of her reforms, lays the foundations for a state where human dignity is respected. Twenty years

before the French Revolution the tsarina brings together a legislative
commission where nobles sit alongside peasants. And when one of the
nobles starts denigrating the people's deputies he is made to apologize to
them in public!"

"So, how would it be if we returned to the subject in hand, Comrade
Luria?"

A mixture of restrained anger and benevolent condescension can
be detected in the voice of the president of the jury.

"But we are at the very heart of the subject, Comrade President.
Audiences will find the past evoked by Comrade Erdmann very topical.
Catherine's advocacy of banning torture. The presumption of innocence
imposed on courts. And the freedom of the press? She creates journals
and expresses her opinions in them . . ."

His words provoke an indignant hiss that modulates into the shrill,
nasal tones of one of the young "judges."

"You seem to worship this great humanist. But it was she who
added to the enslavement of the peasants . . ."

Luria picks up the thread, imitating his contradictor's tones:
". . . while being convinced that serfdom ought to be abolished. She
does not dare do it—'the nobles would sooner see me hanged,' she says.
That's not just a figure of speech: her enemies are waiting in the wings.
Catherine signs a decree that confirms the privileges of the nobility. 'But
I wept as I signed it,' she confesses. We shouldn't forget that Catherine
confronts men who make a habit of plotting and killing. Catherine succeeds in taming them . . ."

"Especially in her private alcove . . . ," guffaws the president with
contrived mirth, which the SCCA members join in and amplify.

"Yes, Comrade President, her body was a weapon in the political
struggle, there among the wild beasts. Comrade Erdmann describes these
creatures well. And also the moments when Catherine hopes that she is
loved. Let us now imagine a film that answers this one question: out of
all these men who took advantage of this exceptional woman, was there
a single one who loved her?"

Luria's voice fades. It seems as though he is softly voicing a truth that is new to himself . . . The "judges" hasten to intervene.

"Wait a minute, we're not going to turn this woman who slaughtered peasants into a Madame Bovary!"

"Agreed about the alcove. But there are also all those fabrications you were denouncing, Comrade Luria!"

The historian seems at a loss, too deeply sunk in his own reverie . . . But he quickly bounces back with the energy of a seasoned debater.

"You're quite right to mention the alcove in question. Comrade Erdmann speaks of pulleys raising the mirror up above this love nest. In point of fact it was on runners: the mirror was slid to one side. A little factual error, easily corrected. But as for the 'fabrications' you mention, do they really need to be corrected? For two centuries these legends have been recounted in the history books. Why not film them? Why not show Catherine as our collective awareness sees her: a nymphomaniac who attracts all the officers of her guard to her bed, a jealous woman who does have a serving maid walled in, a vindictive woman who sends her soldiers to rape a rival."

"But wait a minute, Professor! There can be no place in our cinema for the madness of this historically inaccurate perspective!"

The president bangs on the table with both hands: his cuff links emit a brief, forlorn tinkling sound. Luria's smile seems to take this plaintive sound into account.

"I agree about that, Comrade President. Especially as this 'historically inaccurate perspective' includes that notorious horse of hers. Yes, the stallion whose sexual potency was said to have been employed to satisfy the tsarina's vile instincts. Let us congratulate Comrade Erdmann on his restraint in refusing to make use of that fanciful tale . . ."

The SCCA jury, which had so far been under the thumb of the president, erupts into a mixture of laughter, protests, fragments of arguments. The most unbridled are the four graybeards—they chuckle, pull faces, wave their arms about, imitate a stallion pawing the ground. The young Johnny-come-latelies curl their lips in grimaces of disgust.

The others teeter between severity and lewd merriment, trying to spot which way the president's mood will go. The latter utters a dirty old man's guffaw, then tenses up, reprimands the old men, who are now neighing like horses. His voice is heard above the turmoil: "Comrades Luria and Erdmann, I suggest you wait in the corridor!"

Oleg leaves first, the historian joins him, his arms piled high with his notes. The corridor is empty. The noise of the voices on the other side of the door calms down, drowned by the president's ponderous tones. Luria winks at Oleg: "The enemy is disoriented. That's all I could do . . ."

"It's already a great deal . . . There was I, expecting a summary execution!"

"I pounced on minor mistakes, so the jury might focus on them and let politically risky matters through . . . But the most important thing is this hidden subject: a woman surrounded by an army of lovers but who's never been loved. Were you setting your sights on this paradox?"

"No, quite the reverse. I avoided that aspect of it. I was wary of too psychological an interpretation, along the lines of the emotional loneliness of the great ones of this world. I wanted to exaggerate the cynical side of her reign . . ."

"That's what's the stuff of legend: a century of predators, hungry for female flesh and good living, yet sometimes they have a sense that their triumphant lives are a failure and hanker after quite a different life . . ."

The door opens, one of the "judges" comes out into the corridor.

"The committee will need an additional meeting for further consideration. You will be notified, Comrade Erdmann. Good day to you."

Outside Luria heads toward the entrance to a subway station, stops, shakes his hand . . . And suddenly, as if breaking through a barrier, he asks: "Is Sergei Erdmann your father?"

"Yes . . . He died . . . eight years ago."

"We knew one another in 1948, we were in preventive detention. At the time of the struggle against cosmopolitanism . . . Look after yourself now. Maybe we'll meet again. Maybe at the premiere of your film, who knows?"

Back home Oleg rereads the screenplay with new eyes, in Luria's voice. He regrets not having told him about the saying his parents used to repeat at the toughest moments in their lives. "All this, because a little German princess had the mad idea of going to live in Russia!"

Dressmakers are feverishly stitching away at the gown on this monumental body, pricking their fingers, keeping their heads down under the rain of blows the woman hands out. Broad hips, a bulging stomach—the flashing of the needles draws the silks taut, drapes the flesh, squeezes and tapers it, and, finally, phew, manages to achieve a tight fit around this ponderous graven image. The Empress Elizabeth enters the ballroom . . . The courtiers see her scowling—one of the guests has a more elegant coiffure than her own. Quick, a pair of scissors! The unfortunate woman loses her locks and flees in tears . . . After the ball they cut Elizabeth out of her dress, snip through the brocade, tear away the lace. The empress loathes undressing, all those hooks, all that lace, the farthingales . . . The next night there will be another ball and she has chosen the costumes: on this occasion the women are to be attired as men and the men will wear dresses with hoops. Oh, the walking dolls, tripping over their crinolines and the buxom women squeezed into military tunics! She orders the musicians to increase the tempo—the dancers fall over, lie struggling on the floor . . .

Now another costume change: a torturer tears off the Countess Lopukhina's clothes to expose her back to the burning lash of a whip. The skin bursts open, the leather whip becomes soaked in blood, the woman faints, they open her mouth, the torturer seizes her tongue, a blade flashes . . .

And yet another masquerade: young peasants dressed in uniform charge into a field of barley with fixed bayonets and skewer other peasants clad in uniforms of a different color.

The swift succession of these scenes reflects the viewpoint of a girl in her teens poking her nose in everywhere, listening, watching, guessing. Soon she herself will be drawn into this maelstrom of masks: tsarina, rejected wife, adventuress, mother, lover, regicide . . .

"The only thing that's been retained from my script," Oleg often says to himself during the filming, "is the pace of the action." And then at once he recognizes that this way of filming History was the whole point of his scenario. Its energy, its originality. His screenplay has survived. What could be more important?

Six months earlier, in February, the jury had finally given its verdict: the making of the film about Catherine II was entrusted to a seasoned director, Mikhail Kozin. But "Comrade Erdmann" was not forgotten: he was appointed "artistic assistant." "The wolves are fed but the sheep are still alive," his teacher, Bassov, observed. "You've neither won nor lost. No, that's not true. You've won, because Kozin is a heavyweight. A strange guy, you'll see he's easily offended. And he stammers, which makes communication tough. But a good eye, he knows what he's doing . . . And who'd have thought those slugs at the SCCA would have run scared! A spot of support from the Kremlin comes in handy, wouldn't you think?"

In particular this "support" made it possible to start filming in June. "Her f-f-first s-summer in R-r-ussia," said Kozin. For Oleg his trembling lips were painful to watch—yes, Catherine's very first summer in St. Petersburg. It felt as if Kozin were eager to propel the young German girl without delay into the short-lived paradise of white nights.

Curiously enough, his stammer made relationships on the set easier. Kozin said only what was essential. Unable to describe, he showed.

Miming a scene, he left the actors to infuse it with emotions from their own experience.

This art of silence reconciled Oleg to his secondary status: "I could never direct people the way Kozin does!" Bassov's advice came to mind: "Note every detail of his way of working. You're not so far from him in the way you see things. But he can only speak to other people through the camera."

By now, two months after the start of filming, Oleg's notebook is filled with observations, sketches, jottings. The scenes that worked: the dress being cut off Elizabeth, the men in crinolines crawling about on the floor, Lopukhina and her torturer, the battle in a field of barley . . .

The facts are true. Elizabeth owned fifteen thousand dresses. Catherine herself was once knocked over by a male courtier's skirt when dancing. Lopukhina was mutilated, while her fellow accused, Princess Bestuzheva, slipped a cross studded with diamonds into the torturer's hand, thus saving her own tongue. The bayonet charge in a field of barley is a reconstruction of one of the battles in the Seven Years' War . . .

A Swedish diplomat and the young Poniatowski come to the reception given by Catherine and Peter. The tsarina owns a little grey-hound bitch that snarls at the Swede but nuzzles affectionately up to Poniatowski. "Dogs are the most treacherous of creatures," the diplomat hisses into the blushing favorite's ear.

A similar shortcut is taken in filming the trade in bodies organized by Potemkin: he receives a hundred thousand rubles from each new lover he introduces to Catherine. This is precisely the sum each favorite is given by the tsarina as a "gift of welcome." Kozin telescopes the two transactions together: the young man collects his rich pickings and goes straight to hand it over to Potemkin . . .

Oleg notes even more economical details: Catherine arrives in Moscow, her carriage gets bogged down in the mud, the golden onion dome of a church is reflected in a puddle, a pig lazily contemplates the mired carriage . . . Five seconds of action and Catherine's scorn for Moscow is plain for all to see!

The sequence in which Catherine hides under the bed to escape the anger of her lover, Orlov, is equally brief. "I would have made it a comic scene," thinks Oleg. "Kozin shows a terrified woman confronting males equipped by natural selection for killing, violating, and crushing the weak . . ."

This laconic style is the echo of Kozin's shackled voice.

Poniatowski loves Catherine at the risk of rotting in prison! "At the sight of her beauty one forgets the existence of Siberia." A romantic declaration to which Kozin adds three seconds: the lover returns to Europe, and his grand passion is quickly forgotten.

"Having loved you, how could I love another?" Catherine asks Potemkin, in tears. A moment later the camera catches her in the arms of Vassilchikov, the one who has the courage to admit: "I'm simply a kept woman . . ."

It is at this moment in the filming that a little incident occurs. The actor playing Vassilchikov moves off into a gallery in the palace. Kozin is about to speak, he has his eye on one of the dollies. Tongue-tied, he gasps painfully . . . Suddenly the dolly, badly wedged, begins to slide down its track, then stops. "A tracking shot by telepathy," shouts out one of the technical crew. They all have a strong sense of there being "a drama behind the drama"—of a world that underlies the words spoken.

Oleg goes out, toward the ashen-gray Neva, lights a cigarette. The thought is disturbing: a life beyond the games of power and desire they are in process of filming . . .

He hastens to reassure himself: "But of course not! Kozin's going to make a good, realist film, faithful to the Party line. Catherine's marriage to this great oaf, Peter. Her first lovers, coup d'état, the ferment of great reforms. Wars, festivities, debates with Diderot . . . The apotheosis: Catherine in the Crimea. And the decline—the fall of the Bastille, a tsarina in old age, deserted by Mamonov, weeps at a window . . ."

"They've finished for the day, Oleg! Shall we go home? No, first treat me to an ice cream. Kozin said I was brilliant."

Oleg kisses the pretty face from which the makeup has just been removed: Dina—the young Catherine II. Half an hour ago she was hurrying over to a secret alcove, a mirror slid aside, revealing a bed and Vassilchikov, naked . . .

They stop on the Palace Bridge, embrace, Dina's body is as pliant as a growing plant. A body that lends itself to everything the role demands. And when they embrace this suppleness offers a soothing pleasure, a banal sweetness.

"Did you see that dolly moving all on its own? That was a paranormal phenomenon, wasn't it?"

She laughs with light, childish joy. Everything about this shoot is running so smoothly that their meeting seems to be part of the script. The costumes are delivered on time, the sets are skillfully designed, and the young female star falls in love with the "artistic assistant." All that is needed now is for Kozin to become infatuated with the tsarina *number two*, the "older" Catherine! A handsome couple they'd make: this bear with his stammer and the East German actress who will soon be coming to Leningrad . . .

They walk around the Peter and Paul Fortress, sit down in a café. Dina heaves a comical sigh: "I don't want to put you off your food, but all my lovers smell really bad. Especially Poniatowski. He's the fattest and, what's more, Kozin wants him to wear a lot of things made of fur. Apparently he was an aristocrat terrified of the tiniest draft. Talk about the prince and the pea! And I have to put up with his emanations . . ."

Outside the window the fortress wall can be seen and the bluish expanse above the Neva, lit by a shaft of light . . . A few months ago Oleg's life had been this frozen river, rare meetings with Lessya, sadness, shame. Now, there is this young woman who loves him, the filming, the work with Kozin. An aura of being on vacation. The buoyancy of a life waiting to be explored.

Dina holds out her hand to him, draws him to her. He lets it happen, going along with the sweetness of these human games. At twenty-eight he finally feels he has understood that not loving too much may be a form of wisdom.

In Dina's expression he recognizes the smile with which the young Catherine, in love, greeted Vassilchikov.

Little model soldiers, made of starch, parade across the salon floor. A man kneeling on all fours lines up the regiments, whistles to imitate gunfire . . . A valet enters, announces that dinner is served. Reluctantly the man abandons his game, goes out. And in the salon where the wax from a candle is dripping onto the floor, a rat appears—monstrous by comparison with the size of the little soldiers . . . The scene changes brutally and the tiny figures are being trampled under the boots of giants. Killers hurl themselves at the man we have seen playing his game of soldiers . . .

It was Oleg who had suggested this way of filming Peter's murder. "An artistic assistant can have his uses," he jokes at intervals. Kozin nods in agreement: "S-s-spare w-wheels are the b-b-best."

Another suggestion: Cagliostro. "So much has been written about the elixirs of youth the old rogue used to dispense to the women of St. Petersburg. Why not film Princess Golitsyn's baby instead? The child has just died, Cagliostro carries off the body, and two weeks later the baby is brought back to life! The parents are overjoyed and it is only the child's nurse, an illiterate peasant, who denounces the substitution. She's the only one who's truly fond of this other child."

Oleg has learned Kozin's silent language. He knows its syntax! A whole scene "compressed" in a single detail . . . Catherine gives herself to Grigory Orlov (a dull reflection in a mirror) and, reflected in another mirror, Peter III, with his throat crushed beneath the boot of Aleksey Orlov, Grigory's brother . . .

Kozin has a special gesture of his own to show that a solution pleases him: in one hand he grips an imaginary needle, with the other he slips a thread through the eye. "You've scored a bull's-eye!" he would have said, but, with his halting words, that would take too long.

It feels as if, for Kozin, this film is an exam retake, following an error for which he must earn a pardon. The censors will be lying in wait for him at every turn, especially in the scenes depicting the tsarina's sexual life. Oleg remembers that, according to one biography, the walls of Catherine's vaulted recess were covered in licentious miniatures: nymphs and satyrs in suggestive poses, copulating dancers. Why not film these, instead of the sex scenes, which will, in any case, be censored? Kozin thinks for a moment, then his hands go up. A thread, a needle's eye!

Alcohol liberates Kozin from his stammer. One evening in August he and Oleg are in a restaurant—"to take stock, on reaching the halfway mark." Soon "the young Catherine" (Dina, who has aged on film by thirty years) will pass the baton to Eva Sander, the East German actress who will play the tsarina in her declining years . . . Kozin is now on his fourth glass.

"So that's it, Erdmann. You'll have no more need to be jealous of all those lovers groping Dina . . . Your erotic miniatures have already made her task a lot easier. Just imagine if all those bareback circus tricks had to be acted out for real! And *circus tricks* is the operative word. Apparently the tsarina once fancied a stallion . . . Well, I know it's only gossip. But it speaks volumes about the contempt men feel for women like her! You see, I want to defend her . . ."

Kozin casts furtive glances around him, a vigilance that is second nature to him: on the telephone, in a restaurant, and even when talking to close friends . . .

"I'm not going to put her on a pedestal," he goes on. "It just needs to be shown that she wasn't a pathological nymphomaniac, or totally obsessed with power. Of course the old crocodiles on the SCCA will cut to ribbons anything that goes beyond the official portrait. If it comes to the crunch they'll put up with her bare backside, but not the revolutionary aspects of her reign. Look, she created the House of Education—where any child of a serf, once accepted as a pupil, becomes free. She can't abolish slavery, so she adopts an oblique maneuver. The peasants know that a means of becoming free exists. And that's what is crucial! How can we say this without bringing the crocodiles paddling out of their backwater?"

Kozin drinks slowly, he looks relaxed: he has just revealed the very basis of his thinking and the burden of suspicion falls away. "In our country," thinks Oleg, "rehabilitating Catherine the Second is a subversive enterprise, and one that marks you as a dissident!"

He says this out loud and it is like the password Kozin has been waiting for. If one of them is hiding what his real game is, so be it. When sharing confidences everyone takes the risk of being denounced. The two of them are banking on sincerity.

"Let's copy Luria!" Oleg spells it out, referring to the historian who defied the SCCA. "Let's imitate his method. A flash of truth—the House of Education where slaves become free—and then, immediately after that, a politically unassailable scene. A country landowner reading this advertisement: 'For Sale one light carriage (new) and one female serf, aged twenty . . .'"

"So you mean the crocodiles' suspicions will be lulled by this reminder of the harsh realities of feudal life? The sale of a surrey and a young woman, bundled together in the same lot . . ."

As Kozin says this he makes his gesture of approval: a thread in the eye of a needle.

"And what do we do with the scene where Catherine talks about her *Great Instruction*? A text so in advance of its time that its publication was banned in France. They'll never let us show that."

"We'll tell a story, like Luria did. You film a courtier reciting some verse ponderous enough to put your jaw out of joint. At Catherine's court they made up for lack of taste by declaiming one of Tredyakovsky's poems, clumsy imitations of the classical French poets . . ."

They laugh, picturing Dina, first of all serious and passionate, her manifesto of reforms in her hand ("Rulers should serve the people and not submit them to their whims")—then in a lighthearted mood, smiling, as she listens to the versified mumblings haltingly recited by a sweating courtier.

Kozin pours more wine for himself, then sighs, as if what he now puts to Oleg is a challenge beyond their powers: "Right, we're going to rescue Catherine. But Potemkin? He's a lost cause, isn't he? A tyrant, a crook, an erotomaniac, a warmonger . . . And what's more, a Cyclops. The Orlov brothers put out one of his eyes in a brawl. Such a male-dominated world for our little Cathy, coming from her fairy-tale principality . . . So how about it?"

Oleg draws out his notebook.

"I've got someone to speak up for him: the prince de Ligne. Listen to this: 'Potemkin is the most remarkable man I have ever set eyes on . . . Lazy, but he works incessantly . . . Melancholy in his pleasures, unhappy by dint of being happy, blasé about everything, quickly losing patience with things, morose, inconstant, a profound philosopher, an able minister, a brilliant politician, as thoughtless as a ten-year-old boy, fabulously rich, but without a penny to his name, holding forth about theology to his generals and strategy to his archbishops, never reading, but learning from those he talks to, greedy as a child for everything and, like a great man, capable of doing without anything. What was his secret? Genius, genius, and yet more genius!'"

Kozin waves his glass in the air.

"He hit the nail on the head, the prince de Ligne. That's Potemkin, the whole man, before all those carrion-feeding biographers could chop him up into a thousand little Potemkins, miserly, capricious, boastful, and lecherous. A man's not a man unless he's complex. And if you try to simplify him, you end up idiotically classifying everyone either as good citizens or as enemies of the people . . . I once wanted to do a film about one of these complex characters, a central Asian Party boss. They quickly gagged me! And since then the jailers at the SCCA have kept me . . . Well, I'll tell you about that some other time. But as for Potemkin . . . He was after something apart from riches and power. He owned as much land as all the kings of Europe. The festivities at his Tauride Palace outshone Versailles. Tropical gardens beneath the northern sky, Venetian gondolas, vessels his mistresses dipped into for diamonds. He gave the Crimea to Catherine as a birthday present . . . And he died out in the middle of a steppe—without so much as two kopecks in his pockets to close his eyes with! His genius was to reach the very top by triumphing at all the appallingly complicated games that make up the farce of human existence, and, at the end, to become infinitely simple—a man lying on a bare plain beneath an autumn sky . . ."

He has been speaking too loudly, so Oleg can hear him above the noise of the restaurant. People are turning to stare, mocking or disapproving. Oleg quickly proposes a sotto voce toast: "Well then, here's to Potemkin."

Kozin drinks, absentminded, his face torn this way and that as images arise and fade in his mind. Then he concludes: "All that our cinematographic watchdogs will allow him is his debauchery and his great despot's ugly mug. Oh, and the Potemkin villages, of course! We'll have to throw him to the wolves. Even your Luria couldn't help us here . . ."

"Luria would talk about Petushkov . . ."

"And who's that?"

"A young master sergeant, who one day needed to get Potemkin's signature. A crowd of notables has been waiting in the prince's antechamber for hours. Potemkin is sunk in one of the moods of black depression that follow his excesses. He's lounging about in a dressing gown, gloomy and unshaven, refusing to attend to affairs of state. Petushkov, bold to the point of recklessness, jostles ministers, thrusts aside footmen, goes straight up to the prince, introduces himself, holds out all the papers for him to sign. Astounded by so much impudence, Potemkin remains silent. He hesitates, then picks up the pen . . . Petushkov returns to the antechamber in triumph. 'He's done it!' Everyone crowds round to see the princely signatures . . . And there's a Homeric outburst of laughter! All the documents have been signed the same: 'Petushkov,' 'Petushkov,' 'Petushkov' . . ."

They leave the restaurant with a shared sense, both gleeful and in earnest, that they are up against an invisible machine, one that watches over every word in their country.

"Nowadays they'd send Catherine to the gulag," murmurs Kozin as he shakes Oleg's hand.

The night wind brings with it the scent of cold granite and the sea close at hand. Their drunkenness dissipates, giving way to intoxication with the ideas their film will defend.

At home, already in bed, Dina is studying her part. "It's the last day for me tomorrow," she tells him. "In the script I'm fifty now and I'm due to ditch a faithless lover, that pig, Korsakov!"

Oleg falls asleep unable to banish a smile from his lips: close against him, the empress is already snoring softly.

Their bodies can be made out through the steam. In the Moorish baths the suitor, the young Korsakov, is being put through his paces by Countess Bruce, "her ladyship, the tester," as Catherine calls her. He is tall, strong, has shoulders bulging with muscles. The countess, a slender beauty, gains from this contrast. Dark and petite with the build of a gymnast, slim thighs, breasts firm and round. Her hair is tied back, an amber necklace sets off her olive skin.

Historical facts: Countess Bruce used to test the candidates' sexual vigor. Without being able to allow herself the least deviation . . . The actress achieves an ambiguous performance between seduction and refusal. She offers herself, lets herself be embraced then shies away. Suddenly her attitude changes: she continues to expose her flesh as bait, to simper, to grip the applicant's penis, gauging its strength . . . Their bodies continue with these restrained exercises, while the looks they exchange are lit up by tender and pained expressions . . . Finally the action breaks off, as if they had just discovered a hidden meaning in their nakedness, in their embraces . . .

Filming resumes: Korsakov becomes Countess Bruce's lover. Catherine, informed by Potemkin's spies, conceals her anger beneath mocking disdain, banishes the lovers to Moscow. All they are fit for is to rot in the Asiatic tedium of the former capital.

Kozin bullies Dina, makes her perform the scene of the deceived empress over and over again. Catherine learning of the betrayal: "That young man thinks he's a sultan . . ." Being left alone, as her favorite's carriage drives off beside the Neva and disappears . . . At the umpteenth take Dina is at her breaking point. Oleg is angry with Kozin, for her performance is excellent: jealousy, bitterness, hatred changing into contempt. What more could one imagine? Dina's lips tremble, a drop of moisture glistens on her eyelashes . . . Kozin nods. Catherine has just become the very way he imagined her.

That night Oleg catches Dina weeping in her sleep. She who's forever laughing and joking . . . A young woman who has aged thirty years over two months of filming. And whom he has continued to love from one age to the next.

"Better still, I've loved a Catherine more true than the real thing. Art is a concentration of reality. That was Maxim Gorky's dictum: in a novel steel is steelier than in real life. Yes, Dina has been more Catherine than the tsarina herself!"

He smiles, surveys her profile with its lightly rounded brow. Dina's breathing becomes plaintive. He slips his hand into the young woman's hair—her bad dream will be banished by the arrival of a fearless knight on horseback . . .

This is how actors inspire intensely real dreams in us. Take the actor who plays Potemkin. He travels to the film set on the subway, smoking cheap cigarettes and then, under the camera's eye, is transformed into an arrogant lord, a blasé lover. At every moment of his performance he is the essence of Potemkin. We are all much more complex than the little selves we cling to. And actors' selves have the ability to migrate from one character to another. Hence the egocentricity of artists. They are uncertain of their own identity . . .

The power of this "steelier than steel" in art also applies to the laconic verbal exchanges Kozin requires in the film. Grigory Orlov wants to compel Catherine to marry him. He is the one who put her on the throne! The tsarina knows that, once married, she would lose all her power. In the end Orlov obliges her to submit the marriage plan to the Council of State. The chancellor, Count Nikita Panin, rises to his feet and firmly declares: "The empress is free to marry Prince Orlov. But Lady Orlov will never be our empress." He tilts his head proudly back and his wig leaves a trace of powder on the wooden paneling of the wall. A member of the council goes up to it and presses his brow against this patch of white. The others do the same, as if pledging an oath.

If History can be acted out in this way, does it have the weighty import that is attributed to it? Maybe it is no more than a stage set, upon which wars, conspiracies, dramas of love, the marriages of tsars, and the fading of glory are all played out.

The next day their filming marks time: the East German actress has been delayed in Berlin. ("I expect she's having drinks with Marlon Brando," they joke on the set.) While they are waiting a decision is made to "let the kids do their scene"—Alexander and Constantine, Catherine's grand-sons. The tsarina made little overalls for them herself. Kozin wants to show her wielding a needle.

The actors feel as if they are having a day out in the country and the setting lends itself to this: they are a long way from Leningrad in a wing of the Peterhof Palace, surrounded by its great park. The weather is still summery, all these princes and ministers abandon their wigs and go for a swim in the Gulf of Finland. "It's all right, Kozin. If your Marlene Dietrich does show up we'll be back by the time she's got her makeup on."

The filming has a "summer camp" aspect to it: the cast have been bused out there, actors squabbling like kids, lost costumes, hilarious mistakes—like the eye patch that one-eyed Potemkin accidentally some-times wears over his left eye, sometimes over his right . . .

Dina stops by to take her leave of the cast. Kozin has a word with her about some scenes that need to be shot again, just three very short sequences. "Oh sure, don't tell me. The three Russo-Turkish wars!" she says, with a laugh. For her filming is really over and this departure of the "young Catherine" adds to the end-of-term feeling.

"Why don't we go for a boat trip? Right now, like tourists!"

Oleg was thinking of taking the train back to Leningrad, but Dina carries him off. They run toward the jetty and catch the last ferry of the day. On the deck there is just a small group of senior citizens, all agog with having caught a distant view of a film being shot: "There were aristocrats from past times in costumes embroidered with gold!"

The boat passes a beach where the "aristocrats from past times" are now splashing about.

"History, as a film set," Oleg says to himself, recalling those images that once flashed through his mind at night. He feels an urge to explain this to Dina, to bring her out of her reckless childishness.

"They should mount the camera on this boat," she murmurs. "It's all a ready-made film set . . ." She was the first to say it, as if already sensing what he was about to say to her. "And look, that's a movie too. Well, a totally crazy film . . ."

On the far shore a vast industrial building ornamented with neon letters: "The Party's plans are the people's plans!"

Dina laughs, Oleg tentatively follows suit. No, she's not the rather foolish young woman he has always, feeling vaguely superior, imagined her to be.

"But if that's an illusion, Dina, what's the point of the films we make? And the part you're playing as Catherine? Is all that just more fooling around?"

She smiles, affectionately contrite.

"No . . . But when you're an actor you've got to give a good performance of this phony world . . ."

"Right, ape all the Potemkins and Orlovs who act at being great men. Act the tsarina who acted at being the Semiramis of the North . . ."

With a brisk movement, Dina gives him a little slap on the forehead.

"Excuse me. I was just killing a mosquito . . . Yes, you're right . . . Except that if the actors manage to get right inside these phony characters, we can then see what lies beyond them . . ."

"But what is this mysterious 'beyond'? Does Catherine belong on a shrink's couch? I don't get it . . ."

These questions come to him out of pique at having allowed Dina to say something he had been unable to put into words himself. She answers him in tones of unaccustomed melancholy.

"It was just a way of showing where the frontier lies. Our lives, this film, that neon sign on the building over there . . . And beyond all this . . . A September evening, this last boat of the day . . . Imagine a woman walking beside the sea, over there beneath the trees. She's alone. She's looking at the gray skyline of the Baltic here. She's the empress of an immense country, but she's also quite simply a woman who's just been abandoned by a man. A woman who, at this moment . . ."

The siren of a liner sailing up the Neva sounds with deafening force. Dina's words are drowned out, the truth her lips are speaking is obliterated.

The café where she takes him is decorated with life preservers and model ships—the harbor is not far away. They order cocktails that have maritime names, too: a "Caribbean," an "Arctic" . . . in fact, they are vodka colored with liqueurs . . . "To kid us we are out at sea . . . ," murmurs Dina, and they laugh, happy to have regained their carefree mood.

Between two outbursts of laughter his girlfriend confides, with a pained smile: "I'm sick of all the dreary ideas our egghead friends are always brooding on. They hate the old bastards who run the country, that's understandable—the censorship, the police everywhere. But the upshot is they become even more boring than the Politburo! They're preaching against the regime, but they're still preaching . . . I just want to relax without having to think too much. And if that's an illusion, too bad! . . . Here's to you and to the end of my hard labor! Do you think it was fun playing Catherine the way Kozin fantasized her?"

They drink, kiss, remain for a moment with their brows touching. Oleg has removed his glasses and with his myopic vision he makes out the tiny wrinkles on this well-loved face. Dina pulls away, smiles: "I haven't got my lovely tsarina's makeup on any longer . . ."

That night, making love, they are as lighthearted as actors going mad after the end of filming. Dina is in her element—a life lived as a masked ball, all teasing and frivolity. "Hold on, let me show you Catherine giving herself to Orlov. Ah, ah . . ." She hurls herself at Oleg, feigning an erotic swoon. "And now, with Potemkin . . ."

By the end of it this sexual exuberance becomes a little strained. Dina falls asleep in the middle of a caress, a caress that Oleg, wearily, feels obliged to prolong. This sad, empty feeling is due, Oleg prefers to believe, to their earlier debate: illusion, truth, the impossibility of being understood. His whole childhood was spent in the shadow of that distressing fantasy, the model his father continued to construct in the hope of who knows what revelation . . .

Dina groans, wakes up, apologizes.

"I was in a palace. Walking along corridors, opening doors . . . There were great bay windows, lots of light . . . And no way out! It was terrible . . . Ever since we started filming I haven't been able to get this idea out of my head. She was never able to escape! Yes, she traveled around, down the Volga and in the Crimea. But Catherine never left Russia. She remained in her empire, as if it was a prison. Her courtiers would write to her from Paris, from Rome, from Venice . . . But I just can't picture her walking in the streets of a little Italian town one morning. And what's more, no man ever did suggest escaping to her . . ."

The first morning of frost has transformed the park. Oleg has come ahead of the rest of the crew before the day dawned, and this cold whiteness hypnotizes him—how, beneath the hoarfrost, will they get their bearings, recognize the groves, the pathways, the streams?

The previous day Kozin had asked him to prepare the shots they were going to film—the scenes they would now be planning to shoot, given that the East German actress, the "older Catherine," has still not arrived. The task seemed a simple one: to select places where the tsarina's grandsons, Alexander and Constantine, now several years older, used to play, go fishing with nets, cut down trees . . .

He had pictured them under a summer sun—now it is hard to imagine them running around on these frozen slopes. Two princes educated according to the philosophical precepts of the century, little Voltaireans in a Rousseauistic setting. Alexander is destined to shine as an enlightened monarch. Constantine (a prophetic name) will occupy the throne of Constantinople: as a child he had a Greek nurse, so that, along with her milk, he might imbibe the great Byzantine dream. Meanwhile they are two restless little boys who speak a mixture of Russian and French, have a passion for military parades, and play with their exuberant grandmother's favorite.

This white morning keeps Oleg from thinking about their lively games and the sounds of laughter . . . He reflects on the courses taken by the lives of the two children. Alexander: a dreamy adolescent, a young man teeming with humanistic plans for his empire, but also the betrayer, who will let the conspirators kill his father, Paul I, in 1801. War against Napoleon, defeats, Moscow burned, victories, Paris conquered by the Cossacks, a life overloaded with romantic adventures and undermined by feelings of guilt toward the father he did not seek to save. Constantine: a spoiled child who becomes a capricious brute and a contemptuous despot. Drunken orgies, both soldiers and civilians beaten up, rapes, murders . . .

"So what was the point of it all?" Oleg catches himself whispering the question. Two little boys at play, two adolescent dreamers, two men who wage wars, lie, betray, kill . . . And then, nothing more. This silvered plain, the gold of the leaves beneath the ice, the mist of his breath. Nothing more. "What was the point of it all?"

In the distance, beneath a row of old trees, a dark smudge, hazy at first, then slipping into the rhythm of a figure walking. A workman, to judge from his blue overalls, a plumber coming to protect the fountains against the frost. Or rather a female worker, her hair loosely plaited into a braid, a bag carried on her shoulder, blue overalls . . . No, they are jeans, a jacket, and a scarf around her neck. A tourist who's lost her way?

The woman approaches him, smiles, a little embarrassed. "I'm looking for Mikhail Kozin . . . Or someone from his crew. I have reached Peterhof, haven't I?"

The accent is noticeable—there is a muted hardness about the consonants. But the great surprise is that the stranger's name ("I'm Eva Sander," she introduces herself) does not tally at all with the person they were expecting. The "older" Catherine II . . . The actors had pictured a star arriving in a private jet, bombarded by flash photographers . . . They had dreamed up a variety of mocking explanations for the delay: "Her plane was diverted to the Seychelles . . . A Hollywood studio's just asked her to play Cleopatra . . ."

But now here is this woman. A pale, slightly angular face, big gray eyes in which the white of the trees and the sky's dull light are reflected.

He explains the situation. Behind their conversation, the language whose echoes he detects in Eva's words strikes deep chords within him. German, which, in his infancy, he heard his mother speaking, or rather singing, at his bedside.

"I can speak German, if you like," he suggests.

She laughs softly: "I mustn't forget my Russian. Catherine made such efforts to learn it . . . Would you like some coffee? I have a thermos . . ."

They walk through the park. The silence is evocative of an evening in winter. As the path turns a corner Oleg notices a foreign car whose gray color, overlaid with hoarfrost, is reminiscent of worn velvet. He recalls having seen a station wagon of this type in a film from the sixties. They climb into it as if they were about to drive off. Eva leaves the door open. The smell of coffee mingles with the bitterness of the air . . .

"It's not as strong as Catherine's," she says. "One of her favorites, who wanted a sip of her brew, had a fainting fit. But take care, all the same. This coffee's been keeping me awake all through the night . . ."

She smiles and her eyes betray traces of the weariness of that night and the reflection of a road stretching to infinity in the glow of headlights.

"You've come from Berlin?"

Believing he knows the answer, Oleg feels foolish at not managing to avoid such a trite question.

"No . . . I've been in Italy. I thought I'd be here on time for the filming, but one always underestimates the vigilance of the customs officers in our fellow socialist countries. At the Polish frontier it took long enough. But then, gaining access to Soviet territory . . . I guess I should have worked in a James Bond movie first!"

For people living on their side of the Berlin Wall humor serves as a password.

A minibus carrying the most senior of the actors from Leningrad arrives at the entrance to the park, all the "doddering dignitaries," as Dina calls them. And a few of the dowagers, who, in the film, like museum exhibits, represent the last remnants of the era of Peter the Great. One of them is stepping down painfully, supported by Kozin.

"I hope your director hasn't replaced me as Catherine by that lady. Good, I'll go and make my incompetent motorist's excuses to him. Men like hearing that women are hopeless drivers . . ."

They go to meet the others and very soon, as if through the drowsiness that is catching up with her, Eva softly observes: "On a frosty day like this the tsarina should be left to quietly stitch overalls for her grandchildren."

That first encounter brings together everything that he will observe during the filming when Eva Sander is on the set. She will remain simple, with very little of the star about her, even vaguely disappointing the actors, who had pictured her sitting next to a Hollywood hero in a limousine! Hidden beneath the energy of her performance, Oleg will perceive a certain detachment, moments when, though present, she is far away. He alone will be able to see her again as that unknown woman walking along beneath the trees white with hoarfrost.

The aspirant Mamonov is instructed by Potemkin to hand a watercolor painting to Catherine: a pastoral landscape. He brings back an ambiguous verdict. "Design pretty, but coloration mediocre," is what the empress has written on the verso of the sheet of paper. This Mamonov, a Kalmuck of Asian origin, has yellowish skin. Potemkin is preparing to look for another man when Catherine comes to reassure him: the design (his muscles, his physical vigor . . .) is exceptional, so let's forget the "coloration," that Asiatic flesh tint.

Oleg has checked: several historical accounts confirm the trick with the watercolor.

It is the first scene in which Eva Sander has acted. The minimal style she deploys is highly professional. "Economy of gesture," notes Oleg. "Vocal effects under control. Instead of the lasciviousness of a debauched old woman, just the flaring of her nostrils, a she-wolf scenting her prey . . ."

Two or three times Kozin repeats his sign of approval: a thread in the eye of a needle. Then he abandons the gesture. Eva gives the impression that she is not so much playing a part as recounting an experience of her own. Often she suggests filming a sequence again when she is unhappy with a detail, or when another actor has not won her "needle and thread."

Oleg tries to translate into words of admiration what Kozin would express if he were not tongue-tied. "Gorky would have spoken of 'steely steel.' Well, you are a Catherine to the power of ten!"

Eva replies coolly: "I'm just Catherine as you imagined her. I'm simply playing that Catherine."

He had chosen a bad moment: they are about to film the tsarina going into the alcove where Mamonov awaits her—a body overwhelmingly brutal in its maleness. Their embrace is paced by the dancing of the erotic miniatures on the walls. The breathing of the lovers blends in with a voice-over—one of Catherine's letters in which she speaks about Mamonov: " . . . a most excellent heart, combined with a richly courteous spirit . . . admirably educated . . . with a great penchant for poetry . . ." The man's thick arms can be seen, straining fiercely, the ugly strength of them. And a woman, this aged Catherine, offering her body—a body still beautiful but palpably frail—to a young lover, somewhat crude in the way he possesses her, bending her to his pleasure, thrusting her aside after the climax.

The scene is clear (sex and power) and yet this new Catherine, even more than before, looks like a woman still hoping to be loved . . .

Absorbed by this notion, Oleg fails to notice Eva leaving the set and coming toward him. She seems to regret her curt tone just now. "It's a very good idea, those frescoes in the alcove! They spared me from having to sumo wrestle with Mamonov. Marilyn's partner in *Some Like It Hot* used to say smothering her in kisses was a real chore, comparable to kissing Hitler. With Mamonov, given his elephantine build, I think it might be more like Hermann Goering . . . I've been rereading the script. Especially your marginal notes. It's incredible what you know about St. Petersburg! There are two or three places I'd really like to take a look at . . ."

Their wanderings swiftly take them away from the center of the city. Eva seems more interested in remote districts that were covered in forest in Catherine II's time. Oleg leads her there with very little notion of what

she finds fascinating about all the industrial buildings and canals pol-
luted with hydrocarbons.

One evening in the north of the city, they find themselves in a network of roads and railroad tracks that he knows well—that mountain
crag of an apartment building from his childhood is not far away.

"This is an odd itinerary for a tourist," he remarks. "If you were
from West Germany the KGB would soon be on our tail. They've made
plenty of films here around that theme: a woman from the West who
claims to be a lover of Russian architecture and is seen prowling around
the gates of an arms factory . . ."

She smiles and turns up her jacket collar to look like a secret agent.

"Yes, I know . . . I had a part in a film like that when I was young.
A factory worker who caught an engineer, a traitor to the socialist fatherland, in the act of photographing a top-secret thingamajig made in
their factory . . ."

"OK, but, as we don't have a camera . . ."

"My father had one when he came over here."

"Your father? In Leningrad?"

Eva starts walking more quickly, looking as if she really did want
to throw any surveillance off the scent. Her voice becomes impersonal.
Suddenly Oleg realizes she is speaking in German.

"During the war my father spent two years doing aerial reconnaissance above Leningrad. He was not a pilot, he was a photographer. Using
his intelligence the Luftwaffe bombed the city . . . At the end of 1943
he was taken prisoner by a Soviet unit. He was employed as a builder on
the construction sites in the city he had been observing from his plane.
When he was finally released he settled in East Germany, in Rostock,
where he was born. His conscience was clear: he had not taken part in
any massacres. His work as a photographer had been clean, technical . . .
He went back to the same trade after his return and, up to his retirement,
he took countless pictures that were useful for the country's industry.
When I was young I turned this father of mine into a cross between

Adolf Hitler and one of those German shepherd dogs. Our generation needed these symbolic scapegoats . . . When I confronted him angrily he always remained calm. 'I was a soldier. I obeyed orders. I didn't kill anyone. And I worked for four years rebuilding Russian cities. I spent my life working for the good of the German Democratic Republic . . .' He was the worst caricature of a German: a robot taking orders from other robots . . . A year before his death we became closer. He was ill and his second wife, who was younger than him, had left him. For some time now I had stopped regarding him as a war criminal. He was the one who brought up this past again. 'You were right, I was a robot . . . But one day I . . . I did fail to obey orders. I'd observed a railroad junction from my plane. Trains being boarded by children and old people. As sure as anything, they were being evacuated. It was my duty to photograph the spot, but I didn't do it. And they didn't bomb the place . . . You know, I've never been back into the Soviet Union, but I'd really like to take another look at that district.'"

They scramble across the railroad track, walk beside a canal. Eva smiles: "Now you know the object of my espionage . . ."

Five minutes later they are climbing up into the attic of the crag-building. It is a clear evening and through the transom of the garret there is a good view of the station building, the storage yards, the trains at a standstill . . . Eva spends a long time studying this bleak location, which has the look of an old black-and-white photograph. Then she turns toward the model of the palace that occupies a good third of the room . . .

Oleg begins talking in German about that former life of his and discovers that it no longer chokes him with pain at every word.

In the days that follow, they resume their excursions after filming, now going back to the city as Catherine saw it and whose construction she, to a great extent, initiated. A St. Petersburg that the eye must extricate from the later architectural strata—as one chips out crystals from within a layer of rock . . . This crystallized deposit of the eighteenth century is

well known to Eva. Oleg is even introduced to several new "mysteries of
St. Petersburg," as she calls them with a smile. "At number nine, that's
Prince Naryshkin's house. That's where Diderot stayed . . ."

But what is truly mysterious is simply to pause at one of these
spots, unmindful of the glamour of History, only aware, as they are now,
of the coppery autumn light glinting on the granite of the little Swan
Canal and the buildings that look uninhabited. To linger there, no longer
thinking about the empress, just picturing the woman crossing this foot-
bridge, two centuries ago, on a cool, luminous October evening, suffused
with the sharp tang of the Baltic.

"It's a good thing she's old enough to be your mother, otherwise I'd die of
jealousy!" Dina pulls a face, acting the part of a tragic actress tormented
by the pangs of love betrayed. Then she bursts out laughing. "Besides,
that Sander woman is too fat. She's like an old opera singer. Actually,
no, I'm talking nonsense. After all, she's only thirty-nine. And in any
case, she's meant to be well padded. Catherine filled out a lot toward the
end of her life. When she was young the tsarina was like me: wasp waist,
lily-white complexion. I remember reading that when she got to Russia
she made fun of the Empress Elizabeth: 'Her bosoms spill over the edges
of the coins she's engraved on.' Except that, as she grew older, Catherine
caught up with her . . ."

A month earlier Dina had been offered the leading role in a stage
play, that of a young revolutionary infuriated by her comrades' cowardice. A fiery, ferocious character—and this now rubs off on Dina. Even
in their private moments she continues speaking in the tones of her part.
The way she takes off her blouse has changed—this is how you bare
your breast to a firing squad. Oleg sometimes feels he is making love to
an unknown woman . . . And once more he is struck to notice how easily
life and performance blend into one another, creating an intermediary
world in which everyone is acting out the role of themselves, while at the
same time cribbing from their fellow human beings.

He talks about this one day to Eva . . . She has just finished filming the party thrown by Potemkin at his Tauride Palace in April 1791. Gondolas, gardens like paradise, three thousand guests, silks, gold, jewels. The prince's hat is overloaded with diamonds—Potemkin sheds it and his footman proceeds, bearing this weighty headgear aloft, like a reliquary. In a few months' time Potemkin will die. His hypersensitive intuition warns him of this. At the height of the festivities he bursts into tears, kneels at the feet of the tsarina—she who has made him into more than a tsar, she, whom he had made into Catherine the Great . . .

That evening Oleg meets Eva again. Caught in the rain, they take refuge in a café, "a real Soviet café," she remarks, finding the poverty of the district touching, very different from the restaurants on the Nevsky Prospekt. They talk about the dishes Potemkin's guests gorged themselves on and about his weeping fit. "Pure histrionics!" Oleg insists. "Unconscious histrionics that became second nature to him!" replies Eva. "Where do the Russians get this passion for acting from?"

In Eva's tones Oleg notices a tentative distancing: on the one hand the Russians, on the other, herself and him, the Germans. He tries to smooth over this distinction.

"A love of acting isn't an exclusively Russian foible . . . At Catherine's court everyone wrote plays. And everyone acted in them: Poniatowski, Orlov, Ségur . . . France infected the Russians with the alexandrines of her verse drama. The tsarina herself composed several stage plays. No longer any boundary between living and acting out a life. After all, Potemkin tried out every possible role: tycoon, monk, libertine, student of sacred texts, pimp, writer of delicate love letters . . . And as for Pugachev, that true Cossack and fake Peter the Third, that was some performance!"

"Yes . . . But why this desire to change your identity the whole time?"

"I've studied the language Catherine uses . . . What's astonishing is how often she used the word *theater*." For her everything was theater: diplomacy, wars, the airs and graces of her courtiers . . . And even love. A drama acted out by her lovers . . ."

"So, was there nothing beyond this playacting?"

They feel as if they have come within a hair's breadth of a truth much deeper than the mysteries of a particular reign. Oleg remembers the threshold he had already come close to when talking to Lessya. "Film what Catherine was not," she had said. And that remark of Dina's too: picture Catherine walking along in the streets of a town in Italy . . .

He now says this to Eva, getting into a bit of a muddle, translating the odd word into German.

"Kozin has always stressed this drama behind the drama. The bacchanalia of Catherine and her favorites, the bombastic farce of History, the antics of fashionable society, and suddenly, extreme simplicity, humanity naked beneath the sky . . . And, above all, the fact that you just cannot simulate love!"

"But wait a minute, Oleg. You said that for the tsarina love was simply a theatrical performance."

"Yes, a drama she acts in and applauds at the same time: I love and I am loved! Age will make her more humble, she will often quote Louis the Fourteenth, who wrote to Madame de Maintenon: 'Love me or, at least, act as if you loved me . . .' Catherine's whole life took place in this 'as if.'"

"So, no man ever loved her?"

Mentally Oleg runs through the list of favorites.

"No . . . At least not any of the ones who'll be seen in the film . . . Passionate declarations, fine erotic performances, but nothing that might go beyond such playacting."

Eva speaks softly, perhaps afraid the sound of her voice might distort the truth that suddenly seems so clear to her: "She lived up to the limits of the games humans play, at the peak of what you and I can imagine in terms of power, riches, sexual pleasure. These limits were her daily fare. So she must certainly have wanted to go beyond them and . . ."

"Escape!"

They say it as one. To exclude the noise in the room they have drawn closer—the consistency of the space between them, now restricted, has changed: it has the density of a shared revelation.

Years later all Oleg will retain of this is the memory of an intimacy being born. He will even know why, that evening, this affection did not find expression. "I was still with Dina. And after all, Eva Sander was a star. And there was the difference in our ages . . ." Circumspect reasoning of the kind men console themselves with when they have missed an essential opportunity. And yet it will suffice for him to encounter some echo of that time (yes, that autumn light on the granite beside the little Swan Canal) to relive the immediacy of the perception that united them at that moment. "Escape!"

What also keeps the two of them from growing any closer is a fit of madness that overcomes Kozin—his sudden decision to change the ending of the film. The working script shows the elderly empress in tears: her favorite, Mamonov, has just left her . . . And then the Bastille falls! A panoramic shot: the smoke of the explosions, a crowd of prisoners liberated . . . Kozin calls this version "a barrel of lies in a drop of truth, the censors' favorite dish."

It no longer suits him. The story will not now end in 1789, but in 1796, with Catherine's death. Her last couplings with the Zubov brothers will be shown and the climax will be the scene where she faints at the foot of her commode, the Polish throne installed in her privy.

Aghast, Oleg argues that the film will overrun the prescribed length, that it will be difficult to find two good actors at the drop of a hat capable of playing the roles of the two bad lovers . . . But Kozin's decision seems to be final.

Eva accepts this revised scenario without flinching. Grayish makeup transforms her into an old woman. Her gait becomes more ponderous, her hands shake, she has a whining voice. She is no longer a she-wolf on the alert for prey, she is an old bitch following the scent from habit. Kozin has lost nothing of his feeling for detail: the mirror that hides the alcove now moves aside on its track with a long-drawn-out, sinister grating sound . . .

"C-c-come on. W-we're g-going f-for a d-drink."

As Oleg knows, a half bottle of strong drink is the dose that begins to loosen the knots in Kozin's discourse. Seated at the table, he is quick to put pressure on Kozin, to get him to admit the reasons for his about-face: "We've made every effort to extricate the tsarina from her image as a sexual obsessive. And now you're showing a shameless grandmother going to bed with little whippersnappers aged twenty! There's no longer any logic to the film . . ."

"Yes there is . . . Historical truth! That's what you've always been after, isn't it, Erdmann? . . ."

"But there was more to her life than all the sex she had!"

"What else was there? A couple of dozen favorites and, at the end, those two gigolos. Obscene? Unaesthetic? Maybe, but it's the truth. That's all the world could offer her . . ."

"OK, I understand. You're going to accuse the age, that society, of hypocrisy . . ."

"No, I'm not accusing society!"

"So, who?"

"G-g-god!"

An incredulous whistle freezes on Oleg's lips. Kozin's eyes are closed, his bottom lip is pale, he has been chewing on it so much. "An attack of madness," thinks Oleg. And yet the accusation hits the target: not this "G-g-god," but a sly fate that turns a woman in search of love into this mass of flesh in the arms of a young upstart.

"But all she had to do was . . . ," Oleg says to himself and is surprised to realize that the only option available to Catherine was an imperial marriage and giving birth to a dynasty . . .

Kozin opens his eyes again. They are red and this makes him look like a weary old man. Oleg ventures a conciliatory sally: "You're right . . . It's hopeless. Throughout the whole of her life there wasn't a single man ready to love her . . ."

Kozin gets his breath back in fits and starts.

"Wrong! There was . . . one! That was . . . L-l-l-l . . ."

His face is distorted by the effort. Finally he takes out a pencil and scribbles a name on his napkin.

"Lanskoy," Oleg guesses before the director has traced out even half the letters.

Back from the theater, Dina tells him that Kozin's wife, who worked at a research institute, was exposed to radiation. The latest tests give scant grounds for hope.

So Kozin has accounts to settle with this "G-g-god . . ."

Before Dina's return Oleg had reread his notes. Alexander Lanskoy, favorite from 1780 to 1784. Inconspicuous in the whole list of the lovers. Put in the shade by their brilliance. Orlov and Potemkin violated History. Poniatowski was its victim, but what a victim! Even the Serb, Zorich, only briefly a favorite, did not pass unnoticed—a gambler, a braggart, an adventurer. Others made names for themselves by their greed. Some by their fondness for intrigue. Nothing of this kind with Lanskoy. No monetary covetousness, no whims of a spoiled courtesan, no political designs. Catherine showers praises on him in her letters—but she does that with all her men, including the one-eyed hulk, Potemkin. One difference: after Lanskoy quite a lot of time passes before she takes up with a new companion. The reason for this is simple: in June 1784 young Lanskoy dies, so a kind of mourning period is called for . . .

Oleg tells Dina about this brief life in the shadows. She listens absentmindedly, then remarks softly: "His wife . . . Kozin's wife, saved him. In the sixties he made a film about the corruption of high-ups in the Party in central Asia . . . It was banned before being edited. He spent a year inside . . . His wife stood by him. On top of her job as a university teacher, she went to work at the lab with that radioactive stuff . . . For Kozin, the film about Catherine the Second is a test: the SCCA wants to see if he's become a good boy . . . Don't contradict him too much. This is not a good time to be having fantasies about a man who might have loved our poor Catherine!"

Eva echoes this view: "Let him get on with it. Of course that last scene's pretty awful. But the fall of a cardboard Bastille wasn't much better. Yes, 'a barrel of lies in a drop of truth' . . ."

They are walking along, slipping on the fine hail that whitens the sidewalks. Eva has just completed the final two scenes: Catherine in Zubov's arms and her death agony at the foot of the commode. Grotesque, macabre tiny enclosed spaces, airlessness, Kozin's sadistic perfectionism . . . She inhales the chill air coming from the Neva, reaches up with her brow toward the falling ice crystals.

"I felt closer than ever to Catherine," she says with a sad smile. "The filming was becoming torture and I said to myself: now, at last, this is what she went through. Except that I can take my crinoline off and say *adiòs* to it!"

"She could have said *adiòs* in Russian, got rid of that idiot Zubov, and lived more appropriately for her age . . ."

"Oh sure . . . All she had to do was lie down and die while softly crooning to herself, is that it? People forget that she was a woman. Count Ségur called her 'that woman who was a great man' and Ligne, making her masculine, 'Catherine *le* Grand.' As if all the greatness in her came from her suppressed masculinity . . ."

"They were fine compliments! They emphasized her strong personality, her singularity . . ."

"Her loneliness, more than anything. Yes, a woman, very alone, who had two kinds of men for company: brutes who treated her like a female of the species and striplings for whom she became a mother figure. And when she just wanted to be a woman in love, people talked about her 'uterine rages,' her 'insatiable vagina' . . . They watched out for the least sign of aging in her. At the first wrinkle, a hue and cry! 'Her bosom's sagging,' 'those full Russian garments no longer hide the breadth of her hips,' and other charming observations . . ."

"The biographers are equally hard on the men, Eva . . ."

"Maybe . . . But tell me, what does the word *courtier* mean?

"Mm . . . Well, it's a man at the court . . ."

"And *courtesan*?"

"Well, let's say, a woman of . . . light morals."

"OK, a whore. And a *ladies' man*, like Potemkin?"

"A Don Juan."

"And a *woman with an eye for men*?"

"Well, yes . . . a harlot."

"A *man of reputation* is a celebrity and a *woman with a reputation* is inevitably a slut . . . Language always gives the game away about the laws of this world. And our 'Catherine *le* Grand' could do nothing about it, because those laws did not anticipate her particular case: a woman who sought to be loved. You'd have to imagine her meeting . . . yes, a man sufficiently apart from this world . . ."

"Imagine a man . . ." The idea is at odds with Kozin's determination to make a realist film. He needs to be certain the cast are acting out historical events.

This is their understanding as they set off for the Crimea. The itinerary: Leningrad—Kiev—Black Sea, follows that of Catherine in 1787. Oleg shares a compartment with "Potemkin" and "Ségur." One of them is leafing through satirical magazines, the other is attempting to pick up a female passenger from the next coach . . .

This is a surreal jaunt. The scenes that take place in the Crimea have already been filmed—on location near Leningrad! The Russo-Turkish war, Potemkin's traveling harem . . . All Kozin needs now is a little local color: "We're going in November, the tsarina was there in May. But at the seaside fall and spring look the same . . ."

In fact, a whole host of unlikely elements will create the illusion of reality. Such is the nature of the art . . .

On the second day of their outward journey at about noon, the train stops, a station building can be seen, the empty streets of a small town. Suddenly the howl of a siren makes the air throb, drowning out the sound of voices and doors slamming on the train. One minute, two minutes, five . . .

The silence that follows transforms the significance of every action. "Ségur" runs along the corridor, imitating a newsboy: "Extra, extra! Read all about it!" Then, lowering his voice: "Brezhnev is dead!" The copy of *Pravda* he is waving bears the date November 11, 1982.

Brezhnev was a figure hated, ridiculed in hundreds of comic anecdotes, loved for his kindly appearance. He embodied an era—the later years of the Soviet Empire—an era that has just ended. Is this a cause for rejoicing or concern? Which one of the patriarchs in the Politburo will take the place of the deceased? Andropov, the former head of the KGB? And what kind of touch on the tiller will be given: back toward the past, toward Stalin? Or toward a future almost as alarming as the past?

All this is said, repeated, whispered, shouted from the rooftops. Oleg allows himself to be drawn into the debates, relishes speculating, then grows weary of it, withdraws, watches the forests striding past the windows . . . For months the cast have been acting out History and now History has caught up with them.

Eva is pestered, they are waiting for her predictions, as a Berliner, from East Berlin, to be sure, but someone who has traveled in Europe. She confesses that she has mislaid her crystal ball . . . Oleg winks at her, they weave their way through the groups of debaters, go to the restaurant car.

"Instead of asking me to prophesy," she says, "they should have remembered my death agony in the film. Catherine dies on November sixth, 1796. And within two days everything changes. Zubov, the favorite who terrorized the court and humiliated Paul, the heir to the throne, is on his knees before the tsar, begging for mercy. Paul the First pardons him, but in his worst nightmares could not have imagined that five years later this same Zubov would be in the ranks of his assassins! After that, anyone who can read the future in tea leaves is clever indeed . . ."

. . . Several years later Oleg will still remember that lunch with Eva. The USSR will no longer exist, the Berlin Wall will have come down. But when he tries to define what has not changed since then he will call to mind the silvery gleam over the fields, the autumn sunlight on the bare forests, and the tender look in the eyes of a woman smiling and talking about tea leaves.

"I'd like to show you my old maps," Eva says, as they are leaving the restaurant car.

A dozen sheets of coarse paper. Oleg spreads them out on his bunk bed. The European part of Russia, Poland, Prussia, Brandenburg, northern Italy. Germany is, as yet, nothing more than a scattering of principalities, Italy a patchwork. Europe at the end of the eighteenth century . . .

That evening in the actors' coach the atmosphere heats up. As at a wake, they are drinking. Oleg finds Eva in the open area at the rear of the last car in which Kozin has managed to install his troupe, to protect them from the curiosity of passersby. She is standing right at the back of the train, where one can see the rails unwinding, the tracks dividing at the switches, and coming together again. The coach sways and the snow flurries increase the feeling of an ocean swell.

They remain silent, mesmerized by the swirling flight of the white masses. From time to time they hear a door slam, tipsy laughter.

"Why did you agree to act in this film?"

The moment has come when he can question her so directly. A whole era is on the brink of keeling over!

She answers him without taking her eyes off the snow, as it lashes over the track. "I told this half-truth to my friends in Berlin. Oh, the Soviet cinema, a great tradition, Eisenstein, Pudovkin and company . . . But I've no need to lie to you. What interests me is to see how Kozin will fail . . ."

"That's a bit masochistic, acting in it while thinking it'll be a flop . . ."

"I'm not talking about a flop for audiences. People will like it, I'm sure. But that's a secondary consideration. Kozin's real originality lies in this admission: even if we lived lives on as grand a scale as Catherine, we'd still always lack what is essential . . . I discovered this when I was a young libertarian who wanted to live to the limits of what is humanly possible. One day, at a secondhand book store I stumbled on a biography of Catherine the Great. It was a sobering shock. Beside this giant figure I felt ridiculous. From the depths of her eighteenth century she challenged me: a feminist who appoints the young Princess Dashkova to be president of the Academy—can you picture that in France under Louis the Fifteenth? An autocrat who proclaims her republican sympathies . . ."

"And proposes to publish Diderot's *Encyclopédie* in Russia . . ."

"Yes, a very great reign . . . But if you look at the personal side of that glorious life—a disaster! A whole stable full of lovers greedy for honors, an old age rekindled by young Romeos supplying ejaculations for cash. And then that grotesque death at the foot of a commode."

"And does this sad life have no redeeming feature?"

"There's nothing sad about this life. It's prodigious! Young as I was, I realized I would never experience one-thousandth of what Catherine experienced, as regards fame, wealth, and pleasure. Even with plenty of love affairs and great films to my credit, I would be small potatoes beside her. For a dozen years or so I managed to forget her. And then one day I encountered a descendant of the Lanskoy family . . . She was eighty and lived in Berlin. One evening we met at a library: I was doing research for a part in a historical movie—I'm not a novice, you see—and this lady was returning a book . . . She was the one who gave me those old maps . . ."

"Oh yes, Prussia, Switzerland, Italy. But Catherine never set foot outside Russia. So . . ."

"So are we forbidden to dream of a secret journey?"

"There's no historical evidence for it, Eva . . ."

"Well, what about Paul's tour. He got himself styled 'Prince of the North,' and toured round Europe with his young wife? And Joseph the

Second of Austria, who crossed the continent under the name of 'Count Falkenstein'? And, above all, Catherine's grandson, Alexander the First: in 1825 he dies, too discreetly for a tsar, and . . ."

"And reappears in Siberia! It's an old legend."

"I related these 'legends' to an Italian friend. You must know his films, though he only made a few. Aldo Ranieri. I showed him those maps. The idea of a secret journey fired him up. We wrote a screenplay but . . . As you know, it's the same old story: on one side of the Berlin Wall the censorship is political, on the other side it's financial. Especially as a film was just coming out about the tsarina and her orgies. Alongside scenes of a Catherine with silicone implants being serviced by Charles Atlas types who went under the names of Orlov and Potemkin, our dreamer, Lanskoy looked a little pale . . . This setback played its part in Aldo's death, making him less determined in his fight against cancer . . . But in any case he was aware of the flaws in our project. In our script this journey became a mere escapade. But they were going away, not just for a change of scene, but to change their whole lives . . ."

The train crosses a bridge and the thunder of the wheels drowns out their words. The river is so wide that it looks like a geological fault separating two continents. When the noise subsides, Oleg takes on the role of devil's advocate, without conviction.

"But, honestly, do you find it likely, this incognito flight across Europe by Catherine and Lanskoy?"

Eva gives a little laugh, both sad and affectionate: "A year ago, when you were working on the screenplay, would you have found this conversation of ours likely? And this way of talking about our own lives through the intermediary of a woman who, one day, believed that she was loved?"

The door in the corridor slams—"Poniatowski" and "Ségur" appear and, making operatic bows, invite them to join a "funeral dinner." Oleg turns them away, promising to join their crazy celebration very soon . . .

Outside the window the snow still whirls, the track slips away to infinity. He must dare to give a reply to this silent woman, admit all that is between them now.

The noise from the dinner is increasingly invasive, the corridor is filled with laughter and the white tempest sweeps that still-unspoken admission away into the past. The moment when it might have been possible to put it into words has flashed by, somewhat like a little railroad station buried in snow. As it hurtles through in a frenzy, the train will never stop there now.

. . . Later on everyone will say that from that day forward, time bolted. At Kiev the news breaks: the country will be governed by Andropov, the man from the KGB. People shudder, a return to Stalinesque dictatorship is predicted . . . And people would be very surprised to learn that this future tyrant is no more than a sick old man who has only a year to live and who, from the brink of his own death, will embark on reforms soon to be taken forward by a certain Gorbachev.

"Who would have found it likely?" Oleg will often think, remembering Eva's words.

He is to be one of the victims, not of the tyrant people fantasize, but of the panic that overcomes the bureaucrats of film. They remember that earlier screenplay of his, lacking in ideological correctness . . . The swiftness of the punitive action taken will be commensurate with their fear: the day after his arrival in the Crimea Oleg will learn that his post as artistic assistant has been canceled and that, as a consequence, he simply has to return to Leningrad.

The last image he will retain of Eva Sander will be this moment of filming: a woman walking along a path lined with tall white poplars, a great wind glutted with sunlight, a feeling of the sea beyond the gilded rippling of the foliage. In the film these leaves, dried out by autumn, will be taken for the dazzle of spring.

III

Oleg spends the first few days after his operation noting the subtle details of the new times in which he must learn to live.

From his hospital bed he can hear the sounds of the television set where the patients gather at the far end of the corridor. Matches with hysterical commentaries, films in which the dialogue, without the picture, seems even more stupid, news programs. And this way of addressing other people: no longer "comrade" but *gospodin*—"mister"! An archaic title, resuscitated as a clear mark of the end of the Soviet era.

And this wailing, an unceasing death rattle, involuntary for a long time now: an old man "singing a duet with his cancer," as one of the nurses muttered. Evidently the dying man needs painkillers, but there's a shortage of drugs and injections are expensive. "He'll have to grease the doctor's palm," the man in the next bed to Oleg explains. "Thirty dollars and you're on cloud nine . . ."

Gospodin, dollars . . . Twelve years—a yawning gap, teeming with political upheavals, hatred, hope, lies. Twelve years ago this *gospodin* would have provoked a guffaw, like a horse-drawn carriage arriving at the airport. As for a bribe, and, what's more, in dollars—unthinkable! But, most of all, they would never have left that old man battling all alone against the maddening pain he's attempting to silence by biting on a threadbare sheet.

The name of the country has changed and so have its boundaries, Leningrad has become St. Petersburg once more, and an "Assembly of Nobles" is restoring titles and arranging balls at which counts and princesses are among the dancers. And here at the hospital, the patients, who lack drugs, and who were once "comrades," are getting used to forms of address that were employed by their great-grandparents.

"Would you have found that likely?" Oleg remembers Eva Sander's voice. Their trip to the Crimea . . . That night the snow had swirled over the track, it had seemed as if the world were taking flight. And indeed it did take flight, blending present and past, destroying lives, breaking ties. Without leaving anyone a moment to make sense of the cataclysm. Oleg realizes that now, at last, he has time to think about it. "Thanks to the knife blade that cut a hole in my stomach . . ."

. . . A week before, a gang of men had burst into the offices of the magazine he was working for. Six hooded men beating up the journalists and ransacking the premises. One of the attackers noticed Mila, a young typist. He grabbed her by the neck, forced her to kneel, unbuttoned himself . . . Oleg bounded toward the man, but before he could seize him, received a punch in the face. His glasses broken and his lips bleeding, he returned to the assault. A sharp stabbing pain burned his stomach . . .

Closing his eyes, Oleg tries to forget the old man's moaning . . . Figures cross his mind, both familiar and unrecognizable. Lessya, whom he has only seen twice in twelve years. The first time: he is just back from the Crimea. Laid off. Lessya doesn't know this yet and in her eyes the status of artistic assistant still carries a certain prestige. "I'd like to interview Kozin for my magazine," she says. "But that old bear never talks. So how about you?" An invitation verging on the seductive. She promises to call Oleg but then, on learning that he's nothing anymore, forgets him . . . The second encounter is more recent. Hearing him talking about the little magazine on which he collaborates, Lessya heaves a sigh: "Poor Erdmann! Who's going to read your wretched rag now? The Berlin

Wall's coming down. A fine time to be tilting at windmills . . ." A gentle note has entered her voice. She breaks off, annoyed with herself for this weakness. Oleg changes the subject. "And what about you? What are you planning to do, now things are falling apart?" A certain sharp frankness lights up the look Lessya gives him: "Me, I'm planning to lead the life all Russian women dream of: a house, barbecues, travel to exotic countries. I've just married a Swede . . . Do you have another scenario in mind for me?" Oleg stammers: "No, no . . . To live in Sweden, well that's . . ." And he remembers the remark Lessya once made: think about the moments when Catherine lived what she was not . . .

He has also caught up with his former rival, Valentin Zyamtsev: in a broadcast devoted to the last Soviet Cinematographic Congress. A gathering that proclaims itself to be revolutionary, in response to the new ethos proposed by Gorbachev. The speakers declare that the only films that matter now are those previously banned by the Communist regime. Zyamtsev draws up a list of "enemies of free cinema." The malefactors are named, one by one. Oleg hears Bassov's name mentioned and then, a few seconds later, that of Kozin! Enemies . . .

The old man's cries fade away into shrill moaning, like a child's whimpering. Someone needs to "grease a doctor's palm," obtain a sedative . . . "I could sell my watch," thinks Oleg. "But no one would want it. Everyone's eager for brand names, pretty toys with several dials . . ."

So what other ghost was haunting him? Yes, of course, Kozin . . . The release of "their" film, at a festival in Moscow, which Oleg goes to at his own expense. The bitterness, the humiliation, and the suppressed sobs in the train on the way back to Leningrad—Oleg still remembers this. And the posters quickly warped by the rain. *Travels Around an Alcove* . . . Neither on the posters nor in the film credits was his name mentioned. His memory skips over several years and he feels the shock of a very recent sorrow: a subway station entrance, warm wafts of air mixed with

the cold in the street, a bearded man, drunk, his overcoat shiny with
filth: Kozin! Oleg puts up with this bum's bad breath, as he talks loudly,
breaking off to take a swig from the bottle, then grabbing him by the
lapel. "You, Erdmann, your hands are clean, you goddamned German.
But I made that filthy film, a drop of truth in a barrel of crap! I sold my
soul to win applause at their fucking festival! Catherine the Great . . .
Travels around an alcove . . . Who are you kidding? All they want to see
is how she fucked. As for the rest, they couldn't give a good goddamn!
But the worst of it is, Erdmann . . . because of that crappy movie I didn't
get to see my wife when she was dying. I, I . . ." He starts stammering,
grimaces, whispering through his tears. Oleg thrusts all the money he
has on him into his pocket, promises to come back the next day at the
same time. But on the next day and the day after that Kozin is no longer
there . . .

Who else? Dina. The "young Catherine" . . . There was a time when he
began to loathe this face wreathed in little blond curls. Dina used to appear on TV ten times a day. She was the very first actor to be featured
in commercials, a great novelty in Russia. This young woman embodied the sweetly bland aspirations of the period: the time when the last
days of socialism still guaranteed a certain economic security and the
capitalism people dreamed of seemed like a cost-free Disneyland. One
day he ran into Dina and started to mimic her: "'*Summer Time* brings
sunshine to your sheets'; '*Magic Carpet* toilet tissue, softer than a cloud,'"
he recited. "So, was playing the part of Catherine good preparation for
all this stupid detergent and diapers garbage? Kozin may choose to live
like a bum, but he won't prostitute himself . . ." At these words she took
a deep breath, as if after weeping, then said softly: "Do you have a little
time? I'd like to show you something . . ." They went to the outskirts
of Leningrad (no, already St. Petersburg) and arrived in front of a long,
gray brick building. Children wearing thick jackets, all the same, were
just at that moment emerging. "When I was a little girl I was like them,"
explained Dina. "I was brought up in this orphanage . . . Now all these

'educational institutions' are collapsing, I try to help them, as best I can. By prostituting myself in commercials. And, just so that you can despise me even more, you should know that I live with my boss . . ."

Oleg turns over on his bed, trying not to crush the tube from the drip. Remembering Dina is painful. Reaching into his memory again, he comes up with a merry face, wreathed in russet hair—Zhurbin informing him, with the self-assurance of a big businessman (this was three years ago): "I'm the president of an airline." Oleg assumes the vacuous admiration of a simpleton: "So, tell me, *Gospodin* President, how many planes do you have on the line?" Zhurbin laughs, once more becoming his good friend of long ago. "To tell the truth, only three, and two of them are under repair. But what matters is that I've already managed to get a share of the market. To think there were times when you and I would be happy to steal a couple of pounds of tripe down at the slaughterhouse!" On another occasion they meet on a suburban train: the president of a company on a scruffy local train! And what's more, Zhurbin is wearing a dirty padded jacket and rubber boots and, oddly, a fine mink hat. "No, I'm finished with planes. Too much trouble. Regulations, spare parts. And the cost of the fuel, ruinous! No, I've got a mink farm now. It's a gold mine! I'm even exporting to India. What do you mean, that's the tropics? They've got the Himalayas down there as well . . ." Suddenly he begins yelling: "But what about you, Erdmann? What the hell are you doing here? The Berlin Wall's come down, haven't you heard? They're rolling out the red carpet for Germans who want to return to their historic fatherland . . . *Nach der Heimat!*" People on the train turn around, his words in German are reminiscent of orders barked out by Nazis in the war films of the 1950s. Oleg manages to shut his friend up, tells him the purpose of his journey: he's going to see Bassov. Zhurbin exclaims: "Ah, Bassov! Our master, our idol! My mentor . . . Though I have to admit I skipped quite a lot of his classes. I had my job. At the slaughterhouse, as you know. Yes. 'Three carcasses to go to exit two!' And now my mink farm, do you know what I'm going to use that for? A garment factory?

Oh, you poor, unimaginative Prussian! No, the mink are my start-up capital and then I'm going to make films! A film studio. So it's in your interests not to forget about me the way you generally do . . ."

He'd be happy to stay in Zhurbin's company. But, in memory now, he must leave the train and catch a bus, that takes him on a long, rocking, laborious journey to the estate of dachas where their old teacher lives . . .

He can no longer contrive to recall Bassov's face without thinking about his death. A body discovered in a half-frozen pond. Murder? Suicide? More likely one of the "real estate" crimes that are increasingly common in this new country. The victims: elderly people whose homes in the city somebody covets, or else a house in the country that one of the new rich will raze to the ground in order to build himself a hideous mansion with turrets and a perimeter fence eighteen feet high . . . Oleg screws up his eyelids, tries to picture Bassov alive, as he was two years ago at the end of March, the snow weary, the cawing of rooks in the trees, and this old man on the steps of his house, inhaling the damp, sharp air, elated by the nascent aromas, smiling at the birds' raucous squabbling . . . And now Oleg can see him and hear his words.

"Now that I'm older than Catherine, I understand her better. In Kozin's film, *your* film, there is the scene of Pugachev's execution: they cut off his head first, then his arms and legs, a method more humane than the quartering of Damiens in France under Louis the Fifteenth. Catherine is well informed about Damiens's trial. She even receives this staggering piece of information: the French public prosecutor is approached by three citizens of Paris who've dreamed up highly sophisticated methods of execution. The first suggests inserting wooden splinters covered in sulphur under Damiens's fingernails and toenails and setting fire to them. The second would like them to flay the condemned man's muscles and burn them with acid. The third has fashioned a blade on a spring which makes it possible to enucleate the tortured man's eyeballs, so that they pop out of his head 'like frogs,' as he puts it. Catherine confesses herself to be perplexed. Granted, one must strike down those who endanger the kingdom. But whence comes this infinite meticulousness, with which man is ready to torment his fellow man? She makes a similar observation on the subject of love. Her agents keep her informed about fashionable Paris society, the orgies and the whole circus of bed-hopping at the court, the sexual rivalries . . . Thanks to Damiens, she has learned that for man killing is not enough. Thanks to Versailles, she has discovered that loving is not enough, either. In cruelty, as in pleasure, human beings seek complexity, plot and counterplot. A whole performance. Yes, the 'theater' she refers to in her letters. This performance becomes their only goal. Inventing a thousand ways of killing makes it possible not to think about the pain you're inflicting. Pirouetting your way through a thousand ingenious erotic games makes it possible to avoid loving . . . Now, if you could say that in a film one day!"

Bassov has never criticized Kozin's film. He simply talked about what he had not found in it. A life that is apart from the ingenious farce human beings devise for themselves . . .

Oleg sits up in bed, surprised by the silence—the old man is no longer moaning! No doubt the other patients, appalled, have made a collection to pay for painkillers. They had done that the previous week and when Oleg offered his store of rubles, he had learned that, since he came into the hospital, inflation had eaten half of their value away . . . The newspapers talk about Russia being on the skids, hospitals that can no longer treat patients, factories no longer paying their workers, criminality corrupting society, alcohol carrying off millions of lives . . . Previously Oleg would read such things with the detached curiosity one has for statistics. Now here's that old man who has received his dose of cloud nine. And Kozin huddled in a filthy corner by the subway. And Bassov's body stretched out on the ice of a pond.

Twelve years before, at the film's premiere, Oleg's vanity, his sense of himself as a director had distracted him too much: he was noting his own inventions. When he watched the film later in Leningrad he had focused especially on Dina's and Eva Sander's performances . . .

The third time he saw it he finally concentrated on Kozin's art . . . Rafts surmounted by gallows float down the Volga: after the crushing of the Pugachev rebellion they set these gibbets adrift to frighten the last of the rioters. A child is fishing beside the river—suddenly a cluster of hanged men looms up above the willow groves . . .

Another scene has been added after Oleg left. One of the favorites dies—it is Lanskoy. Catherine is devastated. She refuses food, sinking into a kind of madness. The frailty of this woman of fifty-five is harrowing—her body shrinks like that of a rag doll. And it is this neglected body that Potemkin possesses brutally, reclaiming *his* Catherine, who had almost escaped him.

Oleg also notes which sequences were cut during the editing. Having lost his crown, Peter III asks to be allowed to depart, his only luggage being his violin . . . Ivan VI, imprisoned as a child, has never known anything but the walls of his cell. Catherine grants him fifteen minutes of freedom: on top of the prison watchtower. For the first time in twenty years he sees the sky. For the first time in his life he sees the sea. He inhales until he feels giddy. Catherine lowers her eyelids as the tears flow. She has just given the order for Ivan to be executed if ever he tries to escape . . .

Oleg wakes up: these sights had been mingled with his dreams. The bottle for the drip is empty. What may happen? An air bubble traveling along the tube and causing an embolism? Would that be a painful death? Or liberating, like the moments he has been thinking about?

When they get their morning call he learns that the old man whose moaning he could no longer hear had died at about 3:00 a.m.

The books are arranged in piles along his bed—a slab paved with bindings, reminiscent of a sarcophagus.

He is back in his old room, where he has not lived for several months. He had rented a space with his girlfriend, Tanya. But after the operation she called him. If he wanted to see her again, she said, he would first of all have to "work out his problems." In plain terms, no more getting on the wrong side of the people who had nearly disemboweled him . . .

This expression, "work out your problems," is currently in frequent use; it can cover anything from having to change a lightbulb to a pressing need to liquidate a competitor. Tanya does not want to encounter that hooded gang on her doorstep one day. "You know St. Petersburg holds the record for the number of murders. And by the way, I've already changed the lock . . ."

She is a young, beautiful woman, not prepared to die for the freedom of expression championed by the fly-by-night magazine Oleg works for. And he can understand her.

His return to the communal beehive helps him to take stock of the course Russia has now embarked on. Previously the apartment was lived in by people who were certainly of modest means but who all had a job or a pension. Among them, too, were artists who had come to take

Leningrad by storm, divorced people hoping to find something better quite soon. Now social rejects are crowding in, the losers in the sifting out of the strong from the weak, the only way of life now in this new country. Their poverty can be seen from the laundry they hang out to dry, from the meals cooking on the stove.

Year five, following the fall of the Berlin Wall.

To be ranked among the defeated is unpleasant. He, too, has had his good years! Not an airline, but good jobs and therefore good salaries. During the first years of liberalization a simple cigarette salesman in a plywood kiosk became a "businessman" . . . Oleg has written radio plays, made short films, worked for a theater, even ventured into the field of selling used cars . . . And on Saturdays he filmed weddings: the emerging middle class needed to immortalize the brilliance of their family celebrations. From this nuptial merry-go-round he has moved on to making commissioned documentaries, tracing the rise of oligarchs. Always the same scenario: impoverished youth under the Soviets, first steps taken into the harsh world of business, the awakening of the entrepreneur of genius, and, at the end, a luxurious gilt-and-marble office, where this *self-made man* was telling his story . . . Some of these tycoons would be murdered shortly afterward ("I'm not in this for nothing," Oleg joked). The times Russia was living through pulsated with a frenzy that was pathological. Fortunes were made in a matter of months and lost in a matter of hours. Seeing a man lying in a pool of blood out in the street was as commonplace an occurrence as stepping over a drunkard asleep on the sidewalk had been in the old days. On one occasion Oleg filmed a limousine, the gleaming symbol of a successful career. The next day all that was left of it was a pile of scrap iron with the smell of explosives hanging over it and the police gathering up what remained of its owner into plastic sacks.

He knew he was capable of adapting to this obstacle race. Changing jobs. Hardening his heart. Forgetting his dreams of cinema. Making the videos that gave him a living. And he lived well. He was able to rent fine premises, while still keeping his room in the communal apartment— "my junk room," he called it. At one point he had two girlfriends, and, to crown it all, they looked like one another! In fact, they both looked like Lessya . . .

It was the death of his old teacher, Bassov, that gave him doubts about this new life. He pictured the old man having fallen over at the edge of a frozen pond—a body lying there as passersby skirted around it. The world made no sense if a man could disappear like that: without deserving an inquest into the causes of his death, without so much as a sigh being uttered, beneath the gray sky that heralded the spring.

After that encounter with Kozin he found it impossible to go back into the race. Decline shocks us more than death. Kozin choosing to let himself die slowly, in filth, in full view of the contemptuous looks of others, his long drowning in death, shook Oleg more than a sudden decease would have done . . .

He abandoned his oligarchs and one evening answered an advertisement: the magazine *No Comment* was looking for a photographer.

This magazine published only photographs with short captions. The pictures, presented in pairs, owed their impact to juxtaposition. The first one, for example, might show an old woman sitting in the snow, holding out her hand—the second, taken in the same street, a private town house where guests were stuffing themselves with caviar. The overcrowded dormitory at a poorhouse, pictured opposite the residence of a minister. Children in rags—and a schoolboy getting out of a luxury car accompanied by a bodyguard . . .

Oleg was under no illusions about the effect these contrasting pictures might have. But he was touched by the little team's enthusiasm. The six journalists had faith, something lacking in this new country where the pressure to succeed forced people to adopt the grim rigidity of robots. He was familiar with the circles oligarchs moved in, which, for the editorial team, made him "our man in the world of the rich." He did end up believing that their efforts might alert the crowds embarked on a wild stampede toward nothing.

Every day they received threats. Several times the magazine's vehicle was torched. The response of the police was predictable: "You bring this trouble on yourselves. You're lucky they haven't shot at you." This "they" implied a lot of people: each issue contained photographs aptly designed to displease the powerful.

The attack by the hooded men had not greatly surprised them. What was surprising—Oleg would think about this on his hospital bed—was the extremely natural aspect of this evil. Smashing, punching, and, if a woman attracts you, violating her. And, if an idiot gets in the way, sticking a knife in his guts, just to be rid of him. An unthinking brutality, almost devoid of any malice. "After all," he said to himself, "a wolf tearing open a sheep's throat doesn't hate it." This absence of hatred seemed more distressing than the violence itself.

"The struggle for survival reduces men to their animal nature." He has often repeated this. Now he asks himself sharply, "But what can you offer them? What other life? What other goal?"

The question comes back to him one night, in response to the moaning of the old man with cancer. "What other life?" An image lights up in his mind, between memory and dream: a woman walking along beside tall trees, white with the first snow. A vision that truly does have the clarity of a goal. This beauty, he would like to say, but the notion is driven out by an even more vivid vision: a man walking through a clear night, amid fields. Carrying a violin under his arm . . .

Oleg is back in his old room, thinking about those moments as he rediscovers the piles of books, echoes of distant times. His screenplay, the filming, the journey to the Crimea. Twelve years . . . Wars, crises, revolutions, global disasters and his own petty disasters, breakups, separations, the wound still weeping in his stomach . . . And the steadfast beauty of that moment: a woman walking beside the sea beneath snow-covered trees.

The choice is simple: get rid of all these books, get back into the rat race. Or else . . . He opens a volume. The Seven Years' War, Russia's adversary is the Prussia of Frederick the Great, the Empress Elizabeth discovers Catherine has exchanged several letters with him. Is she a German spy? Count Shuvalov and Prince Trubetskoy, who are heading the investigation, succumb to the young princess's charm. The author of the book claims that she received them together . . . Always this desire to couple Catherine with several males, to turn her into an animal. The same story was told in connection with the Zubov brothers—they were said to hurl themselves at her, both at the same time, of course.

He replaces the book on the tomb-like pile of printed matter. Tales of two kinds: some portraying a female in heat, others showing a mistress of political games. Not much choice: sex or the antics of court life . . . A cage!

He dreams of a volume buried somewhere in the depths of this sarcophagus of words—the tale of a life lived far away from this prison-like existence.

He knows such a story does not exist. Create one? An inspiring plan. But what's certain now is that it is impossible for him to go back— back into that world the books in the sarcophagus are talking about.

That same evening he counts his savings: 2,400,000 rubles, enough to keep going for three months or, rather, given the galloping inflation, six weeks. Sufficient time for an attempt to break the bars of the cage.

In 1762 Catherine's lovers kill her husband, Peter III. In 1801 the last of the tsarina's favorites takes part in the assassination of her son Paul I. Men very close to this woman, who have known her caresses, her kisses. With her lips she has touched the mouths of future killers and future victims . . .

Thinking about it, Oleg reaches a point where scholarly dissertations about Catherine II become devoid of interest. All the historians are doing is piecing together the logic of her reign. But what ought to be expressed is the monumental absurdity of this woman's destiny.

She seeks to relieve the people's sufferings and what she gets is a devastating uprising. Her republican impulses lead only to an increase of slavery. Toward the end of her life the discordant rhythmic accompaniment for her famous refrain "Voltaire brought me into the world" is the clatter of the guillotine in the sweet France she dreamed of . . . One of Catherine's lovers plays with little Paul, the child adores this man, who, later on, will be among his murderers . . . As it happens, Paul I could have escaped his death. His doctors advise him to "put a curb on nature," for his wife is weakened by her pregnancies: the tsar has the doorway sealed up between his wife's bedroom and his own. That exit would have opened up a series of adjoining rooms through which he could have escaped when the conspirators arrived.

Oleg has spread out his books all around the sofa. Lying there, he gathers up these fragments of absurdity that give the lie to the portentous "march of History." Born in 1754, Paul lived among men who entered his mother's bed after killing his father . . . When Catherine dies in 1796, he gives orders for the remains of Peter III to be exhumed. After thirty-four years in the grave the skeleton is laid to rest at the Winter Palace, alongside Catherine's body. Paul defies death with sumptuous, macabre madness: his mother's ex-lovers accompany the two coffins to the imperial burial chamber. The favorites carry the decorations and crown of the man they had killed. This theatrical ceremony exposes the stupidity of men, their bestial appetites, the conceit of their claim to rule the world. Paul feels himself to be God, a sad god, to whom not even the proof that he was right can bring joy. Already present in this funeral procession are the men who will murder him . . .

Once Oleg used to seek out the great events of the reign, its remarkable personalities . . . History of this kind no longer interests him . . . The real story line is much simpler. It is the tale of a pack of human predators, running around, tearing one another apart, coupling, dying . . . Some strong and cunning males massacre a weak male, so as to take possession of his female. Nothing more.

Several books declare that Peter III's death accords with the logic of History. As for his naive hope that he could walk away with his violin under his arm, this proves that he was simply feebleminded.

It is as if there is a tacit agreement among the authors to uphold the laws of this world: strength crushes weakness, sex heightens the appetite for domination, dreaming signifies maladjustment, an inability to survive in the social jungle. And because we are civilized people our language cunningly conceals this bestiality thus: the logic of History, the triumph of Reason . . .

The arrogance of Reason! The arrogance of historians seeking to use chronology to keep chaos at bay. The arrogance of the "Age of the Enlightenment," in making man into a god. The arrogance of the enlightened monarchs who hoped that the veneer of their salons would hold firm over the knotty wood of men's souls . . . In one volume Oleg renews acquaintance with one of these arrogant men—Frederick the Great, the great friend of Voltaire, later his sworn enemy. It is war, the Russians sack his residence at Charlottenburg. The prince de Ligne recognizes that his Austrian hussars are not to be outdone: they are wading "knee-deep in porcelain and fine glassware." A haven of peace designed for tranquil conversations about the benefits of civilization . . .

Arrogance, touching in its fervor, in Catherine herself. Her grandsons, Alexander and Constantine, will have as their tutor the Swiss citizen Frédéric-César de La Harpe. A republican, a Rousseauistic teacher, and, later on, an admirer of the French Revolution. What better way of elevating the young princes' minds? A few years after La Harpe has left, Alexander lets the conspirators kill his father, Paul I. Constantine, at the head of his band of thugs, after many acts of violence, seizes a St. Petersburg woman who had previously resisted his advances. Despite the presence of her two children, this young widow is violated by a dozen men. Her limbs are broken, her ligaments severed, and her mouth, when ripped open, reveals fragments of broken teeth. The rapists fling down her corpse in front of her mother's house . . .

Oleg gets up, begins to pace up and down in the corridor. The episode of the rape is rarely told by the biographers. They never draw parallels between this brutality and the fine ideas of La Harpe, Voltaire, and the doctrines that at that time proclaimed the sacredness of man and liberty. La Harpe returns to Switzerland, just as Catherine is receiving an account from her ambassador in Paris of the revolution in progress. One detail gives her food for thought: the severed heads have their hair curled before being handed over to the victims' relatives. The natural goodness of mankind . . .

As he reads the accounts of wars, Oleg increasingly experiences nausea. "Austria lost thirty thousand men and two hundred million florins. Russia lost two hundred thousand men and two hundred million rubles. The Turks lost three hundred thousand men and two hundred million piastres . . ."

One voice approves of this obscenity—Voltaire! He begs Catherine to confirm to him that fifteen thousand Turks have just been shot down. "Thus," he says, "my happiness will be complete."

You have to read between the lines to discover the truth about this philosophy teacher of the tsarina's. Then you catch Voltaire busy writing letters of denunciation, aimed at sending to the Bastille a young writer who dares to criticize him. He goes to bookshops with the police: the books he disapproves of will be seized, the bookshops closed, the printers put in prison. The hatred he exudes finally comes to annoy Catherine herself. "War is an ugly thing, Monsieur," she replies to this humanist exhorting her to massacre the Turks.

At the end of a month comes this astonishment: how could he ever have been enthusiastic about all this tomfoolery? One country invades another. This king bumps off his rival. A royal mistress conspires for a war to break out. Frederick the Great nicknames his favorite dog "Pompadour." Furious, the marquise de Pompadour engineers the alliance between France and Austria. The result is the Seven Years' War, the war "of the three petticoats," Pompadour, Elizabeth of Russia, and Maria Theresa of Austria. Frederick is defeated by these ladies—the Austrian hussars wade "knee-deep in porcelain and fine glassware." But Elizabeth dies, Peter III comes to the Russian throne and rescues Frederick, whom he idolizes. For the Russians, this tsar needs to be toppled. Catherine accomplishes this task and . . . And the story continues—a bloody farce with endless new developments. It leads to nothing other than perpetual repeat performances of killings, political juggling acts, utopias, petty intrigues . . .

And as for the sequel to all this madness, Oleg can see it on television: a specialist explains the war in Chechnya by Catherine II's refusal, in her day, to invade the Caucasian provinces. Houses burned, corpses of soldiers . . . Then the news bulletin is interrupted by a commercial: "Villas on the Baltic coast with full access to a private golf course."

He goes to the kitchen to make himself coffee. In the corridor a woman is scurrying along with a big, steaming cooking pot. Zhenya, who lives with her three children in a room nine by twelve feet. "A villa" . . .

Oleg says to himself. Zhenya's husband was jailed for four years after stealing a chicken from a refrigerated truck.

While he is looking for matches Oleg discovers an old kettle in a closet . . . In the old days he often used to see it on the stove. Its owner was Zoya, a woman in her fifties of whom he knows nothing. When did she leave that communal apartment? And where did she go? He has an almost fond memory of those evenings when he would see Zoya sitting, looking out of the window, adrift in a time where no one could reach her . . . Her fine face was worn with weariness, she had very bright eyes, as if washed by a shower of rain. "Your boozy neighbor," his girlfriend Lessya used to call her, somewhat scornfully . . .

The following day he sees Zhenya, dressing her children to take them to school. She is shouting, hitting them, threatening them. "Just you wait till your dad comes home from his travels . . ." Oleg asks her if she knew Zoya.

"The fat one who was always on the bottle? Yes, we used to talk sometimes at the stove . . . Well, anyhow, no one knows how it happened. Sure, that train driver should have been on the lookout . . . But as she drank . . ."

The death is recounted in between the clips around the ear Zhenya hands out to her sons. The "fat one who was always on the bottle" worked on the railroad and was knocked down by a train—between one swig of vodka and the next, so they said. Did she have any family? "In two years, no one came to see her . . . And, do you know, you're the first person to ask me about her. OK. I've got to go now . . ."

Oleg settles on his sofa swamped by books. Thousands of pages spelling out every step Catherine took. Compared with this plethora, Zoya's life is not even a shadow. The memory of a face, the echo, now silent, of a voice. And these scraps recounted by Zhenya: a woman who drank, worked at night, and failed to dodge a train. That's all there is— nothing more!

His rebellion is physically violent, a challenge in the face of death. "No! There was also that morning!"

. . . Yes, a morning in February. A first spell of milder weather, snow that, as it fell against one's face, seemed filled with warmth. They met in the entrance hall, both of them returning from their night work: he at the slaughterhouse, Zoya at her railroad depot. Their coats were caked in snow. With somewhat clumsy gestures they each knocked the snowflakes off the other's clothing. Oleg saw this woman's face, which, on account of a sleepless night, was still unburdened with the cares of the day. She must have seen the same distant dreaminess in his own eyes . . . They parted, Zoya went to put her kettle on the stove, Oleg went back to his drafts. "That woman's beautiful," he said to himself. "What a shame that . . ." He had no time to clarify this regret. There on his worktable were his typewriter, the pages of his screenplay, the little pocket mirror Lessya had looked at herself in, a few weeks before, as she put on lipstick . . . "That's funny," he thought, already in ironic mode, "Zoya looks quite like Catherine around 1780." And he brushed aside any vague tenderness for a woman whose beauty he had always ignored . . .

He leafs through the pages of the books spread out at his feet and suddenly, with a mixture of joy and amazement, he realizes that, thanks to that moment in February, Zoya's life is infinitely better known to him than that of the tsarina. That one morning, with its scent of snow and the spring, is more real than all these historical summaries. And it is the tsarina, entombed in her sarcophagus of words, of whom we are totally ignorant, for not one of these volumes captures the freshness of a winter's morning as Catherine one day lived it.

They become lovers in the spring of 1780. Alexander Lanskoy is twenty-two, Catherine fifty. Unlike the previous favorites, Lanskoy turns out to be selfless. He does not angle for titles or seek jobs for his family. Intrigues bore him, he is indifferent to the influence he might have. At the apex of an empire that dominates half of Europe and half of Asia, he seems impervious to the reach of such power, setting little store by the history that is dictated by the caliber of cannons. He seems sincerely fond of this woman who is still beautiful and lively and maintains a very strict physical discipline. The other favorites, once at the palace, felt like prisoners and veered off into power games, plots, and debauchery at the first opportunity. Lanskoy is only happy in his long tête-à-têtes with Catherine, their walks along the pathways of the Peterhof, their evenings beside the Baltic . . .

It looks as if he loves this woman . . . which is both logical and totally impossible. Logical, since every favorite owes it to himself to declare his passion to the empress. Impossible, given that these men are not made to last—very soon they start to throw their weight around and try to turn their own whims into the policies of the State, deceive the tsarina, and then, overnight, disappear from her life. A letter of dismissal, a parting gift (land, serfs, gold), and a ban on appearing at court. Often a new favorite takes over the empty apartments the following day.

With Lanskoy it all happens differently. Catherine sees him for the first time in December 1779, but only the following spring does she invite him to the palace. The rhythm of the tsarina's life is changing.

This new lover appears to be calming the fever of the great reign. At last Catherine can catch her breath. This doubtless relates to her age, to her physical ripeness. Furthermore, during these years she has reached the stage of a "cruising flight," when her power, firmly established, weighs less heavily upon her. The peasant revolts are in the past, the conspirators have laid down their arms, disdainful Europe has finally accepted this vast country that can still be reproached for its Asiatic ponderousness, but must now be reckoned with. Catherine's creation is like a bronze statue that has just been removed from its mold: it still needs to be cleaned and polished, but the sculptor knows that the essential work has been done.

For historians Lanskoy is a mere interlude of sweetness in the ongoing struggle of a woman destined to assert herself, to reign, and, in the absence of love, to purchase sex. A transient Prince Charming.

Yet he remains at the tsarina's side for more than four years. The breakup is not caused by dismissal but by his death.

And it is he who prepares the way for the greatest change in the life of the one he loves—escape.

Oleg remembers Eva Sander. She was fervently attached to this version. A late love affair that Catherine finally comes upon, an unexpected tenderness on the part of a woman who has always contrived to organize her sexual life like a government department.

"What they were living through was so foreign to the way of the world that in order to love one another they had to erase that world. Escape. Be reborn . . ."

Eva had said this with a passionate conviction that was based on almost nothing. A dozen old maps of Europe and a brief note that historians occasionally quote: a note from Lanskoy to the tsarina in which he talks about "our journey" . . .

This probably referred to their visit to Finland in 1783, where

Catherine met the king of Sweden, Gustav III. The only long journey the two lovers ever undertook.

If Oleg does not abandon the idea of an "escape," it is because of a calm, steadfast certainty: without the hope of such a secret journey Catherine's life no longer makes sense. Or at least it makes no more sense than the chronicle of wars, rebellions, and political intrigues, the tangle of bloody, brilliant vanities that goes by the name of History . . .

He thinks about Zoya, too. Without that February morning long ago, when they met in the entrance hall, all covered in snow, yes, without that dizzy, luminous moment Zoya's life would be no more than a tale of which no trace remains: a woman fond of drink, a lonely soul heating the water for her tea in a huge kettle, a worker who, one night, had a fatal accident at her place of work. This epitaph and then oblivion.

Almost no trace of that journey exists, although Oleg tries to detect some of them in the intervals between major historical events. Catherine negotiates with Gustav III while the Russian armies are fighting close to the Caspian Sea. But amid all this how does she live? What is the flavor of the hours, what sun shines on the seasons that give a rhythm to her love for Lanskoy?

Often they read together. Catherine no longer hesitates to put on her glasses, which she never did in front of the previous favorites for fear of showing her age. It is also from these years that she begins to wear flowing clothes—not to hide the roundness of her figure, but in the certainty of no longer needing to wear corsets in order to please.

She gets Lanskoy to read over those of her letters she writes in Russian: he corrects the verbs of motion, which are the principal hazard in this language. On the tsarina's advice, he is learning Italian . . . In their conversations he often tells her how politics disgust him.

A few scattered clues, from one published account to the next, make it possible to guess at the nature of their love affair: after the highly volatile passions Catherine has always experienced comes a serene harmony of hearts and bodies, the feeling that they have all eternity for their mutual love. "With him, the flow of my days is like a handful of sand I can take up again and again," she writes. "Before, it was always an hourglass that I would turn over repeatedly, terrified by the way the grains ran through."

Catherine seems not only rejuvenated but ageless. Lanskoy gives the lie to the insipidity of the portrait a court painter made of him. He matures, his presence gains substance, it is as if he were protecting this woman who is at once so powerful and so vulnerable. "When he gave his arm to the empress," Catherine's librarian notes, "Lanskoy walked with his shoulder thrust a little forward, like a shield."

Oleg pictures the loving couple. They walk through the connecting rooms of the Peterhof Palace, then mount horses, and ride slowly along the Baltic shore in the pale light of a June evening.

The evidence that they may be preparing to go away is tenuous. Lanskoy learns Italian? But then Catherine encouraged all her favorites to speak foreign languages. Nor do the books they read (Algaritti, Voltaire, Swedenborg) offer any indication of their developing an escape plan.

The maps? Placed end to end, the routes underlined in ink that is barely visible could be tracing a journey that would link St. Petersburg with northern Italy. But there is nothing to show that the maps should be brought together in this way.

One evening Oleg realizes that his investigations have already taken up two months and it is only the memory of Eva Sander that drives him to continue. The idea of a tsarina abandoning everything, the wonderful madness of such an escape, is exhilarating. But he can now see where it comes from: Eva and her Italian friend, Aldo Ranieri, their love illuminated by the legend of Catherine and Lanskoy.

The jealousy he feels makes him smile: that was all so long ago! Walks through a city that was still called Leningrad, the filming, the Crimea . . . Since then the Berlin Wall has fallen, Germany has been reunified, and Eva must be quietly continuing her career as an actor. Has she any memory of an "artistic assistant" she convinced about Catherine's secret journey? A madman who, for the thousandth time, is leafing through these dusty volumes, in search of a word whose resonance would evoke the sound of hoofbeats on a road at night?

The next morning he is woken by the whine of a saw. He glances out the kitchen window: the building opposite seems to be swaying. No, it is the tree at the center of the courtyard; it shudders, traces a great curve in the air, and falls, throwing up a cloud of snow.

 Dressing in haste, he goes down, shouts, as if something could still be done to negate this fall. Four men look at him with relaxed contempt. "Was that tree in someone's way?" he asks, aware that his voice does not carry. A scornful grin: "Well, it ain't in no one's way now. And if you don't like it, buster, I can give you a bit of a trim yourself." The man holding the saw spits out his cigarette butt. The others erupt into guffaws. And they begin cutting up the trunk . . . An hour later two big four-wheel-drives are parked where the tree stood. Oleg hates the build of these vehicles: they are like great beasts confident of their right to run you over. "The clatter of hoofbeats on a road at night . . . ," he says to himself as he crosses the courtyard.

At the central library in St. Petersburg his inquiries provoke contrasting reactions: admiration for his obstinacy and the wariness a fanatical scholar always attracts. The staff member who hands over the document he has requested informs him he will be consulting materials nobody has looked at since September 24, 1932!

 The memoirs of a nephew of the favorite, Yermolov . . . Lanskoy dies on June 25, 1784. After an exceptionally long period of solitude— eight months—Catherine chooses as her lover Alexander Yermolov, who acquires the nickname at court of the "White Negro," on account of his blond curly hair and thick lips. Catherine buys back the deceased man's decorations from Lanskoy's family in order to give them to the new favorite. The nephew relates this incident and also the excursion he took part in. It is a fine Midsummers' Day at Peterhof. The empress walks on Yermolov's arm, a little retinue accompanies them. A violin can be heard and the sound of a melodious voice. Two Italians: a blind old man playing, a youth singing. Yermolov throws them money. The courtiers grumble about these barefoot beggars who have one hand on their hearts and the other in your pocket. They are still at a distance when the youth's voice suddenly rings out with passionate force: *"Il prim' amore non si scorda mai . . ."* The empress laughs, everyone follows suit, mocking these Italians who, beneath their hot sun, cheerfully experience their "never forgotten" first love every day of the week . . . Suddenly they realize Catherine is weeping . . . The next day Yermolov is dismissed.

In front of the library building stands the statue of Catherine II. Oleg has studied it a hundred times, scanning the bronze contours for the key to the mystery of this woman . . . There she stands, a symbol of power, of Reason, of the inevitability of History. Around her are the men who supported her in her titanic endeavors. No trace of Lanskoy. A pigeon is asleep on Potemkin's head.

In the courtyard at his apartment building Oleg is already getting used to the presence of huge vehicles where the tree stood. "History on the move," he says to himself. "The boorishness we call the logic of progress . . ." There are lights on in the windows of the building opposite, workmen can be seen tearing down wallpaper. These former communal dwellings are being transformed into luxury apartments.

From the kitchen Oleg glances outside, as Zoya used to do: the two four-wheel-drives, sawdust, a cement mixer grinding away at the base of the wall. A life forging ahead—oblivious of the shade of a slightly drunk woman sitting at this window, her gaze lost in the slow fluttering of the snowflakes.

He understands it more clearly than ever: to write the history of a life or a reign you have to sacrifice those eyes fixed on the falling snow.

And to sacrifice, too, the daydream two lovers hid from everybody, that secret journey across Europe.

The next day another "historic" event! New banknotes arrive to replace the old ones. The population was given twenty-four hours to change their money. Deep in his archives, Oleg became aware of this too late. He had little money left, in any case. Thousands of retired people, not very robust when it comes to elbowing their way up to the desk, lost all their savings.

This financial swindle is only one detail of the great postsocialist rummage sale. But it is from this day that Oleg abdicates. "My phone is off the hook," he says to himself. This phrase applies to everything he wants to avoid contact with: the frenzied rush of people in the street, the noise of the cement mixer, the potbellied owners of four-wheel-drives, television programs (an expert demonstrates how monetary reform will save Russia). He would also like to break the link with himself, with the prudent "ego" urging him to get out there and resume his place in the rat race, to go back to making short films for the new rich . . .

And yet he still believes in a life in which a tsarina abandons her throne and escapes with the man she loves. One in which a woman stares out at a great tree at the winter's end amid the swirling snow.

Going back to those old books was simply an attempt to rediscover his youth, he knows this. When he was writing his screenplay he was twenty-six (Lessya, their days on the beaches of the Gulf of Finland . . .), now he has just celebrated his fortieth birthday. Well, not exactly celebrated . . . A call from Tanya: "So have you worked out your problems with organized crime? Who? Me? I've got too much to do this week . . . I'll call you . . . Happy birthday, anyway!"

Nostalgia is deceptive. There was nothing very wonderful about those years when they were filming. He recalls the contortions Kozin used to go through to foil the censorship. The boldness of what they dared to show now seems derisory. Anything can be written about Catherine, you can portray her as a monster or a humanist, show her being served by a horde of lovers—there is no SCCA to wield its scissors.

This freedom has an unexpected effect: it removes the desire to explore her life. A tsarina struggling between power and sex, it's not a hard nut to crack. Unthinkable now to write a screenplay in which she was planning to escape so as not to be the woman everybody thought they knew.

If he still regrets that past, it is for the passion with which he dreamed of showing that other Catherine . . .

He rediscovers the past by going to sell his books. The transaction is simple: one volume brings in enough to live on for a day . . . Time stands still amid these shelves collapsing under piles of yellowed pages. The bookseller does not seem to have changed since the days when he used to come here in search of texts about Catherine. She is pale and thin, her hair held back by a band that looks like the faded fabric of a bookmark. "What people are really buying these days," she explains, "is fine bindings. You know, they furnish a room . . ." Oleg has often seen these "books furnishing a room" at the homes of oligarchs. Indeed, one of them had been saved by the thickness of such volumes when an attempt was made on his life: he used to show his visitors an encyclopedia riddled with fragments of metal . . .

From this bookshop outside of time, Oleg goes to another place hidden away from the world. In an alley behind the Cathedral of St. Nicholas, "the sailors' church," an Armenian grocery store where, from time immemorial, they have been selling the same kinds of food. Big, highly spiced olives, salted cucumbers, unleavened bread, dried meat, and brandy in bottles with labels that have passed unchanged through all wars and revolutions . . .

Drunkenness comes slowly, in drowsy waves, and the slices of dried meat take time to reveal their flavor. His memories soar above the confusion of the past, no longer becoming snagged on a thousand brambles, resentments, and regrets. He smiles, a draft of Armenian brandy helps him to remain aloft above his life, levitating.

Vestiges he believed sunk without trace rise to the surface. That fragment the censors cut from Kozin's film: Catherine talking about the Russians. "The universe has never produced an individual more male, more self-possessed, more frank, more human, more generous than the Russian . . . By his nature far removed from any kind of deception and artifice, his directness and honesty find all such devices abhorrent . . ." In Kozin's film, this exuberant praise was presented as a voice-over, behind images of the massacres during the Pugachev rebellion. The censors had spotted the hidden irony . . . Another memory—that mound sixty feet high starting to belch fire. An imitation of Vesuvius during one of the parties at Peterhof. Always these Italian echoes. The theater at the Hermitage is copied from that at Vicenza. A whole area between St. Petersburg and Moscow is covered with canals, to become a "Russian Venice." And that *Barber of Seville* by Paisiello, which Catherine listens to in Lanskoy's company . . .

The evening always ends with Oleg encountering that pair of lovers! They return to remind him of the appointment he has failed to keep. Two souls in torment whose suffering he had no means of assuaging.

He pours himself more brandy, hoping that another drink will banish these phantoms . . . No, they are still there—a bright night in June, Catherine's bedroom is suffused with a bluish light. The tsarina is seated, naked, on the edge of the bed. She has let down her hair, Lanskoy strokes her hair and her back, which shivers gently at his caress . . .

The tenderness he pictures is so intense that Oleg closes his eyes, lost amid the beauty of this nocturnal moment. This is what Kozin should have filmed. It was at such moments that the lovers spoke to one another of their desire to escape.

He hastens to erase the vision of the journey they dreamed of. A night in June? Not possible! At the end of June 1784 Lanskoy falls ill. The historians offer two versions, both equally tempting to writers of fiction. The first: Potemkin learns of Catherine's plan to marry Lanskoy and decides to crush the marriage. The second: seeking to satisfy the tsarina's sexual cravings, Lanskoy overdoses on aphrodisiacs, cantharides in particular. But since in Russia this "Spanish fly" is prepared in a vinegar base, the ulcerating effect of the brew combines with the toxicity of the cantharides.

In this death, fate went into overdrive, as if History did not wish to give Catherine any chance. If Potemkin's poison had not worked, Lanskoy was destined to be poisoned by his own hand . . .

Drunkenness no longer ensures that his detached flight soaring in memory over the past can continue. Again Oleg sees a night in June, the two lovers, their tenderness. And all at once—death.

After a month this mode of existence ceases to seem contemptible, something that had distressed him at first. That was when he made an effort to get back into the race. The magazine *No Comment* still existed, but the photographs of rich and poor were no longer juxtaposed. On the contrary, each pictorial indictment of poverty went hand in hand with an article praising the philanthropic activities of a tycoon . . .

Next he made another attempt to become involved in making films glorifying oligarchs. But in this field, too, the situation had changed. The new rich no longer wanted to flaunt their wealth—the documentaries now showed them visiting the old people's homes they were funding. Filming these gangster benefactors would have been even more hypo-critical than celebrating the bandits gloating selfishly about their worldly success.

Most of all, what Oleg realized was that there were limits to the freedom of maneuver offered by the cut and thrust of this new life: step on other people or be downtrodden yourself. For a time, thanks to the Armenian brandy, he still managed to keep his distance from the general melee.

One day, recognizing himself as one of the "downtrodden" becomes a matter of indifference to him. The sale of a book pays for a little food and the torpor of the drink, a familiar sequence of visions that makes possible that road where a couple are riding along on horseback through the night . . . For a time he can inhale the cool of the air in the pathway they are following and . . . And then reality takes over: the horseman dies and his mistress once more becomes that aging tsarina who loves power, honors, flesh . . .

This merry-go-round of ghosts finally leads to a palace constructed from little scraps of wood, the model his father made. The pain of this memory is sharp: Oleg fills a glass and knocks it back, attempting to

fend off an even more tormenting recollection: his mother's night table,
the cup, a little pearl necklace, a book with a worn cover . . . And at the
center that empty space where his memory has never succeeded in identifying the trinket that nevertheless was definitely there, registered by his
childish gaze.

The empty space in his memory grows larger every day, a pale expanse
blotting out well-loved faces. Sometimes a remnant of pride shakes him:
look at me, Oleg Erdmann in this room that smells of dirty clothes and
tobacco, me, waiting in line to buy a cheap bottle of drink, now that the
Armenian's brandy is too dear, me selling my typewriter and seeing it
on display, like a prehistoric object, in the window of a store that sells
computers! Me . . . But after all, I'm just part and parcel of that string of
losers who are out on the streets selling the pathetic relics of their lives,
a spoon, a pair of shoes, a tarnished military medal . . .

   A glass of vodka banishes first the shame, then the need to think.
What remains is the childhood memory he carries with him into his
sleep. His mother stroking his head, softly singing a lullaby in German,
and before he falls asleep he has time to see those objects set out on that
night table. He knows them by heart: a cup, a necklace, a book . . .

Walking along he discovers just how weak he is—he gets out of breath
on the staircases in the subway, then makes an exhausting trek along the
railroad track. One last surge of energy, a wager: if he could get as far as
the crag-building of his childhood, his life would take off again, would
give him back a reason for running, for fighting on.

   The day before he had restored a little order to his room, washed
some of his things, left the bottle alone. He unearthed the old maps of
Europe, the ones for the "secret journey" he no longer believes in, he
thought of sending them to Eva Sander, whose address he has kept. But
at the thought of this he was overwhelmed by a feeling of cosmic remote-
ness. Then he remembered Luria, the historian who had once supported

his screenplay . . . So the parcel of maps went off to him and, calculating his age, Oleg reflected that Luria might well be dead and therefore even more out of reach than the remote galaxy where Eva dwelled . . .

At first it seems as if in his exhausted state he has confused the network of streets, his route to the crag-building. The rows of warehouses and run-down housing developments no longer exist. In their place is a forest of concrete pilings, fences around construction sites, sections of walls revealing the interior of a room, the intimacy of a former life ripped open . . .

He hurries on, fearing he will come upon his childhood home in ruins as well. He is out of breath, the air smells of steel, the bitter exhaust from trucks, snow mingled with mud. The alleyway that used to lead onto the railroad tracks has turned into a river of earth. The light is already fading. Feeling his way amid fragments of scrap iron, he leaps from one patch of asphalt to the next. The tracks have been taken up, a trench some sixty feet wide has been dug to replace them—probably a future tunnel.

Finally, through the jungle of steel girders he catches sight of the crag-building: no longer ringed by the rolling stock of trains but by a high metal fence.

"Even so, there must be a way in," Oleg says to himself. "The people who live there must have to slip through somewhere . . ."

Walking along outside this fence becomes a challenge, he flounders around amid muddy ice, gets out of breath, unbuttons his coat, ignores the lumps of clay clinging to his boots. The fence follows a curve and at each corner appears to offer an opening that would lead to the building whose outline he can see. But, inexplicably, its windows continue to remain on the other side of the barrier . . . Dusk engulfs the path, he stumbles, his vision blurred with sweat, his breathing raw from the wind . . . Then he stops, colliding with a pile of old railroad ties, and sits down, exhausted—hearing nothing now beyond the pounding of the blood in his temples. At his feet, behind the fence, a huge cavity opens out, a pit destined to accommodate the foundations for a structure. The nature of the project is spelled out on a sign: "Prestige development, from studios to six-room apartments, penthouses, swimming pools, parking lots, fitness rooms . . ." He pictures the apartments, how they will be teeming with every modern convenience, children, hugs and kisses, satisfaction fulfilled. All this sited over a hole from which the cold smell of earth, of damp wood—of the grave—will arise. But the happy residents will be unaware of this. Nor will they ever see the old railroad ties where a little boy once hopped along, hurrying to return to an attic half taken up with a model of a castle . . .

His return journey is a flight in darkness amid mud. His way is barred by ditches, great steel pipes, rolls of fiberglass. His eyes are hot with tears, tears of disgust at his inability to be anything other than this forty-year-old man, his feet caked with mud, gasping for breath in a way that reaches right down into his chest in a stinging rush. He would like to push this dummy to the limit, make it fall, roll it in the earth soiled with the remnants of lives destroyed. Or knock it out with long drafts of alcohol. Then for a few minutes it could live in harmony with that child of ten who used to walk along, counting the ties, until he reached the crag-building, climbed up, undressed, and crouched down in a little zinc bathtub, beneath a stream of warm water.

The crag-building, a little zinc tub, a stream of warm water, his father softly whistling a tune . . . During his illness, recalling this childhood happiness will be the only reality that keeps him in contact with life.

He sees a doctor visiting, an elderly woman whose weariness he can sense. "They earn nothing these days, these local doctors," he thinks in his listless state, but he lacks the strength to thank her or to feel indignation. He remains silent, too, in the presence of Zhenya, his neighbor, not from ingratitude, but on account of the cough that is choking him. She brings him broth and he notices her three children poking their heads in at the door, curious to see the dying man their mother is feeding. Oleg remembers that during his years of success he had never once given a thought to Zhenya, forgotten here in this communal cavern. The idea pains him more than the burning in his chest.

There is also an old man whom he recognizes through the mists of the fever and whose face, at first, makes him weep. It is Luria, leaner and paler than the man who, long ago, made his stand against the State Committee . . .

Half alive and lethargic as he is, Oleg recognizes the already spring-like chill given off by the coat Luria hangs up on the door and the faintly smoky aroma of the tea he prepares, boiling up water in Zoya's antique kettle . . .

These comradely actions recall the collective life of the old days, though Oleg always detested its poverty. What he is experiencing now is the lingering echo of that life: the humble, patient solidarity of the losers.

He is too weak to carry on a conversation. Besides, Luria says little, thanks him for the old maps of Europe ("Lanskoy's maps"), advises a diet of honey. For Oleg, the taste of this honey merges into the stirrings of life being reborn.

One evening, amid the drowsiness of his illness, a troop of shadows appears, processing across the wall opposite his bed. Men in frock coats, women in crinolines . . . It takes Oleg a moment to guess the source of this theater of phantoms: Luria has managed to repair the magic lantern. The historian murmurs a commentary, in an ironic and mysterious voice, like someone embellishing a tale of adventure. On the wall the silhouettes of a man and a woman in each other's arms: "The abbé de Boismont in bed with a duchess. Suddenly they hear the husband's footfalls: 'Pretend to be asleep,' whispers the abbé. The duke appears beside the adulterous woman's bed. 'Hush,' the abbé orders him. 'I call on you to bear witness!' The duke is dumbfounded. 'Witness? But . . .' The abbé gives him no time to react: 'Silence! Let me explain. Yesterday the duchess claimed she slept so lightly that a fly could rouse her. I wagered her fifty louis d'or that I myself could slip into her bed without disturbing her dreams. She laughed in my face. But you can see for yourself that my arrival has not disturbed her sleep at all.' The duke sighs: 'What a ridiculous wager . . .' The abbé gets dressed and, before leaving, persuades the duke to agree that the duchess shall not be told. The next morning he returns. The duke bears witness to what he saw during the night and, like a gentleman, pays out fifty louis to the winner of the bet . . . who has cuckolded him."

There may have been other stories projected on the wall, but this is the first one Oleg has grasped completely, without interrupting it by his coughing fits. The first that makes him laugh.

The shadows get up to more of their little games. June 1770, the

comtesse de Valentinois prepares her guests for a somewhat special dinner party: with each new dish the diners will remove one item of clothing.
After dessert those who are now naked will indulge in the pleasures of
their choice . . . Excitement takes hold of the table companions, a menu
of a dozen dishes offers them the prospect of catching the object of their
desire in the act of shedding all her—or his—petals. With the crème
caramel the countess's own beautiful breasts make their appearance and
she bares all just as half a dozen of the men have stripped naked as old
Adam. Madame de Valentinois, if a memoir of the time is to be believed,
"made of her own flesh a dessert a great deal more tasty than the crème
caramel these gentlemen had just been savoring."

No, Luria is not just trying to cheer him up. These shadows
remind Oleg of his original screenplay about Catherine. The tsarina
watched France with a feverish mixture of jealousy, fascination, and
wounded pride. Paris was the looking glass in which she studied herself
every day, closely observing the fashions, the currents of thought, and the
art of seduction . . . Her correspondents kept her abreast of the city's
latest gossip, her secret agents unmasked for her the plots that were being
hatched at Versailles. As for the diplomatic briefings being sent to the
French Embassy in St. Petersburg, she was aware of their contents before
the ambassador himself. She knew all about the vortex of mistresses
around Louis XV, about the adolescent girls groomed for the king's
pleasure in his Parc-aux-Cerfs hideaway at Versailles . . .

On the wall a man with a wig is pursuing the silhouette of a
woman. Luria comments: "They've wagged their tongues so much about
Catherine's sexual appetite. But was the old king's taste for very young
girls any more moral? Take a look at this character: Lebel, the footman
who 'tried out' the king's future mistress, Madame du Barry. Always two
yardsticks, a double standard. In Catherine's case, people blush. Would
you credit it? She has Countess Bruce, the 'tester,' check out the favorites
for their sexual vigor. While Lebel's 'trial run' is held to be an elegant
amorous exploit."

This shadow theater does not seek to clear the tsarina's name but to situate her once more in the Europe of her age. And at that time the quintessence of Europe was French.

"And now we have this plump gentleman, let's say he's the regent of France, Philippe d'Orléans. He's with his mistress, Madame de Parabère, the archbishop of Cambrai, and the famous financier John Law. A paper is brought for the regent to sign. But he's so drunk he can't manage the pen. So he holds it out to Madame de Parabère: 'Sign, whore!' She declines the honor. Then, to the archbishop: 'Sign, pimp!' The latter abstains. Finally, to Law: 'Sign, thief!' Law refuses. The regent sums up: 'See how well the kingdom is governed: by a whore, a pimp, a thief, and a drunkard!'"

Luria removes the cardboard silhouettes, switches off the lantern. "Tales like these were, if you like, as much the political background to Catherine's life as the chatter on television is for us today. We rub our eyes when we see someone like Potemkin neglecting the business of the empire on account of a hangover. How shameful! But he would have been perfectly familiar with the anecdote of Philippe d'Orléans making fun of himself. Oh and, by the way, Catherine one day got word of a new diversion for the Parisian aristocracy: the magic lantern! Oh yes. Except that these were plates of glass on which painters depicted scenes of debauchery. The blue films of their day. One of these performances at the home of the marquise de Travenart caused a scandal: the beautiful nudes her magic lantern projected on the walls bore a strong resemblance to Marie Antoinette . . . Before we judge Catherine we must always remember the background to that apocalypse of joy . . . Right, I'm leaving you now. Here's your doctor. And eat more honey, Catherine adored it. See you tomorrow."

One day Luria talks to him about Kozin's film, about the scene where, in flashback, we see Peter the Great witnessing the beheading of his unfaithful mistress, Marie Hamilton. The tsar goes up onto the scaffold and picks up the head that has just been cut off . . .

"The film turns that execution into the symbol of Russian history. Just think, Peter the First picks up the severed head and kisses it on the mouth! Horror! Barbarism! Slavic savagery! Kozin forgets that Peter didn't stop at that kiss. We're in the eighteenth century and he is passionate about science. After kissing the lips that are starting to turn pale, the tsar flourishes the head and gives a learned lecture on the functioning of the blood vessels now dangling down from the severed neck. Yes, an anatomy lesson, right there on the scaffold!"

Oleg feels a debater's energy awakening within him. Luria's argument was there to provoke him.

"But, hold on, that's just what Kozin did show. That's all there is in our history—tyranny combined with a hunger for scientific progress. Space rockets invented by scientists whom Stalin kept locked up in laboratories that were prisons! Violence plus utopia, a very Russian formula. Peter the Great often employed it . . ."

"And what would you say about this other execution, perpetrated in the name of a utopia? A woman receives a sword blow in the back of her neck and, barely alive, is forced to walk over the bodies of the victims who have preceded her. She's finished off with pike thrusts and then they amuse themselves by undressing her and washing her, the better to mutilate her body. One of her legs is thrust into the mouth of a cannon, her breasts are ripped off, her genitals reduced to pulp. Finally she's beheaded and her head, with the hair curled by a hairdresser, is presented to her best friend. Yes, you've guessed it. We're not talking about the customs of Russians under Ivan the Terrible, but the pastimes of citizens in a highly civilized country. This was how, in the twilight years of her life, Catherine learned of the death of the princess de Lamballe, the friend of Marie Antoinette. So the Russians invented nothing. It's a shame Kozin didn't allude to that French looking glass Catherine used to glance at in alarm . . ."

"But he does, in the final scenes. The taking of the Bastille, the freeing of prisoners . . ."

"Yes, a total of seven were held there. That's all. Under Louis the Sixteenth their meals consisted of three dishes and a choice of wine. A few years later, in the hell of the revolutionary prisons, such treatment would have seemed like a dream of paradise. As for the prison where I met your father, the famous Butyrka in Moscow, there were over sixty of us detainees crammed in there, standing up, in a cell four feet by twelve. Packed in so tightly against one another that we had to take it in turns to breathe, if I can put it like that: one of us breathing in to take advantage of the little space left by his neighbor breathing out. Soon there was not a breath of air left in that dungeon. Your father asked two fellows to lift him up and he managed to break the glass in a skylight close to the ceiling. His hand bled a good deal but we were able to survive. My limbs were shattered after the interrogations, your father let me lean on his shoulder. That vertical torture lasted more than twenty-four hours. And as always, in that kind of situation, there was an element of black humor. They accused Sergei Erdmann, your father, a German, of being a member of a Zionist organization. And me, a Jew, of being an agent of the German spy services. They'd unearthed letters I once exchanged with a professor in Tübingen . . ."

Luria breaks off but his hands go on moving as if he were still telling the story of this life long ago to someone invisible. Oleg feels a sudden surge of deeply painful sympathy. And realizes he is cured, he is once more capable of sharing in other people's sufferings.

He gets up, goes to the kitchen, makes some tea. Outside it is a spring evening, the air is faintly blue, there is drizzle, gilded by the sunset. Zhenya's children are playing near the four-wheel-drives parked in the courtyard. A window opens, a man with a shaven head yells out. They scatter . . . The smallest of them stops, dazzled by a late ray of sunlight, slanting down, that has contrived to slip into this dark courtyard.

Back in his room Oleg sees Luria bent over the maps spread out on the sofa. "Lanskoy's maps."

"I didn't mean to bore you with that stuff about prison," Luria remarks softly. "But here's the question that diverted me from my profession as a historian. There came a time, maybe when I was about thirty, when I began to feel a bit of a fool: I was spending my life recording the follies and atrocities committed by our beloved fellow human beings.

What an enviable vocation! That was when I began to turn my attention to the circulation of money under Catherine the Second. A neutral, technical subject and one that absolved me from heaping upon the tsarina all the insults a good Soviet historian was supposed to bestow onto her: upholder of slavery, autocrat, Russian Messalina . . . When I read your screenplay the question I had sought to repress came back to me in all its impertinence. Who is to blame for the torrent of grandiose crimes that are called 'historical events'?"

"Is there really one guilty party to be singled out?"

"Yes. Us."

"You mean, humanity?"

"No! Us. You, me, thinkers, historians, artists. We who accept this caricature of Catherine: a debauched woman on the throne, the seducer of French philosophers, Bonaparte in skirts . . ."

"So there's a hidden side to her that people try to obliterate . . ."

"Well, there are these maps and the mystery of them. And archive documents that bear witness to the preparations Catherine and Lanskoy undertook for their escape. But above all, if you believe in this plan, then Catherine's life appears in a different light."

"Agreed. An unknown life. But how could Kozin have shown it in his film, since no historian speaks of it? I made no mention of it in my screenplay . . ."

"I'm no screenwriter, but I'd begin like this: the start of winter, a German town, a coach with four horses is about to depart. Standing in front of the carriage, a young man of twenty-four and a young girl of fourteen. The future Catherine the Great and her uncle Georg Ludwig, her first love. History separates them: the girl will go on to win the throne of Russia. Her beloved departs for Italy. Snow, the sound of hoofbeats, and in the girl's loving imagination we see the road Georg Ludwig will follow, valleys, mountains, sleepy villages, and, finally, on the far side of the Alps, the first breath of spring in Italy. The light of a country she will never see during her glorious reign . . ."

"Do you think she clung to the memory of the man who loved her?"

"I even think she rediscovered this lover again forty years later—in the figure of Alexander Lanskoy. That young Russian officer of Polish descent looked very like Georg Ludwig: the same blond hair, a similar build, the same age. This time Catherine really hoped to go away with the man she loved."

"But then why hadn't she done it before? With Potemkin, or Korsakov . . ."

"For a very simple reason: none of her favorites loved her. They were fond of her power, her wealth. Those things didn't interest Lanskoy . . . Georg Ludwig wrote one day to the future Catherine the Second: 'Just one night on the roads of Italy would be worth more, for us, than the thrones of all the kingdoms in the universe.' And he added: '*Die Zukunft wird zeigen . . .*' Yes. The future will prove it."

Luria gets up, puts his coat back on again. Oleg walks to the entrance hall with him.

"That version of the facts may seem too romantic to you. But the evidence exists—those maps, among other things . . . And besides, it was by thinking about those two lovers escaping to Italy that I managed to survive eight years in the camps . . ."

Two bodyguards hurl themselves out of a car and block the sidewalk. The passersby, brought to a standstill, see a man emerging from a restaurant with his arm around the waist of a very young blond woman. Oleg stops, too, waiting for this individual and his companion to settle into their sedan. Such a scene, which a few years ago would have seemed improbable, no longer surprises. A rich man, a youthful mistress, their right to hold up the traffic, heavies keeping inquisitive bystanders at bay. In the old days behavior like that was only permissible if you were a senior Party boss. And even then . . . Now you just have to have a lot of money. "A historic change," Oleg says to himself. During his illness History has been signing up a new cast of actors, rewriting the script for its farce . . . This is the first time he has taken an evening stroll without having to pace himself to match his fatigue. This resumption of his place among his fellow humans in the mild spring warmth sharpens his perception of everything. That man, dressed like a playboy, his girlfriend, a teenager's face, her lips curled in a contemptuous pout . . .

Before getting into the car the man turns his head . . . Oleg exclaims with impulsive fury: "Hey, Zhurbin, you old son of a bitch! It's you!"

One of the bodyguards bounds toward him, but already the "playboy" has turned around and his blasé expression now looks less convincing under the gaze of an old comrade.

"Erdmann! Didn't you get my letters? Why not? I wrote to the address where you were living with Tanya . . . Oh, I get it! She loves me, she loves me not . . . OK, get in. I'll drop you off. That way I'll have time to explain . . ."

And that is how, somewhat squeezed between Zhurbin and the young woman, Oleg learns about the existence of a "mega-project."

Zhurbin already owns several restaurants in Moscow and St. Petersburg. He is part owner of three luxury hotels on the Black Sea coast. His idea, he explains, has the simplicity all ideas of genius do.

"I've just bought a film studio. We've already made two excellent thrillers. But the audiences are not coming. Russian audiences like their crooks to be American, as you well know. So I need a project on a grand scale. You know, a TV series people will get hooked on, stars whose faces they recognize in the street. And not only in the street—in my restaurants and hotels! Do you get the idea, Erdmann? Audiences will come to eat in my restaurants hoping to see the young hero from the series at the next table. And they'll go and stay at one of my hotels so they can say they've swum in the very pool where the bimbo from the latest episode was doing the breaststroke . . . Not bad, eh? I just need a big subject. You once worked on the life of Catherine the Great. That's who I want! Not the old relic you find in the history books, no. A Catherine who's been dusted down, a bombshell who explodes in our faces!"

Oleg learns that his friend's newfound wealth is based on a number of very diverse enterprises, ranging from the sale of reinforcement steel to eel fisheries in the salt marshes of the Caspian Sea. One of Zhurbin's businesses makes hair dryers, another, refrigerators, and yet another, furniture and bedding. This only appears to be too many irons in the fire, for the eels are delivered to Zhurbin's restaurants and the hair dryers hum away in the bedrooms of his hotels, as do the refrigerators. In a word, the Chinese who come to buy his steel also sleep in his beds, dine off his eels in his restaurants, and extract their cans of beer from his fridges.

"And soon, I guess, they're going to be watching films produced by your studios," jokes Oleg.

Zhurbin laughs, happy to be able to relax, no longer acting the part of an aggressive, domineering millionaire: "And what's more, I've just bought a whole lot of shares in a big liquor factory, in Kiev . . ."

This expression, "bought a whole lot of shares," often recurs as he is talking. Oleg imagines him being shared out, divided up into dozens of little Zhurbins, lively, nimble, altering according to the functions they have to carry out, then becoming joined together again into one massive whole, protected by bodyguards. Everyone in this new country is fragmented, among a variety of professions and types of status, and wears several masks. Beneath the tycoon's front that Zhurbin puts on, Oleg occasionally detects a frailty: a lost, bewildered look that reminds him of a dog he once saw as a child, escaping from the wagon where they were cramming in stray animals to be put down.

This fragmented life of Zhurbin's is visibly trying to knit itself together again in a cinematic "mega-project" that will bring back memories of his years as an actor at the start of his career.

The ease with which the series is launched leaves Oleg with a feeling of intoxication, weightlessness. No SCCA to be consulted, no ideological inquisition to be undergone. Absolute freedom! He is almost unsettled by this. So this new life, as a compensation for its ruthlessness, offers this emancipation . . . To make a series all they need is sufficient finance, and this will be provided by the steel and the eels!

Before Oleg has written a word of the shooting script, Zhurbin's staff are already recruiting a cast of actors. Following the collapse of the state film studios, unemployment is rife in the profession. Oleg is panic-stricken: these former stars are prepared to take part in a series for which not one line of a treatment exists. Zhurbin reassures him: "You know Catherine's life by heart! Create a basic outline, that's all we need. And don't forget, it's a TV series: this week we film, and next week it's on people's screens. Sure! We're not back in the good old Soviet days when you needed ten rubber stamps from the censor for every scrap of dialogue.

Go ahead, get going! I don't want the two of us to find ourselves back lugging pigs' carcasses around!"

Oleg is not sure whether Zhurbin's urgings are giving him confidence or, on the contrary, inhibiting him. Grudgingly, he recognizes that his friend offers him one last chance to find himself a place amid the whirlwind of the new times.

He discovers that they are liberated not only from censorship but also from the straitjacket imposed by the length of a film. Kozin had a hundred minutes to tell Catherine's life, he has this marathon of television episodes, a series, which, if it is successful, will keep running indefinitely. "Three hundred and a half episodes, if you like," declares Zhurbin, remembering his old joke. *"Festina lente:* make haste slowly. Fire out one episode a week, but be thrifty with your ammo. In a year's time I hope Catherine will still be up there galloping on her favorite horse, Orlik, and choosing lovers! Tomorrow I want to see you with the script for the opening scenes. Good luck!"

Oleg knows what scene the series will open with: a girl of fourteen watching a carriage disappearing in the distance as the snow falls. The future Catherine II separated from the love of her youth . . .

Zhurbin reads the first pages of the draft in his office. Oleg, both nervous and excited at the same time, looks around at the heavy furnishings, the profusion of statuettes, pictures, books in fine bindings. Everything he used to see in the homes of oligarchs in earlier times. The only original detail, a huge aquarium in which the famous eels from the salt marshes are swimming sinuously . . . Without breaking off from reading, Zhurbin suggests: "Put a chair in front of the window and stand on it. You can see the Admiralty spire . . . Breathtaking, isn't it?"

Standing on the chair, Oleg catches sight of the gilded spire and, looking down, the seething throng in the street, an old woman beside a kiosk, counting small coins in her palm . . .

"OK, get down, Erdmann. We need to have a talk, man to man."

Zhurbin leaves his director's chair, gestures to Oleg to join him on a semicircular sofa, pours them each a whiskey. He takes a deep breath as he prepares to speak, but his cell phone rings and his stern expression softens. "No, no, my little fish," he murmurs softly, "I'm not with my accountant. I'm with an old friend . . . Yes, he's almost as brilliant as me. He's going to write us a great script . . . Yes, all about the tsarina, like I told you . . . You're right, honey, it's very difficult. Things are hard right now, but my pal is a very gifted fellow. I'm going to tell him what to do and he'll do a super great job, I promise you. You're going to be glued to your screen, my little eel . . . OK, love you. See you tonight . . ."

For a few moments his face retains a radiant and rather foolish expression. In it Oleg seems to see the reflection of the young blond woman from the other evening. "You know, I can't tell you how sweet she is . . ." Zhurbin smiles, lost in a dream. Then he pulls himself together.

"Your script, Erdmann, it's no good at all! No, now listen. These chaste farewells in the snow, your little Catherine having a fainting fit— the viewers are going to start channel surfing! They'd rather see any old garbage of game shows. No. I'm not a total ignoramus, contrary to what you think. I've read books about Catherine's youth and I know that, as a teenager, she was already obsessed by sex. Look, I'm not inventing anything, I've read her *Memoirs*, I've got them here, right in front of me. And it's down there in black and white: she used to straddle a cushion and ride up and down, thrashing about, working herself up until she was exhausted. And you're asking us to believe she spent her time reading fairy stories for little choirgirls with her uncle Georg Ludwig? It's perfectly clear she slept with him. Yes, at the age of fourteen, so what? She loved him carnally with all the passion of the future nymphomaniac she was. That's what we have to film! Otherwise you'll just be doing another Kozin—a Soviet-style movie where the screen goes dark every time the lovers start to kiss. No, my friend, the State Committee's finished. Now, if the stars of the picture kiss, it goes right through to the orgasm. And no coitus interruptus, thank you very much!"

Oleg has a powerful urge to get up and walk out, slamming the door, but he stays, does not argue, listens. He senses that there is a lot of truth in what Zhurbin is saying. Yes, in the old days censorship forced them to sacrifice scenes that, in close-up or in long shot, touched upon the sexual act. Why avoid them now?

He almost manages to be convinced. And then, suddenly, he understands what has given him pause. The daylight is fading, Zhurbin switches on a lamp. Oleg notices that his old friend's hair is no longer red but gray and that occasionally a shadow of distress flits across his authoritarian expression, just as it did in the eyes of that stray dog that had escaped being put down.

He will rewrite the first episode: the Lutheran tediousness of a tiny German principality, a princess precociously aroused, scenes of her making love in her uncle's arms and suddenly—a letter comes from Russia! Destiny calls. The Empress Elizabeth is inviting the lovesick young woman to the court of St. Petersburg.

When it is shown it attracts a more-than-average audience. "Our little Catherine has cut herself a good slice of the ratings pie!" Zhurbin exclaims delightedly. "You see, I've simply adhered to Lenin's principles: art must be accessible to the popular masses . . . We'll meet tomorrow and talk about episode two."

Their meetings always follow the same lines: Zhurbin reads through the text with sighs of vexation, there's a shouting match in which Oleg is accused of being a gutless intellectual and Zhurbin of being an oligarch whose brain is stuffed with goose fat. Finally, after three glasses of whiskey, a reconciliation, based as much on their old friendship as on this certainty: Zhurbin knows that only Oleg will be capable of giving this jumble of scenes the logic of a narrative in the space of a few days, while Oleg admits that Zhurbin's brain, "stuffed" as it is, enables them to stay in touch with economic reality, yes, always the "shares" on which the survival of their characters on the screen depends.

The greatest surprise comes from the actors: Oleg finds them unbelievably disciplined, devoid of all caprice. On the set with Kozin, he remembers, a colorfully easygoing atmosphere prevailed, actresses would burst into tears, railing against the director's "tyrannical" demands, actors flew into rages, threw their wigs on the ground, threatened to walk off the set. And in the breaks between takes, mockery could be heard, teasing and laughter, directed now at the fat actor playing "Potemkin" for being unable to mount his horse, now at "Catherine" for stumbling on the steps of her throne . . . Here there is nothing like that: they work fast, do exactly what Oleg asks of them, never venturing to improvise. The tension is perceptible. One senses that they are watching one another closely, conscious of their good fortune in having found a series to act in, apprehensive of the idea that they could be replaced, thrust back into the unemployment where so many of their former colleagues are stagnating. "Freedom of artistic creation . . . ," Oleg says to himself, unable to banish a sly uneasiness.

The young Catherine and one of her first lovers, Saltykov, show no reluctance over what the shooting script requires of them: a wild coupling on an island in a fisherman's cottage lashed by the waves of the Baltic. The scene is improbable, as any one of her biographers would agree. But they perform, agree to be filmed naked, simulate a noisy, ferocious orgasm . . .

It is Zhurbin who wants this scene. Oleg argued against it, quoting the history books: that trip to an island, in an icy rainstorm, was unsuited to volcanic passion. "Just let Saltykov pay court to Catherine a little. Then they can act out their love later on . . ." The reply is unequivocal, spelling out the whole thrust of the series: "Erdmann, the viewers are not going to wait till episode twenty-five for Catherine's orgasm. They need one now! And when it comes to episode twenty-five, don't you worry, there'll be more. Otherwise they'll be watching another series on a different channel. Yes, my friend, art, these days, is just as simple as that."

The next day they are at loggerheads again: at the height of the coup d'état Catherine goes into hiding at an inn on the road to St. Petersburg. There is a shortage of beds, she sleeps squeezed up against her young friend, the Princess Dashkova. Zhurbin rubs his hands, they are going to have a carnal relationship! Oleg is up in arms, hotly rejects the legend of Catherine's bisexuality, and ends up feeling that he sounds like a Soviet prude. To avoid moralizing he invokes physiology: Catherine is pregnant. "But we're not going to show her belly!" retorts Zhurbin. Oleg sticks to his guns. "But the inn's full of soldiers . . ." "Better still. Intimacy between the two girls will be all the more spicy!" Finally, Oleg plays his last card: that night, all the historians agree, Dashkova was suffering from severe influenza. Zhurbin's logic leaves him speechless. "At your age, Erdmann, you ought to know that a touch of flu has never stopped a pair of chicks from making out!"

The stunning foolishness of the assertion vaguely comforts Oleg. Zhurbin does not falsify the facts of history, but he exaggerates them, lays it all on with a trowel, he wants everything to be shown. Does the Countess Bruce test the future favorites for Catherine? Well then, the famous Moorish baths will be seen on the screen, a naked woman arousing a young man, gripping his penis to assess his virility, avoiding his embraces until finally, no longer holding back, he throws himself upon her and takes her by force, forgetting the tsarina . . .

After this episode, transmitted during the first week of May, their show is hailed in a long article in a film magazine. The one Lessya worked on in the old days, Oleg notes.

Oleg is not aware of the moment when his work becomes what Zhurbin calls "Stakhanovite filmmaking." He contrives to film a number of episodes in advance and thus no longer has the feeling of writing with the guillotine blade of the current week's episode hanging over him.

Then, in June, their series rises to number three in the ratings . . . A morning in winter. Catherine gets up well before dawn, as was her custom, and in front of the stove she would like to see lit she encounters a giant carrying an armful of logs. "Who are you, my good sir?" The tsarina addresses all her servants as equals. "The stoker of Your Majesty's stoves, my Little Mother Empress," the giant replies, using this droll but historically accurate form of address. "Excellent. Go ahead and stoke away, it's very cold this morning!" The man lights a big fire, checks the draft, is about to leave. Catherine stops him. "Wait, I'm really shivering." He piles in more logs, the flames roar, the stove is red-hot. "I'm frozen," the tsarina insists. "I need warmth . . ." The heating specialist throws up his hands in despair and suddenly guesses. The woman stands there, pretending to tremble: he folds her in an embrace . . . At the first orgasm she names him "Lieutenant." At the second, "Captain." Finally, at the third, overwhelmed, she promotes him to the rank of colonel, grants him a title, and awards him an estate on lands taken from the Turks. He will now bear the name of Teplov, Milord Warmingpan . . .

Zhurbin pretends to be repentant. "I'm sorry, Erdmann. I know that morning she spent in Teplov's arms is only a piece of gossip. But . . . after all, it's included in some of the biographies . . . In any case, if it's not true, as they say, it's a damned good story! *Se non è vero . . . è molto ben trovato.* Have a piece of candy. It's based on wild roses, excellent for the throat . . . The stove in that episode is an 'Old Dutch': fine china tiles with pretty designs on them. The very model my factory is just putting on the market. Do you know how many orders we've received since that episode went out? More than five thousand! And we're in the middle of summer. Imagine if we repeated it, say, in November. No, your film's not a crude commercial. It's like this candy. It's up to us to add the wild rose syrup, or caramel . . . Or a stove. Would you like an 'Old Dutch' stove for your villa? What? You don't have a villa? Ha, ha, I'm only joking. Just you wait. By episode fifty you'll be buying yourself a small castle."

This conversation marks the fact that a certain stage has been reached: Oleg realizes he has now allowed himself to be integrated into the new life. Work on the scripts has left him no time to be aware of it. But the facts are these. He earns a lot of money, rents a fine apartment a few steps away from the Nevsky Prospekt, and three months before, Tanya returned to live with him. She was the one who called to congratulate him on his success, commenting that their show was "a bit kitschy, but nothing to be ashamed of." He ends up thinking this himself.

His reentry into life as other people live it has passed unnoticed thanks to Zhurbin's great cunning in always pretending to take nothing seriously—neither his factories in all four corners of Russia, nor this series: "It's good entertainment for all the proletarians who are being exploited by capitalists like me," he would say. "The cannabis of the people . . ." This was his way of soothing any reservations Oleg might have. "You mustn't take all this literally, Erdmann. We're not here to delve deep into the archives. Otherwise the dust would make the viewers sneeze. So take care!" Oleg resigned himself, recognizing that what he was filming was no worse than any other television series. "The competition," Zhurbin remarked jokingly, "has ten murders per episode. We have the same number of sex scenes. Make love, not war, ha, ha . . ."

The speed at which the weekly episodes had to be filmed caused conscience to be disconnected. Oleg preferred to think of them working with "the sangfroid of true professionals."

At the end of September there is this letter from Sweden . . . "Ingmar Bergman's written to you. He needs your advice," jokes Tanya. A card with a view of a fjord, slanting handwriting . . . A note from Lessya! "I'm thrilled that your series is such a success and your dream has finally been realized." Oleg cannot tell whether these are words of praise or of mockery. "My dream . . ." Despite the brevity of the communication there is a perceptible hint of regret—at not being part of the new Russian reality, with its sharp tang of adventure. On the picture of the fjord a little arrow drawn in by pen: the house where the family vacations are spent, a verdant riverbank, everything beautiful, the air pure; tranquillity and affluence reign there . . . But real life is elsewhere, Lessya must be thinking, in those Russian cities where she left her youth, a world where she feels she will never grow old . . .

The next day, early in the morning, he sets off for Peterhof. A space has been hired for half a day of filming, every minute counts. He remembers those long weeks when Kozin had a whole wing of this vast palace at his disposal . . .

He leaves his car, walks through the park, which is petrified in a milky pallor. For the exterior scenes it'll be hopeless, too much mist. OK, they'll film in a gallery or a salon, what does it matter?

The silence of the tall trees, the dull gilding of the leaves, the scent of the Baltic close at hand. And this pathway slowly extending, looking as if one could follow it forever. He notices a figure in the distance and it makes him slow down. Memory is more alive than the present. The same park, the silvery white of the hoarfrost and a still unknown woman walking along, all alone in this sleeping kingdom. Eva Sander . . . Oleg shakes himself, recognizes his actors emerging here and there from the mist. They all arrive on time, with an almost military discipline that will enable them, after this bout of filming, to dash over to another film set to act in a commercial . . .

And it has started: Catherine is surprised at the lack of vigor her favorite, Zorich, displays in love. The young man invents imaginary grievances, becomes confused, and finally throws himself at the tsarina's feet and confesses: he loves another woman . . .

Suddenly Oleg stops the filming: "We'll start again tomorrow. We can't film with this mist in the park." The actors gather up their belongings and disperse, uncomplaining.

An hour later he seeks out Zhurbin in his office. To rule out any compromise, he declares in an almost threatening voice: "Ivan, I'm stopping there. Hire somebody else. As far as I'm concerned, I'm through with this Catherine the Great shambles!"

He suddenly notices a visitor standing just inside the door. Zhurbin is on his feet with an opened package in his hand. With a vague gesture he invites Oleg to sit down, then, turning to the man: "OK, Sasha. Do the same as before. Put in a complaint to the police, but say nothing to our colleagues. We don't want to alarm them . . ."

Sasha goes out. Oleg returns to the assault. "It's best for us to leave it there, Ivan. It's becoming a total mess! Catherine never accused Zorich of being sexually inadequate. And he never told Catherine he was going to marry one of her maids of honor. That doesn't come till later, with Mamonov in 1789. And we're in 1778 . . ."

He expects a retort, a volley of arguments. But Zhurbin reacts mildly, as if in order to make quite sure: "But I thought we'd agreed about that scene. And in any case . . . All Catherine's lovers deceived her. So, Zorich or Mamonov, what's the difference?"

"The difference is that tomorrow I'm supposed to be filming this hybrid of Zorich and Mamonov in the arms of his wife. And you know what follows: Catherine's henchmen tie him up and rape his young wife in front of his eyes. It's a total lie, but . . ."

"But you agreed to put it in the script . . ."

"Well, I don't agree anymore!"

Oleg stands up, towering over his friend as he crouches in his boss's chair. Zhurbin's arguments are easy to predict, the same as in their last dispute: the series cannot be made without these shock images, the public at large is not interested in dusty archives . . .

Zhurbin is silent, absently he smooths out the brown wrapping paper with his hands. Surprised by this lack of reaction, Oleg leans forward to see the contents of the box . . .

"My goodness! That's some gift!"

The sight of the rag doll is so striking that he emits a whistle. An old-fashioned toy that Zhurbin is removing from the wrapping in a somewhat hesitant manner. The doll has been ripped open and the cotton stuffing is colored red . . .

"I receive several of these every month. They're generally toy bears, ripped open, with my name written on them in felt pen. The red is paint, but one day there was blood as well. And on this one it's no longer my name. It's my daughter's . . ."

He talks in a toneless voice, his eyes fixed on the parcel. His marriage, the birth of a child who is somewhat . . . His voice falters. She's not "feebleminded," he spits the word out bitterly, no, she just has an unusual attitude, no sense of danger, no awareness that people are not all brimming with goodwill . . . His wife died two years before, hit by a car. No, nothing suspicious, apparently. Although . . .

"That's the hardest thing at the moment. You have to expect anything, at any time, coming from anyone. And this doll, I don't know where they found it. It's very old. My sister had one like that when we were children . . ."

He puts the doll back in the box, begins wrapping it in paper, as if he wanted to hide the contents. The telephone rings, Zhurbin's tone of voice changes midsentence: "Who? . . . Yes . . . But of course, my dear friend, I'll be with you in just a minute . . ."

Oleg hastens to ask the question he knows he should have asked long ago.

"So why this series, Ivan? Was it just to sell your 'Old Dutch' stoves? A page of advertising would have been enough . . ."

Zhurbin clears his throat, tries to smile.

"This'll make you laugh, but I was hoping to convey a message. In this new country where people no longer have any idea what men are capable of, one where they can threaten a child, kill her, a child like my daughter, who's even more frail than the rest . . . Yes, I said to myself, we must show that it's all been tried before: violence, wealth, sex, power . . . Catherine tested it to the hilt: wars, authority, the flesh. There's nothing new about catharsis. Yes, the viewer who sees this theater of cruelty and desire will see that it's a path that doesn't lead to anywhere very much. A tsarina has a whole army of lovers, she owns the fattest slice of the planet, and she dies unnoticed, at the foot of her commode. I thought people would make the connection: here's a life where you can kill, seek pleasure, dominate others and it's all empty, because there's something else that we need to be looking for . . ."

"But what 'else,' Ivan?"

"I thought you'd be the one to know that . . ."

A secretary puts her head around the door, whispers a visitor's name. Oleg takes his leave and goes. In the subway he tells himself that next time he absolutely must talk to Zhurbin about the old maps on which Catherine and Lanskoy had traced the route for a secret journey.

The episode portraying the rape of the young bride is broadcast a week later. Brutal images, nudity, rapid switches between harsh lighting and the dark shadows of soldiers. At one moment the camera cuts away: in among some cushions, a rag doll with its sad smile . . .

The series hauls itself up to number two in the ratings, a whisker behind the Argentinian series *The Rich Weep Too.* Zhurbin avoids congratulating Oleg on this achievement.

Oleg meets Luria in a little local café that it takes him awhile to recognize. Precisely because the place has not changed. All the restaurants have been adopting fashions that are thought of as Western, making a show of a "design"—sometimes cold and metallic, sometimes overloaded with deep red velvet and mirrors. Here they still serve the ravioli he so often used to eat with Eva Sander after their wanderings . . .

"And still at affordable prices for us poor casualties from the wreck of the Communist paradise," murmurs Luria, winking at Oleg. "Although in your case you've made a very successful transition into capitalism. Bravo! I've seen several episodes of your series, a fine example of the recycling of the historic past by mass culture . . ."

Oleg puts down his spoon, heaves a sigh, tries to avoid Luria's smiling gaze.

"I feel really ashamed! But . . . I had no choice. Zhurbin, my producer, is no . . . Tarkovsky. For him film has to make money, so it has to please the greatest number. Of course, I shouldn't have filmed that rape. Catherine's reputation's bad enough as it is. But how can you show historic truth without both light and shadow?"

Luria nods in a manner both ironic and understanding.

"Eat up, otherwise your ravioli will get cold. As for 'historic truth,' how can you show what doesn't exist?"

Oleg thinks he must have misheard. "No, I meant, the history that really happened . . ."

"No one knows what 'really happened.' We know facts, dates, who was involved. Historians put forward interpretations. Some of them think they are God Almighty and insist on their view being recognized as beyond dispute. In my youth I myself saw the October Revolution as a final liberation of humanity! Since then 1917 has been rewritten so many times . . . Absolute horror for some, a promise of paradise for others. Maybe up there in the autumn sky there's a god who could read Stalin's mind when he was signing off lists of people to be shot. Maybe . . . But we poor mortals can only speculate. Did the Seven Years' War start because Frederick the Great nicknamed his dog 'Pompadour'? Or was Elizabeth trying to punish the Prussian for his arrogance? Did Maria Theresa really want whatever part of Bohemia it was?"

"Yes, but in the series, I simply invent certain scenes, like Catherine sending in a squad of rapists . . ."

"You're making a work of fiction . . . I once came upon a very serious mistake in an old novel. Well, that's how it seemed to me, because it concerned the circulation of money, my pet subject as a historian. In the middle of the fifteenth century, somewhere on the frontier between France and Spain, the hero dug up a chest filled with gold. The author specified that they were doubloons. What an idiot! Those doubloons, double gold coins, were minted much later, after the wealth of the Incas had been pillaged by the conquistadors, when gold became plentiful, and the Spaniards could indulge in this lavish currency. I was seething with rage, until I finally admitted that for readers of a book these mysterious 'gold doubloons' would be much more exciting than a simple heap of coins, which are the same from one novel to the next . . ."

"So why film history? We've made at least thirty episodes! Wars against the Turks, the Poles, the Prussians, the Persians, peasant revolts, people having their tongues cut out, conspiracies . . . And that alcove that's beginning to make my head spin. We have to work so fast I confuse one actor with the next . . . What's the point of this masquerade?"

"You've given the answer yourself: to show just how hollow the masquerade of history is. And to make people understand that a life does exist beyond all this circus . . ."

"You mean the escape Catherine and Lanskoy were planning? But there's very little evidence . . ."

"Among my notes from long ago I've unearthed a piece of evidence . . . monetary evidence, if I may call it that. Yes, it's my numismatic penchant, as usual. In the spring of 1784, Lanskoy makes an inventory of his coin collection, all the biographers speak of this passion of his. But, to judge from his account book, he was chiefly collecting the currencies that circulated in the countries we saw on your old maps: Poland, the German principalities, Italy. You don't have to be psychic to surmise that this was money that would be used to pay for the costs of a journey. Apologies for showing you the financial underpinning for this beautiful dream, but the detail is revelatory: they wanted to travel incognito. Russian currency would have given them away . . ."

Before leaving, already out in the street, Luria says softly on a note of somewhat melancholy encouragement: "In the old days we had to hoodwink our beloved Soviet censors in order to introduce dissident ideas into a film. These days the censorship is commercial. Use our old methods. This series is meant to entertain the masses, but you can always find a moment to express what seems to you to be an essential truth. It's even more exciting than our battle with the SCCA, do you remember that?"

A moment to express an essential truth . . . Oleg pictures it with great simplicity: a light night at the start of summer, a road leading out of St. Petersburg, the silhouettes of two riders, the dull sound of horses' hooves.

The conversation with Luria liberates him, Oleg no longer has to wage war on Zhurbin. More favorites in the alcove, more Russians and Turks making mincemeat of one another, one more dinner with Potemkin and his mistresses, spooning precious stones out of crystal vases, yes, the "dessert" the prince paid for with the hundred thousand rubles he had received from the latest favorite . . .

The filmed series that Zhurbin desires certainly presents the most eye-catching aspects of history. But not gratuitous inventions. The books speak of the Princess Golitsyn, a debauched woman who boasts of three hundred guardsmen on her list of conquests. Her story is generally alluded to in a footnote. Zhurbin demands a whole scene: a mishmash of uniforms open on hairy chests, sweating nude bodies, swords feverishly unbuckled, sounds of spurs, hoarse breathing . . .

After the ball the Empress Elizabeth has her dress cut off her so as to undress more quickly. In the film the fabric snipped away by the scissors opens out onto an exuberant body with great, heavy breasts. Her haste is all of a piece with her desire to be with her lovers. Their frolics are filmed through peepholes cut in a door to which two adolescents have their eyes glued: the future Peter III and Catherine.

It transpires that Peter is homosexual. His admiration for Frederick the Great is thus not military but amorous, and that is what drives Peter to come to his rescue when the "three petticoats" were giving him a hard time in the Seven Years' War . . .

Oleg no longer argues. He adopts the most direct style possible, filming now "with a handheld bazooka," as Zhurbin puts it. The speed they work at lays bare what a perfectionist cinematographer would have covered up: history, too, is made with a bazooka, in its improbably farcical twists and turns. Zhurbin wants the viewers to learn the cause of Peter III's impotence: phimosis. "Broadly speaking, his foreskin is strangling the glans of his peepee . . . ," he observes, lapsing into nursery language. Peter's friends, including Saltykov, who is cuckolding him, beg the future tsar on their knees to have an operation. Saltykov is the most ardent advocate of such a circumcision—he has just made Catherine pregnant and can already see himself being banished to Siberia. Once operated on, Peter could be recognized as the father . . .

That scene accentuates the farcical humor of what passes for History on a grand scale. A gang of buddies in a pickle from sleeping around, a schoolboy prank, a vaudeville comedy that will soon lead to bloody coups d'état, vile betrayals, wars, tortures, banishment . . .

The new episode is a great success, bringing the ratings close to those for the series *The Rich Weep Too.* The word *phimosis* enjoys a brief hour of glory, especially as a way of casting aspersions on a man's virility. Several times Oleg overhears the oath "you pathetic little phimosis" in altercations between teenagers. "Our series is educating the populace," declares Zhurbin with a laugh.

There is, of course, plenty of posturing, a lot of showy costumes, crude eroticism, but in his great historical circus Zhurbin knows how to capture hidden nuances. Is the Empress Elizabeth suspicious and vindictive? When young, she was despised by the court of the fearsome Tsarina Anne. With the nervous fervor of a debutante she attends a grand dinner. Her gown, her only party frock, will dazzle the guests. She walks into the vast, brilliantly lit hall . . . A moment of silence and then peals of laughter break out: the fabric of the tablecloth is the same as that

of Elizabeth's gown! Her enemies had consulted her dressmaker . . .
Later on, once she comes to the throne, she will own fifteen thousand
dresses and after each ball they will cut her sumptuous costume off her.
Countess Lopukhina, who had chosen the fabric for the tablecloth, will
have her tongue cut out . . .

There is no doubt that Zhurbin reads, in secret, boning up on the
biographies, and thinks a lot, while still posing as a dilettante. He suggests that Peter III's assassins should be half naked. This perception is
not groundless: beneath their bodies these brawny men are crushing a
tsar reputed to be a homosexual—an intentional merging of the violence
of the killing with the sexual aspect of the struggle.

"They murdered him on June twenty-eighth. At that time of year
it's hot, that's why they stripped," Zhurbin adds, pretending to be naive.
And he is the one who advises the actress playing the part of the tsarina
to behave with male vigor in the sex scenes: "Oh yes. Catherine chooses
her lovers, she dominates them by her intelligence, but also by her sexual
appetite . . ."

In the end Oleg even accepts the incessant flashbacks Zhurbin insists
on. First, Peter the Great looming up sixty years after his death, kissing
his mistress's severed head. Then Anne, having vast castles of ice built
in which to imprison her courtiers as punishment. Zhurbin unearths
these scenes in the course of his reading and they have to be shoehorned
into the shooting script at the last minute: these ghosts of his appear in
a grayish blur of memories . . . At first Oleg gnashes his teeth, then ac-
knowledges that this ragbag is less grotesque than it seems. These characters are the living dead Catherine sees marching past in her own memory,
in stories told to her by her intimates, in tales of them that linger on
within the palaces at St. Petersburg. Zhurbin's perception is correct: we
live among the departed, our minds are filled with their words. How
many times (thousands of times!) in the night during her old age must
Catherine have had a recurring vision of Potemkin lying there on the
steppe, Elizabeth shedding a dress cut to rags, Louis XV dying amid the

hideous decay of his flesh, Peter the Great holding up Marie Hamilton's severed head by the hair . . . They came without permission, without logic, with the unruly unpredictability of willful phantoms. "A bit like in our series, in fact," thinks Oleg.

The only matter over which he still differs with Zhurbin is Catherine's femininity. In the series the tsarina is dominating, brutal, hungry for sex—an immensely virile spirit in a voluptuous body. Oleg finds this body hard to tolerate. To play the part of the mature Catherine, Zhurbin has engaged Zara, a Ukrainian actress who has performed in erotic films: outrageously thickened lips, breasts "bulging with silicone," as Tanya puts it. Oleg objects, quotes the testimony of contemporaries . . . Zhurbin sighs, adopting a contrite air: "I guess you're right. We should have had something other than this sex bomb. Oh, and, as it happens, I've found this description of Catherine at the age of fifty . . ."

He produces an old leather-bound volume, locates the bookmark, recites: "What is surprising about her face is her fresh complexion, one that a very young woman might envy: the only mark the years seem to have left there is the perfection, the overwhelming beauty, that men know promises ineffable delights . . . She possesses the most majestic, most supple, most regular figure at court, her throat could have served as a model for Francesco Albani: and no finer hand than hers has ever inspired admiration for the elegant gesture that is the one she favors. One could find fault with a little too much portliness in her shapely form and yet the very volume of it must be admired for its dazzling whiteness . . ."

Zhurbin laughs. "Portliness! Volume! There you are! So don't despise Zara, she's got everything that's needed. Oh, and if you recognized your dear Catherine in that, here's a little surprise for you. It wasn't her at all, it was Madame de Maintenon, beloved of Louis the Fourteenth! I just changed the names . . ." He sticks his tongue out at Oleg. "You see, I do a bit of research from time to time! And now, guess where I found this book."

Oleg takes the volume, opens it at the flyleaf, pages through it. And suddenly, in the pencil notes, recognizes his own handwriting . . .

His friend is jubilant: "I bought up all the books you sold off cheap to that secondhand book store, Erdmann. Look, they're all there."

One section of the wall in Zhurbin's office is taken up with a set of shelves on which Oleg can immediately recognize the volumes he long ago traded in for food and drink.

He cannot contrive to understand what moves him more: Zhurbin's gesture or . . . He feels tears pricking his eyelids. In fact, it is the whole flavor of those days that overwhelms him, the time when, beyond these yellowed pages, he had a vision of the silhouettes of two riders on horseback on a road at night . . .

Sensing his distress, Zhurbin hastens to conclude on a flippant note: "Since, in any event, we shall never know Catherine's true measurements, we might as well make her a turn on, no? Like Zara with her big boobs . . ."

For once his laughter sounds forced. He, too, must be recalling those early dreams of filming a little German princess as she watches the snow falling over the Baltic Sea.

The dinner Zhurbin throws at the end of the year wipes the slate clean on their old life. The new world is there, embodied in a score of guests who live in the here and now, no longer content to focus their minds on some vague nostalgia, but on useful, pressing, and pleasant reality. Two couples across from Oleg are discussing the respective delights of islands they have just visited, which he would have difficulty in placing on a map, Baa Atoll and Ari Atoll. Eventually he gathers that they are talking about the Maldives . . . Another great discussion revolves around the sexual identification of different makes of car, or rather what type of woman one would expect to see driving this or that model. A Jaguar, it appears, is only fit for ball-breakers with too much testosterone . . . At the other end of the table, through the haze of tobacco smoke, Oleg can see two fair-haired men, quite physically similar, occasionally exchanging a quick kiss . . . This dinner party on December 20, 1995, is Zhurbin's "pre-Christmas" and he tells the company he will be spending the holiday in Switzerland with his daughter. He passes around a photograph that gives rise to enthusiastic compliments: what a pretty little girl, oh, how she's grown!

The fare is abundant, excessive even, and the quantity of it is intended to demonstrate not only Zhurbin's generosity but also how commonplace such a display of food and drink is: porcelain dishes piled high with salmon, raw, marinated, and smoked; venison; boar; loins of beef; bowls of caviar ringed with ice cubes; orange mounds of seafood overhung with lobsters' dangling claws, as big as a man's hand . . . Bottles from all continents reminding the guests, as they remark—of many a trip, or anniversary . . .

"Ten years ago all this was inconceivable," Oleg reflects, unable to find a better way to express the turning of the page on an era. The Maldives, expertise in choosing a brand of car, the two gays kissing, and Lugano, where Zhurbin is off to, just as if he were going to spend a weekend in the country . . . The theater of History has put on a new production with new costumes and a freshly scripted soundtrack. A few seats away from Oleg is a tall dark-haired man with a receding hairline and a very tanned face—Zyamtsev! Yes, the one who used to refer to him as a "Siberian peasant," his rival for the role of male juvenile lead, who stole Lessya from him. "That series of yours, Erdmann," he had exclaimed earlier, "is a masterstroke. And do you know, your touch is unmistakable." And Oleg had nearly replied: "You mean my peasant's touch?" Zyamtsev has his fiancée, a Dane, with him—"his entry visa to Europe," Tanya mutters scornfully.

Oleg smiles in response to his girlfriend's rigid mask. Tanya has recently undergone a face-lift. Her eyes are still wide open, the shape of her lips, now more prominent, is adjusting badly to the articulation of words. Oleg murmurs a toast: "Here's to you. You're my visa to happiness." He drinks, trying to silence the painful thought now forming in his mind. Tanya is wearing a suit, the revealing cut of her jacket shows off the shapely curves of her breasts . . . "Just as false as her lips," whispers the thought Oleg has been at pains to suppress. Yes, his girlfriend has had her bust reshaped as well, despite having referred to Zara, the actress playing the part of Catherine, and her bosom, in such mocking terms. For three weeks now they have not been making love—to Oleg it feels as if a frail convalescent were sleeping beside him, strips of bandages protect her bruised breasts, a thick layer of cream forbids kissing . . .

A bell rings! Everyone jumps, they have still not got used to the cell phones that are just beginning to colonize pockets and purses. Tanya takes hers out in a somewhat exaggeratedly relaxed way, extricates herself from the chair and slips out of the private room where the dinner is being held. The sounds from the main dining room filter in through the door, the voices of waiters.

Conversations resume. Ngorongoro Crater Safari Park is well worth a visit, but the snows of Kilimanjaro are a bit of a letdown. Yes, it's global warming. It's really easier to buy a cottage in Finland—ecologically sound and not many thieves. The Trust Bank offers an 8 percent return on dollar-denominated investments . . . Zyamtsev embarks on a funny story: Yeltsin is drunk and calls the Ukrainian president: "Tell me, Leonid, those war planes of mine. Did I send them to bomb cities in your neck of the woods or was it in Chechnya?"

The laughter erupts. Oleg turns in his chair, goes out into the corridor, stops beneath an open transom. The icy air, after the stifling tobacco smoke, seems like a substance never before inhaled. The tension in his temples relaxes. "A deep sea diver who's been brought back to the surface too quickly," he thinks. "I've emerged too suddenly into this new world . . ."

He sees Tanya reflected in a mirror at the end of the passage that leads to the main dining room. With her head down, concentrating on the little device pressed against her cheek, she does not see him. It's hard to hear what she's saying. There is something about her face that strikes Oleg as both touching and disturbing—the face-lifted skin striving to register an expression, tender, disarmed . . . "A relative, a colleague, a girlfriend, a lover?" Oleg wonders, realizing that this portable means of communication adds to the number of conceivable situations. Everything is becoming conceivable. Every combination of bodies, feelings, lives. Absolute freedom to act out this new life. The only limiting factor is the impossibility of picturing two riders on a road at night, two beings who, for the love of one another, abandon the games of this world.

He returns to the private room, where the discussions have broken off—Zhurbin, a glass of champagne in his hand, is holding forth: "And here I'm addressing my friends in the press, in particular. When you tell your readers about this dinner, don't forget to pass on the message loud and clear. Starting next year the guests in our chain's five-star hotels will be staying in specially themed suites of rooms. A Potemkin Suite, that's got a bit of class, don't you think? Furnished in period style. The Empress Suite will contain an alcove that's a precise copy of the love nest where Catherine received her favorites. And, by the way, our menu today is a replica of the selection of dishes the guests enjoyed at the Winter Palace. Our expert can confirm this. It's true, isn't it, Erdmann?"

Oleg agrees, his reply lost in the hubbub of voices, the conversations are incoherent now, heavy with alcohol. Tanya takes her place again, her thoughts elsewhere, picks up her fork, looks along the table to see what stage the succession of courses has reached. Oleg has an impulse to show her the photograph of Zhurbin's daughter, then changes his mind, nervous of exposing the child to her indifferent gaze.

Zhurbin appears behind them, already quite tipsy, leans forward, putting his arms around their shoulders. "Tomorrow, Erdmann, you're going to shoot us a real peach of a scene in the alcove. Now let me tell you how I see it. OK! So far, I guess, our Catherine's been much too good a girl. Now she needs to let herself go. We need heavy. We need *hard.* Tanya agrees with me." He hiccups and laughs, tries to kiss Tanya on the neck. She pushes him away and her taut face settles once more into a vague, indefinite grimace. Zhurbin straightens up and makes a tour of the table, staggering as he goes, and embracing his guests.

Oleg unobtrusively slips the photograph of the child back into his jacket pocket, still convinced he is protecting the little girl from what he sees around him. She was photographed near a place where there are swings and slides and, despite the clever choice of background, seems very remote from that setting. Oleg senses that this child, with her sad smile, would understand what his own feelings are amid this new life.

They ought not to have met the next day. Zhurbin has a yellowish look, and a furred tongue. Oleg has a vise-like headache, he wishes he could press his forehead against the corner of the black marble desk, injure himself to ease the grip.

The pain would be bearable if there were not this shared awareness neither will admit to: yesterday's celebration had been a failure, despite the laughter, the jokes, the lavishness of the blowout. There they had been, all vaguely despising one another, everyone feeling that the whole thing was a banquet for the well-to-do in the middle of a country that has been pillaged. And, to crown it all, they were not even the most bloated profiteers, just medium-sized predators. As they eyed Zhurbin's young mistress, a blonde hardly out of her teens, everyone was mentally calling her "a little slut." And Tanya, with her smooth, frozen face, was provoking sarcastic remarks in whispers among the female side of the company ("Poor girl, her skin is so stretched that when she closes her eyes, her mouth opens . . ."). Zyamtsev's Danish companion understood very little Russian and, overcome with drink, was speaking in a rudimentary English that gave eloquent expression to the emptiness of the chatter all around her . . .

Zhurbin remains in his armchair. Oleg, seated on a visitor's chair, feels like a naughty boy summoned for a thrashing.

"If you don't advance, Erdmann, you lose ground. That's the law of television. I know you're trying to rescue my commercial turkey with your aesthete's brilliance. But I have to tell you that the viewers don't give a rat's ass about your clever little touches. In the scene where the soldiers are raping the young bride you included a shot of a doll. What the hell for? Well, I know why: the brutality of the rape and alongside it this hint of childhood. Now how subtle is that? Except that none of the viewers noticed your little trick. The woman with her thighs open, yes. The husband tied up and sobbing, that too. But as for your stupid goddamned refinements, what the hell do they care about them? Do you want people to call you Tarkovsky or what? Too late, my friend. Tarkovsky was a dissident and that's why they praised him to the skies in Europe. He could have filmed dog shit and they'd have called it a masterpiece. That's all finished. You don't make films for goddamned eggheads now. You make them for millions of men and women who've come home from work and who want to take a break, have a thrill, have a laugh. Yes, and there's nothing wrong with that . . ."

"That's great, Ivan, your theories of cinema are fascinating. But I've got a very bad headache: you really should get a different champagne supplier . . . And, in practical terms, what are we doing?"

"What we're doing is *light* eroticism in general and *hard* sex scenes in particular. That's a clear enough program, isn't it?"

"So, blue movies. And as the series is on at ten-thirty p.m., peak viewing time, it'll be banned."

"Sure, that's possible. Happily, I've engaged a first-rate director, a certain Oleg Erdmann, who, by the way, is beginning to be a pain in the ass, and this very gifted guy will know how to . . ."

The telephone rings. Zhurbin picks it up and speaks in rising tones of fury: "No, Sasha. Tell them Zhurbin's not selling his shares . . . What if they insist? Then I guess you'll have to explain to them that one of my bodyguards is a top professional marksman. He won't kill them, because we're nice guys. He'll just aim for their balls. Either the right or the left, whichever suits them best. That's it, Sasha. That's what you'll tell them, word for word. OK? Ciao!"

The look he gives Oleg is filled with hate, even though his hatred is directed at others.

"So, as I was saying . . . Yes, a director of genius, this Erdmann, a virtuoso, like my marksman. He'll know how to film the most risqué scenes without anyone coming and accusing us of marketing porn on television. There you are, buddy. Now it's up to you. And, stop acting like a halfhearted virgin! To film the episode I'm going to tell you about, you'll need to have balls, preferably two of them. Catherine's going to be making out with her horse, Orlik . . ."

Oleg bursts out laughing and the jolting from this hurts him so much that he really does press his head down against the cold edge of the desk. Then he sits up again, grimacing with pain.

"Listen, Ivan. I appreciate your sense of humor, but . . . Well, no comment . . ."

"But it's your comments I want to hear. I'd like to know how you're going to go about it."

"Phew! . . . We drank too much yesterday. Why don't you go and lie down?"

"Erdmann, the horse will be ready at eleven o'clock tomorrow morning . . ."

"You're out of your mind. At least give me time to pinch myself, so I know I'm not dreaming."

"I'm not out of my mind. That scene will be filmed! Either by you or by someone else . . ."

"That scene's a ridiculous lie, Ivan. In 1917 they invented lots of them, to discredit the Romanovs . . ."

"I don't give a good goddamm about the Romanovs! We need that scene and it needs to be both shocking and acceptable to the bosses of the channel. You're going to do it!"

"You bet I'm not. You can start looking for a madman who'll take over from me. And you'll need to find a woman sick enough to play Catherine having an affair with her horse . . ."

"Don't you worry, Erdmann. Zara's already agreed to it. And let's get this straight. There are going to be no images of bestiality. It'll all be allusive, but very physical. I know you want to stay pure. It's the reflex of an egghead who's afraid of getting his hands dirty. Oh yes, a good little German, with all your lace handkerchiefs. Oh dear! A horse! That stinks! And when the stallion gets a hard-on it's not a pretty sight. And then, horror of horrors, a naked chick wrapping her arms around it. You're all the same: you, Zyamtsev, and the rest—cold pasta instead of guts! And that's why the cute little crap stories that you guys film will be forgotten! When the Marquis de Sade wrote about Catherine he showed her being served by a whole battalion of brutes. Or rather, she was the one who was violating and torturing the men. And Sacher-Masoch? Oh, I've read him, too, don't worry. He has Catherine as a dominatrix, whipping Diderot, who's dressed up as a monkey. And you're scared shitless about showing a horse . . . Right, that's it. You're fired! I know who I'm going to hire. A guy who'll film Catherine being fucked by a rhinoceros if necessary!"

Zhurbin yells that last sentence standing in the doorway of his office—Oleg had already stood up and walked out without saying anything. Zhurbin's secretary does not react. Two visitors waiting to see him exchange quizzical, but not really uneasy, looks. The Russia of these days blunts all capacity for amazement. The country is run by a president who, at the conclusion of his trips abroad, is frequently brought home dead drunk. So, a rhinoceros . . .

Returning home on foot, Oleg reflects on this indifference in the face of outrageous events, such as Diderot, naked, being whipped by a woman in thigh boots or indeed a tsarina coupling with her favorite horse . . . Madness! But as nothing surprises anymore . . .

In his jacket pocket he comes across the photograph he had forgotten to give back to Zhurbin: his daughter beside a plastic slide.

. . . Later on he will sense that Zhurbin's rage was an expression of the inevitable postrevolutionary syndrome. Russia had been stirred by so many hopes during the past ten years! The goal was achieved: political parties proliferated, the economy was privatized, frontiers were opened . . . And Zhurbin had even been able to organize a dinner very much like the ones to be seen in films made in the West. And yet inwardly he must be asking himself: "What's the point of all this, if I'm forced to produce this sleazy television series and the only reason for its success is its dreary sensationalism?"

Over the next two days Oleg sees no sign of Tanya. He begins to worry—in this unpredictable country anything could have happened: a bomb attack on a train, a kidnapping . . . Or maybe another installment of plastic surgery, but what's left to be chopped?

Tanya reappears on the evening of the third day, avoids his embrace, sets down two suitcases in the entrance hall, and opens them. They are empty.

"Are you going away? And by the way, where have you been?"

He is not sure what tone to adopt, settles for mild grumpiness.

"Yes, I am going away . . . I can't take any more, Oleg. You're never there, always stuck behind your camera. So why don't you go ahead and marry your Catherine, your great, fat Zara, while you're about it? You spend more time with her than you do with me . . ."

"Well, as it happens, I've just been fired. So now you may risk seeing a bit too much of me . . ."

"And then there's your artistic selfishness! Ready to sacrifice everything for your filming. Well, I'm sick and tired of it! I've had enough of being bossed around. I'm not a German, you know!"

Oleg realizes that all the points in her indictment had been prepared in advance—it was just that Tanya had not anticipated his losing his job. The parade of her grievances continues, his work on the series is blamed, even though he no longer has any work. Oleg reiterates this, assures her that their life can now be less frenetic, talks about the New Year holiday, vacations they can take . . .

The suitcases are filling up, mainly with clothes and cosmetic products. The reproaches take their course, directed at the person he no longer is. The scene seems strangely familiar to him, as if he had already lived through it . . . But when?

Each case snaps shut with a definitive click.

"I wish you all the success you deserve. I guess it's the one thing in life you care about . . ."

That's it. He's got it. This scene of a breakup is modeled on those in films made in the West! The suitcases, the ping-pong of the dialogue, the tone of voice adopted by the woman as she walks out. All those psychological dramas have gone to their heads, they've been convinced that this is how couples in civilized countries tear themselves apart . . . The cinema is one hell of a brainwashing device! Or rather, one for laundering people's emotions . . .

"If there's any stuff I've forgotten, don't throw it out straightaway . . . No, the cases aren't heavy. I'm off. Bye!"

From his window Oleg sees Tanya opening the trunk of a four-wheel-drive. The windows are smoked glass, it's impossible to make out the face of the man at the wheel. Is he hiding? Or has Tanya told him not to show himself? Just a driver? Or the man she's going to live with?

"He's the one she's had her face lifted and her breasts inflated for . . ." Oleg realizes that he's never known this new body of hers, never kissed the rictus of the reshaped mouth. A new costume change for a richer, more brilliant life, one that calls for these fleshy lips, a smooth skin, a firm bosom . . .

"Maybe she's even found herself an oligarch," he thinks, with a smile. "Yes, the tycoon who long ago sent in his henchmen to beat up the journalists at *No Comment*. Or, if not him, one of Zhurbin's competitors, the one who's going to be emasculated one day by a marksman! Everything's possible in this country. Absolute freedom . . . !"

He gives a little laugh, moves to close the wardrobe doors: bare hangers, empty plastic bags . . . Standing on tiptoe, he feels at the back of the highest shelf—nothing. In her haste, Tanya has gone off with the gift he had planned to give her at Christmas . . .

At the start of their argument he had been expecting her to insist on his leaving the two-bedroom apartment they were renting together. This idea had given him a feeling of relief as he pictured himself back in his room in the communal apartment, as in the old days. That place, for all its poverty, seems endowed with a truth that cannot be found elsewhere.

On the evening of December 31, Oleg accompanies Luria to the station. Given the date, the trip the old man is undertaking is a somewhat odd one: he will be seeing the new year in somewhere amid the frozen lands that lie between St. Petersburg and Moscow. Luria has obtained permission to visit the prison at Butyrka . . .

"This crucial moment when it's possible to consult the archives from the Stalin era, this blessed reprieve for historians, will soon come to an end," he explains. "Yeltsin will emerge from his alcoholic coma and a turn of the screw will be given, by him, or by his successor . . . The head of the prison administration, to whom I wrote, a liberal, advised me to come on January first, when the prison bosses are resting after the holiday . . ."

They arrive at the station very early, Luria is afraid of being late for a departure he has been looking forward to for such a long time. "Ever since they let me out," he remarks, as he and Oleg pace up and down in the station hall.

He laughs softly: "No, it's not that I wanted to go back to jail. Just to return there as a free man, to figure out how threescore men could remain standing there for long hours in a cell four by twelve feet, without a breath of air. Yes, just to see that cell . . ."

He breaks off, embarrassed at having inflicted this past life from the camps on Oleg. "Let's go out. Maybe the train's already there . . ."

The platform is deserted and there surely will be few passengers. Who would want to spend New Year's Eve in a railroad car?

"Why not tell me about your Catherine? Where have you got to in her adventures?"

Oleg sighs: "Sadly, Catherine has left me. Serious aesthetic differences with my producer."

"So her trip with Lanskoy has been scrapped? I was hoping you might find a way—on film—of letting them escape to Italy . . ."

"But that would have been even more fanciful than the regiments of guardsmen parading through her alcove. Lanskoy died and Catherine quickly found consolation in the arms of Yermolov . . . When you're sitting on the throne do you really want to escape?"

On the opposite platform a train has arrived from the North and is spilling out its stream of passengers. Old friends reunited, relatives calling out to one another, suitcases put down in the snow and, above all, the joy of a festive dinner in prospect . . .

Luria smiles: "At a certain moment all the tsars wanted to escape. Take Ivan the Terrible . . . People picture him clinging to the Kremlin like a burr to a dog's coat. Wrong! In the first place, he wants to move the capital a long way from Moscow, to Vologda—just where that train has come from. Then he runs away to a monastery, refusing to govern. And ultimately he's obsessed with the idea of marrying the queen of England and settling in London. The diplomatic moves made in this direction are well known. And then there's Peter the Great, who spends half his reign abroad . . ."

"That couldn't be said of Catherine. She never really left Russia and clung to her scepter with both hands . . ."

"Well, that, Oleg, was because she frequently nearly lost it. If I try to snatch your bag from you, you're instinctively going to tighten your grip. Catherine has the same reflex . . . But the throne weighed heavily on her. Hence her reforms for redistributing the ruler's load. And also those favorites. Yes, yes. They were there to relieve her of part of the burden. After Lanskoy's death she withdraws—for long months. That, too, was a way of running away . . ."

"Not everyone had this urge toward renunciation. When Paul the First is killed, and the murderers are still in the palace, his spouse bellows in her maternal tongue: *'Ich will regieren!'* Yes, she's eager to reign."

"Those who've once tasted of this fruit become much more inclined to hold back. When Peter the Third is driven out by Catherine, he asks only to be allowed to leave, his violin under his arm and his dog at his heels. And Catherine's grandson, Alexander the First. How many times did he not curse his responsibility as an autocrat! He stages his own death and goes on the run disguised as a peasant. A legend? Perhaps . . . But it says a good deal about the state of mind that has always prevailed in Russia. Alexander the Second wanted to abdicate after giving the Russians their constitution. And he would have done so if he'd not died in a bomb attack. And Nicholas the Second? They've told us thousands of times how powerful the Bolshevik revolutionaries were. Bullshit! In February 1917 the tsar was at the head of an army of fifteen million soldiers who believed he was God . . . At that level of power, I believe an irresistible desire to disappear must arise, to be nothing after having been everything. If you don't detect this desire in Catherine, you've not understood her. People don't understand that she was a woman who had come close to the limit of what life can offer in terms of power, glory, pleasure . . . Yes, everything. And this everything suddenly seems so incomplete, compared with . . . how did you put it? A snowy morning, a woman walking along beside the Baltic . . . But the cinema is interested in History on a grand scale and not in such daydreaming, wouldn't you say?"

The train comes in at a slow, muffled pace, as if the rails, covered in thick snowflakes, were muting the clatter of the wheels. The passengers scattered across the platform are few, adrift in this last night of the year.

Oleg goes with Luria to his car, climbs in, puts his suitcase on the luggage rack. Back down on the platform he sees a face smiling through the window, a hand gesture: "Don't wait for the train to leave!" Luria's features have a strangely youthful look.

In the subway Oleg thinks over their conversation: a snowy morning, a woman walking along beside the sea . . . He guesses that Luria, too, is driven by an old dream: tomorrow he will walk out of the prison, stroll along snow-covered alleys in a town drowsy after a night of celebration—a stranger exploring another life.

Without the bustle of all the filming it seems as if time has come to a halt. Early in January, after the days of holiday, life runs out of steam and the empty hours restore Oleg to himself. He decides to watch his series under the conditions of an ordinary viewer: an armchair, a drink, a healthy desire to be entertained . . .

A bad start! In a scene from the Russo-Turkish war, to save money, the same actors sometimes appear as Turks, sometimes as Catherine's brave warriors. There is a lapse that gives him a shock: one of the Turks, now a Russian, has forgotten to change his boots! Oh well, he's only in shot for a second . . . On the other hand that janissary's eye as he goes in to the attack, high as a kite on opium, excellent! And Zara's not bad, either, especially when she gives up squinting languidly, trying to look like a sex symbol.

Oleg is surprised to find he doesn't altogether dislike the series. Catherine's journey to the Crimea in 1787 is almost a triumph. Especially if you think that to film a convoy of eighty barges all he had available was two launches hastily decorated and gilded! The illusion is convincing: veritable floating palaces, three thousand passengers, musicians, banquets, riverbanks covered in "Potemkin villages" and lit up by fireworks. On board, the fine flower of Europe: the inevitable prince de Ligne, the French, English, and Austrian ambassadors, the wretched king of Poland, Poniatowski, Emperor Joseph II of Austria . . . The whole vast public relations campaign—"Catherine II, Semiramis of the North, the Scythian Cleopatra, the liberal tsarina, heiress of the Enlightenment, quoting Voltaire and Diderot amid the steppes of the Khanate of the Tatars!" The triumph of Europe over Asia, of science over ignorance, of humanism over barbarism, of Reason over superstition and so on. All this within the exquisitely delicate setting of a salon: the guests exchanging the latest news from Paris, Vienna, and St. Petersburg, amusing themselves with rhyming verse, their gluttony satisfied thanks to an endless stream of cooks; they indulge in escapades and make picturesque discoveries on trips ashore, like that of the three Tatar women who had removed their veils and were splashing one another in a stream and whom the prince de Ligne and Joseph II spied hiding in a bush. "Mahomet was right to impose the veil on them," observes the prince, noting these naiads' meager charms . . .

Oleg smiles—the viewers will guffaw at the sight of the three formidably mustached ugly ducklings. The whole narrative aims only to provide such moments of laughter, relief, excitement, and fear, and, then again, of mild relaxation, for this is like the tales in the *Thousand and One Nights,* comic, cruel, bawdy, repetitive in its countless adventures . . . In the end, much like the history of mankind. So, Zhurbin was not wrong.

On the contrary, he's completely wrong! For there is this scene Oleg managed to add: Catherine and her guests are strolling through an oriental market, dazzled by the variety of colors, deafened by all the languages that match them, elated by the sunlight. The tsarina pauses—amid the vivid abundance of spices, fruits, and fabrics, one particular merchant's display is modest: lace that resembles the fronds of hoarfrost you see on windowpanes in the depths of winter. A man and his adolescent daughter offer the tsarina collars, table mats, headdresses . . . they speak Italian. Catherine thanks them, moves swiftly on.

The sequence lasts ten seconds. Oleg is certain that not one viewer will have grasped the point of it. For the journey to the Crimea, three

years after Lanskoy's death, marks a new stage. Catherine has forgotten
their plan of escape. She is once more living in the present, in a mood of
affirmation, of triumph. Europe has been seduced, Turkey beaten, and
the chaos of Russia brought to heel. And the young favorite, Mamonov,
is evidently naively in love with his sovereign. This visit to the Crimea is
an apotheosis! Suddenly, this appearance of the Italians is a reminder of
those two riders leaving St. Petersburg one night in June . . .

"But that belongs in a different film," Oleg says to himself. "Or
rather, a different life. One she dreamed of but did not have time to
live . . ."

He switches channels several times, notes that his own series is far
from being the worst that this garbage dump has to offer. After watching
some political discussions (one speaker throws his orange juice in his
opponent's face), a few game shows, sports matches, and other series, he
hits upon a more serious program: filmmakers talking about the artistic revolution of recent years. One of them asserts: "My film, *Little Vera*,
destroyed the USSR aesthetically. For the first time in seventy years the
cinema showed the act of sex . . ."

Oleg switches off the television. So a pair of bare buttocks brought
down the Soviet empire . . . What strikes him is not even the stupidity of such claims, but the fact that freedom is measured by the animal
brutality a woman is subjected to. True enough, since *Little Vera* there has
been progress. Zhurbin dreams of coupling Catherine with a horse . . .

That evening he spends several hours in his old room in the communal apartment. Among the drafts still lying around here and there,
he finds a copy of the lines Catherine and Lanskoy read together. A text
by Swedenborg, the thinker who fascinated them, a scholar, a mystic,
and the son of that bellicose Sweden whose warlike shadow had often
threatened St. Petersburg. The fragment was translated by Lanskoy: "I
was walking in the streets of a familiar town and I knew perfectly well
that I was wide awake, I saw everything around me with an ordinary

gaze. But at the end of that walk I suddenly became aware that I was in an unknown town . . ."

These words allow Oleg to appreciate how naive he had been in the days when he was hoping to use them in his film: a June evening, the two lovers looking out over the Baltic and reading these pages from the *Journal of Dreams*. An "unknown" town giving rise to their plan for an escape.

The telephone wakes him the next day at six o'clock in the morning. A surge of hope: tortured by remorse, Tanya is going to tell him that their breakup was a mistake . . . No, it's Zhurbin! A telegraphic, impersonal voice: "I'm calling you from the street. Take your car. Come to the office. Park behind the building. Very important." And he hangs up.

Impossible to refuse someone who has hurt you, a point of honor. Oleg grins at this old-fashioned psychology as he gulps down his coffee. Outside it is thirty below, his car is in a deep freeze. The Neva stretches out, as smooth as a snow-covered steppe. "With any luck Zhurbin's going to tell me the role of the horse will now be taken by a mare, yes, a kind of lesbian bestiality . . . He's quite capable of suggesting a deal like that." Oleg laughs, mainly so as not to fall asleep at the wheel.

Zhurbin emerges from the service entrance, like an ambush. "Can you keep this stuff at your place?" Without understanding, Oleg helps him to carry half a dozen large cardboard boxes. "Don't worry. It's mainly paperwork to do with our series . . ." The flaps on the last of the boxes are not stuck down and by the hazy light of a lamppost, Oleg can make out the curved shapes of several cartridge clips, for Kalashnikov rifles. "Equipment for Catherine's guardsmen, I presume," he jokes. Zhurbin makes no reply, a blank look, an angry abruptness in his gestures. "Hide all this, OK? And come see me this evening. If they haven't put me inside by then . . ."

That evening they meet, not in his office, which has been sealed off, but in the reception area from which everything has disappeared, even the secretary's computer. Zurbin grumbles: "It's the rules of the game. You want them to leave you alone and what happens? They slap a revenue department check on you . . ."

This remark has doubtless been repeated to a lot of people and Zhurbin utters it without conviction—a truth overtaken by the seriousness of the situation.

"The fact is, it's even more stupid than that. A lot of idiots like me took the bait. Go ahead, capitalists of the future, bring out your savings, invest, sell, resell, work day and night, make yourselves rich and put the money you make into holding companies for eels from the salt marshes, five-star hotels, and unlicensed liquor. Cretins like me believed in it. We slaved away worse than convicts. Ask me if I remember a single day when I had an hour to myself—zero! No, I tell a lie. I remember those days they were sending me mutilated toy bears. That's all . . . We amassed fortunes, we thought we were hunters on the trail of billions. But we weren't really the hunters at all, we were merely the hounds, tracking down the quarry. And now the hunters have arrived. They're snatching the prey from us and kicking us out. And these are not the lot who were sending me toy bears. The real hunters don't need to use threats. They're the ones with the power! They're in the Kremlin, in the Parliament, in the ministries. We've done the dirty work and they're going to dine off the quarry. And when I start complaining, a team of inspectors turns up, armed like an assault commando. The public prosecutor will find enough in the computers they've taken away to award me a long stay north of the Arctic Circle . . . He's one of the hunters too. And the quarry they've bagged, Erdmann, is the whole country!"

He fills his glass, smiles wryly, shows the label on the bottle. *Empress Vodka.* The portrait of a tsarina in a gilded frame and underneath, two guardsmen lying beside a campfire.

"It was this distillery that they got their hands on first. Hooch. That pays. Now they're going to grab the rest . . ."

"But I guess you'll hold on to a few good bits and pieces . . ."

Oleg makes an effort to sound positive, clinks glasses with him, drinks. Zhurbin responds with an old man's grimace, blinking rapidly. His voice is tense, weak.

"As you know, I can live off nothing, that's how we lived when we were young. But the thing is . . . I've got my daughter. I went to see her in Lugano. The place where she lives is a paradise. The countryside, teachers, she has a big room that looks out over the mountains . . . A pond with fish and turtles. Wonderfully peaceful. That costs a lot. And that's my only problem at the moment. I can go and sell cigarettes at a kiosk in the street, it's all the same to me. But that wouldn't bring in enough to pay for that paradise. She's . . . quite a special child . . . As I already told you. She's not mentally handicapped, no. But she doesn't understand that somebody might want to harm her. That some people have the impulse to strike out, to say hurtful things, to hit for the pleasure of hitting. And yet that's what people do all the time. How can you expect her to live here among these mutilated toy bears and the sick people who send them to me? She's already given names to each of the fish and the turtles, she talks to them . . ."

A chime rings out in Zhurbin's office—twelve brief notes that sound like those of a harpsichord. Oleg remembers the big clock in a mahogany case that stands on a malachite pedestal . . . The expression on Zhurbin's face has not changed—the same aged grimace and the tears that seem to be flowing independently of what he is saying. Belatedly the striking of the clock rouses him, he stares at Oleg as if he were a stranger. His voice breaks off, then strengthens.

"Our series has got to continue, Erdmann! If they were to put me behind bars you'd have enough money to send what's needed for my daughter. You'll do it, won't you? I know you'll keep your word. But the series about Catherine has to keep going, even if you loathe it. I promise you that at the end we'll surprise everybody. Here's my idea: Catherine dies on the commode, her death throes, the pretenders cutting up rough, and then suddenly, a historian appears, a bit like your . . . what's his name? . . . oh yes, Luria. And he says to the viewers: 'You've really been gorging yourselves on this hash of sex and cruelty. You've had a great time watching that caricature in a petticoat jiggling about in her alcove. And you didn't give a good goddamn about what this woman's dreams might be. Well, now, in this very last episode, you'll see the man who truly loved her . . .' And then you can film what you like, her meeting with Lanskoy, their love, and their dream of escaping . . ."

They meet again two days later in a subway station, "like secret agents," Oleg thinks. Zhurbin says he wants to keep him out of trouble but, no doubt, he is also trying to protect his production company, the only enterprise he hopes to be able to hold on to.

"We already have a good many episodes in the can. Enough to last two months, if not three. So we don't need to do any more filming. OK, that scene with the horse . . . I was unfair to you, Erdmann. I admit it. But I was on edge, I knew they were bound to come and take me away. Now you can take two months' vacation. Go and visit Germany in the meantime. You could look up that guy who made an erotic film about Catherine. He was the one who showed the horse . . . Yes, Max Pfister. *The Red-Blooded Tsarina,* I think it was called. Travel a bit, it'll do you good. A visa? But you're an 'ethnic German'! They're sure to give you one in a few days . . ."

At the moment when they part Zhurbin hands him his card. "No, I'm not the president of all that anymore . . . But I've made a note on it of the place in Lugano where they're looking after my daughter. When you're in Berlin, send her a postcard. She'll be thrilled. She never gets any mail . . ."

Before going to the consulate Oleg nervously pictured his "return" to the land of his ancestors. The people he would be dealing with would be elderly, marked by the war. He would be speaking to them in German, and in their voices he would recognize the intonations of his father . . .

The person who hands him an application form is very young, barely twenty, an intern, certainly, and she addresses him in Russian. Her youthful chirping is painful. Oleg switches to German, the young woman follows suit with a smile. She must see this Russian German, who has retained some words of his mother tongue, as a strange survivor, like the man in the *Hibernatus* movie, still young after sixty years in cold storage.

While he is filling in the form the intern takes out her cell phone: an audio bombardment of onomatopoeia, giggles, and place-names. Broadly speaking, Oleg gathers she is talking about a visit to London during the vacation that has just finished.

He hands back his form and hears himself expressing the hope that for an "ethnic German" receiving a visa will not take more than a couple of weeks. The intern adds, in almost wheedling tones, that he might also like to consider moving there, yes, settling permanently in his "historic fatherland" . . .

This suggestion enables him to measure, with some force, the extent to which he feels Russian.

The days of waiting are marked by a feeling of dualism: over forty years of living in Russia and suddenly a German identity concocted for him with a wave of her hand by the young woman in charge of the forms— like those salesmen who drape a garment over your shoulders and, with a bit of sales talk, make it inseparable from your body. He knew from his reading that a short time after her arrival in Russia Catherine fell seriously ill. Thanks to being bled several times (or in spite of this), the princess survived. She even prided herself on what happened to her: "I've lost the last drop of my German blood!"

Oleg tells himself that the notion of having foreign blood has never occurred to him. And yet for families like his, the course Catherine's life took has always counted. This distant Germanic kinship did indeed become a "family secret," a private past, sometimes alluded to in that ironic saying ("all this on account of that little German princess") sometimes by a disillusioned observation: whatever we try to do to be Russian, our origins will be against us, people will always see us as potential traitors . . .

After nine days he obtains his visa. The speed of the response ironically underlines his renascent identity: he's one of the elect, an almost Westerner! The ticket he buys enhances the paradox. The date of February 3, printed in drab official type, signals a journey into a country his ancestors had left more than two centuries earlier.

The giddy feeling inspired by this notion prompts him to make one last visit to the crag-building.

The day, halfway through January, is vibrant with cold and sunlight. The suburbs he passes through are wreathed in columns of smoke, the industrial life breath of the big city. He is no longer amazed by the transformation wrought in this district, once squeezed up against the railroad tracks. The little alleyways have been replaced by broad traf-

fic circles and residential enclaves. He encounters the luxury apartment
buildings he had come across under construction the year before: penthouses, swimming pools . . . Wrought iron gates surmounted with gilded
spikes, surveillance cameras, sentry boxes for security guards, pathways
scrupulously swept . . .

A track through the snow skirts the enclosure, he follows it for a
hundred yards or so and at first has trouble recognizing the structure he
is looking for. The crag-building is still there, but its facade is blackened
by fire. Dominated by tall new towers, its four stories look as if they are
being thrust back down toward the earth. It is rather skimpily fenced off
with strands of barbed wire attached to posts. "Danger! Building under
demolition," a signboard proclaims.

He is beginning to look for an opening when an old man, out
walking with a husky dog, calls out to him: "Watch out, there are lots of
hypodermic needles in there. Those goddamned druggies set fire to the
place. Or maybe the developers did it, so as to take over the site without
compensating the people who live there . . ." Pulled along by his dog the
man trots off in the snow. Oleg parts two strands of barbed wire, per-
forms contortions, manages to squeeze through.

The inside of the building is layered with soot, the wooden hand-
rail has burned, but the staircases between the floors are intact. Oleg
climbs up, stepping over bundles of charred clothing and the carcasses
of furniture. The door to the attic consists of charred timbers. He pushes
it gently with the toe of his boot, it opens, spilling long threads of ash.

The skylight window is broken, a draft sets the snowflakes whirl-
ing as they tumble in from the snow-covered roof. Everything has burned
without collapsing—Oleg recognizes the black silhouettes of the chairs
and the two couches. The zinc bathtub, equally blackened, is filled with a
strange substance. The little child's bath is full of potatoes, as hard as
anthracite! The thought that somebody has been staying there does not
distress him. On the contrary, he is touched by this pathetic effort at
survival, establishing a supply of potatoes, breathing the snowy air coming through the skylight.

The table his father worked on has not moved. However, all that is left of the model is an irregular pyramid of dead embers. Ruins. The very things his father dreamed of. "Their existence freed at last from time's petty frenzies," he used to say. Oleg also recalls the lines of poetry his father used to murmur as he gazed at his strange edifice: *"So hab ich dieses Schloss erbaut / Ihm mein Erworbnes anvertraut . . ."* (Yes, he had built himself a castle and committed his worldly wealth to it . . .). These words, in the attic of an empty apartment building, have a poignantly ridiculous ring to them. That "worldly wealth," this mountain of cinders!

Using a knife retrieved from the kitchen, Oleg prods the remnants of the burned model. The panels of its charred architecture crumble, revealing fragments of wood that the flames did not consume. Suddenly the metal encounters a more solid object. Oleg probes carefully, pushing aside the little mounds of charcoal. Finally he puts down the knife and extracts what was hidden at the heart of the ruin: two little porcelain figures. A musician with his violin tucked under his arm, and a singer with her hands clasped to her breast. Those objects that in the old days he mistook for a fragment of coral . . .

Two naive figurines that, as a tiny child, he used to see on his mother's night table.

IV

The day after his arrival in Berlin he meets Max Pfister, the director of the film *The Red-Blooded Tsarina.* The filmmaker, now in his sixties, lives in former East Berlin. "I moved here from Cologne right after the Wall came down. My friends said I was mad and now they envy me. It's much more *in* here. You'll see. There's a lot going on. Soon all the avant-garde in the arts will be moving into these socialist slums they're renovating . . ."

Pfister has fixed himself up an apartment in a building that is a cross between a greenhouse and a gym. A glass roof eighteen feet from the ground affords a pallid light, the inordinate height makes everything seem small—the furniture, the pictures, and Pfister himself, who is, in any case, rather short, bald, and wears tiny round spectacles. His partner appears, a young blond woman who is a head taller than him. She greets Oleg with a sullen gesture and begins wrapping a scarf around her neck. "Would you like to have a drink with us?" Pfister asks and receives a cantankerous snort in reply, followed by a swift slam of the door.

"She's a Czech," he explains. This elucidation is somewhat elliptical and he adds, with a little laugh: "I'm not sure if she's got a grudge against the Germans for '38, or the Russians for '68, ha, ha, ha . . ."

Oleg nods without understanding too well. The language he hears is familiar to him but he cannot keep up with the topics under discussion. After all, he's been doing nothing but walking about all day in the

hope of grasping the essence of his phantom fatherland in one long panoramic survey . . . He collapses onto a sofa in a lethargic mix of hunger,
exhaustion, and disorientation. He has a vague sense that the Czech must
be fed up with hangers-on like him coming to see her Max. And that,
like all women from Eastern Europe, she would be happier in cozier and
more affluent surroundings, rather than this aircraft hangar with its glass
roof soiled by pigeons. And that . . . yes, she's young and Max is old and
rather ugly . . .

He has always had a vision of Germany as a tragic digest of History,
the history of the Erdmann family, among others. The most disorient-
ing thing at the moment is coming upon a couple and their petty tiffs, a
banal domestic situation: an aging artist and a young woman from the
former socialist bloc who hopes, thanks to this "old man," to become
integrated into life in the West . . .

He gets a grip on himself, grasps the glass of whiskey Pfister hands
him, seizes a good fistful of salted almonds. "Don't worry, Oleg, we'll go
and eat soon. But first I'd like to show you my film . . ."

The Red-Blooded Tsarina dates from the midseventies, one can tell this
without looking at the credits. From the first sequences the period shows
through—not so much in the technical quality as in the choice of
shots, the rhythm. But especially in this mix of the claims it lays to sexual
freedom and an overemphatic striving for formal novelty . . . Catherine
is played by an actress who wears clothes totally unsuited to the rigors of
Russian winters: highly revealing silk dressing gowns and shifts . . . And
when she appears swathed in fur coats one can be sure that their panels
are about to burst open to reveal thrusting breasts with scarlet nipples . . .

"It's the archetype of woman as animal," comments Pfister. "I wanted
to step back from history a little, so as to bring the animal nature of
desire into prominence, its immediacy, its *Dasein* . . ."

Oleg notices that the German language is particularly well equipped
for giving expression to these abstractions. But at the same time this
"bringing into prominence" seems to him comic, for instead of a nebulous
Dasein, it is, above all, a big pair of breasts that achieves "prominence" . . .

He hastens to avoid denigrating the film: no, it's far from being crap! In fact, the story line is reminiscent of that very first screenplay he wrote himself. The technique of the animated cartoon—the mirror goes up, a naked lover is seen in the alcove, Catherine moves sinuously to accentuate every curve . . . The mirror comes down and there she is, very much the Semiramis of the North, in the process of signing a decree or receiving Diderot, the comte de Ségur, or Casanova . . .

There are happy inventions that even Kozin would not have scorned! The mirror has just covered up the alcove and there is the French ambassador, baron de Breteuil, coming into the salon. They embark on a discussion, Catherine sets out her view of the situation in Europe, the Frenchman gives his rejoinder. Suddenly his eyes grow wider: there in an armchair, like half a man cut in two, "sits" a pair of the favorite's breeches. "I had a good consultant," Pfister explains. "He told me they made very rigid leather breeches at that time . . . But here, of course, it's a metaphor for the utter emptiness of the whole diplomatic circus . . ."

The filmmaker is visibly moved: the film must be plunging him back into his life of twenty years ago, not really his youth, but an age when so many hopes were still possible . . . So as not to disappoint him, Oleg begins to express his reactions more animatedly and even to applaud from time to time. The film's key scene is close at hand—the empress in love with her stallion! The imminence of this absurdity makes Oleg nervous. He'll have to give a verdict without wounding his German host, who's being so friendly.

"Here, it's just starting!" Pfister announces, becoming almost portentous. It is clear that, twenty years on, he still believes his style of filming was innovative.

Horses gallop across the screen, white, like Orlik, Catherine's favorite stallion. The music is similar to Ravel's *Boléro,* but even more insistent. Whinnying, reworked by mixing, blends into the sound of a woman moaning. The white bodies collide, forming a nuptial round dance. The tsarina appears, clothed in silk. Lying back on a sheet? No, it's a trick of the camera—she's standing upright, her eyes half-closed, her back pressed against Orlik's flank. She turns around, puts her arms about the stallion's neck, kisses it, moans. The violet eye of the horse, filmed in close-up, becomes hazy, blends with the woman's eye. Back to the horses—rearing up, their necks twisting, their manes lashing, gleaming light on their hindquarters. Two horses coupling, then two others. Back to the tsarina, naked, her breasts crushed rhythmically against Orlik's chest . . . And again the galloping horses . . . And again the tsarina—a rapid tracking shot makes her disappear beneath Orlik's muscular bulk, then finds her again, exhausted, her arms outstretched, her hair mingled with the horse's mane . . .

At the restaurant Pfister maintains the solemn air that Oleg has often observed in directors after a premiere.

"Even for its time it was very daring. Imagine that nowadays! Since then we've been steeped in puritanism for years. Try filming a penis in a vagina now, which is, after all, what happens when two people make love, and you'll get an 'X' rating right away. And in my film it was a horse!"

The food is brought—great plates edged with geometric patterns: red stars, hammers and sickles, all the socialist kitsch that is becoming fashionable. The restaurant, located in former East Berlin, seems to be following the trend. On the walls, Soviet flags, no doubt retrieved after the troops left, a few East German propaganda posters, and in one corner a dummy dressed in a long military greatcoat.

Oleg eats without concealing how hungry he was. "People might think I'm part of the decor," he says to himself, "a starving Russian." Pfister smokes, drinks, hardly touches the food. He is happy with his "premiere," pleased with this enthusiastic spectator, now wolfing down his filet of veal in bread crumbs.

"Yes, how to film the tsarina and her beloved Orlik in a way that avoided outraged cries of bestiality! I rewrote that sequence a thousand times. And then, suddenly! Eureka! The trick was to cut the scene in half. In one half the horses mating (something that's not forbidden) and alongside that, just hinted at, Catherine's transports. And visually it was irreproachable, don't you think?"

Oleg agrees, and even manages to make a reference to the "onto-
logical ambivalence of human impulses," while at the same time spearing
the last few french fries with his fork, which a waiter is on the point of
whisking away. He throws in one or two compliments for the sake of
politeness and assures him that the work of a truly creative filmmaker
can clearly be sensed in the film . . .

But this praise is too much. Pfister grows tense, suddenly narrows his
shoulders. The excitement of the premiere is gradually wearing off. From
being the forty-year-old director of twenty years ago, Max is turning back
into what he is now, a little man whose bald pate gleams beneath a vast
overhead lampshade acquired during the postsocialist rummage sales.

To rescue him from his slide down a slippery slope, Oleg renews
his compliments more emphatically. Yes, filming that equine love affair
was one hell of a challenge. Pfister must have really had to cudgel his
brains . . . But privately he knows that it's the weak spot in the film: the
whole time one is aware of a straining after tricks in order to portray this
absurd coupling. All that effort, and the result is this not-terribly-good,
flashy, phony film. An army of extras, that poor Catherine, no doubt
made uncomfortable by the weight of her bloated breasts, and a whole
herd of horses, whose erotic moods had to be kept under surveillance.
All that, just for that!

Pfister attempts an uneasy grin. At first, walking into the restaurant, he had posed as a condescending regular, a West German turning
up here in the now collapsed German Democratic Republic. With the
benevolent loftiness of a colonizer, he had addressed the waiters famil-
iarly, shaken hands with the chef . . . Now he is no longer acting the part,
guessing what this Russian who has finished gulping down his dinner
must be thinking: all that, just for that . . .

In a last effort at social poise Pfister announces between two swigs
of vodka: "By the way, I came across your Tarkovsky a number of times.
An original guy, a bit crazy, a mystic—"

He breaks off, sensing that he has struck a false note. His voice
becomes tinged with bitter sarcasm.

"Oh yes, Tarkovsky, a true icon. A victim of the Kremlin dictatorship. That's how they portray him in the media. He posed as a persecuted
man, as if he were some ex-convict from the Kolyma camps—and all this
in his miserable exile in Venice, where he went to live and was welcomed
with open arms by generous patrons. The first time I felt like kneeling: a
saint, a genius, muzzled by totalitarianism! Then I thought about it . . .
That was in the days when I was trying to scrape together a few million
marks to make one of my own films. You know the old story: you beg,
you prostitute yourself, you kill yourself to assemble a pittance, three
candle ends offered by one producer and a pair of old socks graciously
granted by a television channel . . . And so, I see Tarkovsky, this crucified
martyr, I listen to his lamentations about the calvary he suffered to bring
out his films in the USSR. And all at once, I ask myself, but wait a minute, who financed them? Well, I'll tell you who . . . It was the Soviet State,
goddamn it! Yes, those torturers allocated him a budget, often a rather
substantial one, you know Tarkovsky didn't skimp on his decor. So these
enemies of liberty were supporting a director who made pictures that
were maybe not hostile to, but certainly indifferent to, the ideals of communism. And what's more these pretentiously complex films were often
quite inaccessible to . . . let's say the toiling masses. All that aesthetic
monkey business in his film *The Mirror*, I always found it a bit tedious,
not to say boring as hell . . . But that's not the main point. There, I say
to myself, you have somebody who's forever moaning, but whose films
have been made thanks to the taxes paid by poor kolkhozniks who can't
make head or tail of these movies designed for a little blasé elite. And,
lo and behold, when this crucified martyr turns up on the Grand Canal
it's the same story all over again! The West doesn't suit him either and
he swamps us with his *Nostalghia*, which is even more deadly dull than the
rest. But there are still idiots ready to take over from the kolkhozniks
the financing of our martyr's latest films of his moods and whims . . ."

Pfister rounds off his indictment in the street. He walks along
swaying and gesticulating. "He's a dead ringer for Woody Allen," Oleg
says to himself. With selfish, bitter glee he realizes that his trip to Berlin

will have been helpful: Pfister's film is, in part, what Zhurbin was trying to do. And it's a clear failure.

They arrive in front of the building where the filmmaker lives. "Freedom to create, ha, ha, ha! But who'll let me film another Catherine— that little girl of fourteen who goes off to Russia never to return? I found dough for my *Tsarina* because everyone wanted to see her lovers screwing her, that was all that interested them—a big German woman being served by horny guardsmen. And as we were right in the middle of the sexual revolution, we had to show the horse as well . . ."

He stops, gives Oleg a pained glance. "I went on fighting. Even after that film I still dreamed of rewriting her life. But time passed and it's too late now. You can stay the night, if you like. What? My girlfriend? We'll tell her you're a KGB agent. People always suspect Russians, you know. Oh well. Here's to the next time . . ."

They pause in the snow for a moment more, somewhat hesitant now, both of them aware there's little likelihood of their ever meeting again and that their encounter has brought together countries now swallowed up, eras now obliterated. And that for Oleg (as Pfister knows), it has been his first real evening in company on his "native soil."

In order to avoid painful farewells, Oleg asks: "In Kozin's film Eva Sander played Catherine. You don't know what she's working on now do you?"

Pfister whispers, as if sharing a secret: "Take some advice from an old man. Never go back to women from the past. It only leads to unhappiness. Live in the present. It tells better lies because it's always changing . . . Ah, here comes my present!"

Oleg turns around and recognizes the Czech. He thanks Pfister, beats a retreat. The latter, no doubt sobered up by the chilly air, bellows in astonishingly solemn tones: "And forget about Catherine. Impossible to film a woman no man ever loved . . ."

Those words of Pfister's—"a woman no man ever loved"—change everything.

The next day Oleg was planning to take the train to Kiel, somewhere he has often pictured: a boy of eleven and a little girl a year younger than him, holding hands and watching the snow falling on the sea. The future Peter III's first meeting with the future Catherine II . . . He would like to see this place, so as to convince himself that the tsarina's life could be summed up in these two stories: the young dreamer in her German fairy tale, the "red-blooded" empress in her cruel Russian saga . . .

The next morning he locates Eva Sander's address on the map of Berlin. The likelihood of her still living in the same place is scant, he knows, but he might as well eliminate that hope, too.

The district, near Heinersdorf in former East Berlin, reminds him of Russian towns—low-rise buildings, streets lined with trees, streetcar tracks, patches of wasteland. A similarity no doubt connected to the war that shaped the towns in the two countries.

An old apartment building, a courtyard covered in snow. Oleg stops, observes the windows—the stunted plants behind the glass, you would see them in any small Russian town. The main door opens, an old man emerges, turns to greet a woman, a neighbor, who comes out after him . . . A moment of panic prevents Oleg from recognizing her. On seeing him she makes an about-face and retreats into the entrance hall!

For a split second he believed she was avoiding him. Then the woman reappears, pulling a shopping cart on wheels. Oleg plucks up courage, struck by the banal nature of the situation: a woman going back up to her apartment to collect a cart and now setting off as she intended.

Eva Sander, whom he has not seen for fourteen years . . .

At this first glimpse, confused by his emotion, he notes that she seems to have grown younger, which is illogical, and yet her face has a vulnerable simplicity, a hint of childlike frailty.

Oleg lets her move forward, then calls out to her softly in Russian: "Your Majesty, where are you off to, with that conqueror's stride?"

He is expecting a great "Oh" of astonishment, a burst of enthusiasm, and, possibly, tears. Eva turns her head, raises her eyebrows. "Oh, but it's Herr Erdmann in person."

She shakes his hand, asks in a matter-of-fact way, "So when did you get here? Are you spending a bit of time in Berlin?"

Oleg is just starting to reply, with a fixed smile on his lips, feeling the slight pique one experiences after telling a joke to which the listener already knew the punch line. "Perfect," Eva cuts in. "We'll have some tea in a little while. I'm just off to do my shopping . . . If you have no other plans, come with me . . ."

He finds himself pushing a shopping cart and notices Eva is adding a few odds and ends to her list for "their" tea. This detail seems to him both comic and irritating: an extra packet of biscuits, the only change occasioned by his coming. At the checkout Eva takes out a handful of coins and lays them out in a row to count them. Oleg cannot tell if this is a case of Western stinginess, or quite simply a lack of cash in former socialist Germany, as it comes up against economic reality.

On the return journey he learns why his coming caused Eva so little surprise. When the borders were opened the Russians hurried into Europe. "I've seen several people from Kozin's team," she confides. "They come hoping to find work . . . When they get here they do what they always used to do in the old days: find my address and ring at my door."

"I was going to do just that. Forgive me. I know that in the West you have to telephone your friends six months in advance . . ."

Hard to avoid this acid note. But they try to get over it and act out a scene of old comrades reunited.

Eva's apartment is large, two vast rooms, but the traces of the former socialist life show through—in the look of the furniture, the tired colors, the kitchen reminiscent of Soviet apartments. The objects from Italy that can be seen here and there look like tourist trinkets.

They drink tea, making a pretense of casualness, but the tension is there, from the effort they are making to put the past behind them, that time when Kozin was shooting his film in Leningrad. The long walks they went on after the day's filming, far away from the crowded parts of the city . . . It was the period of the Wall, of watertight frontiers. A world of prisons. And one filled with dreams . . .

"Guess what masterpiece I saw last night," says Oleg, rolling his eyes. He tells her about his visit to Max Pfister and *The Red-Blooded Tsarina* . . . "A very athletic scenario: the sex was filmed like a bout between two wrestlers. And then, that horse!"

He speaks with heavy sarcasm, portraying Pfister as a sexual obsessive, a bitter old man who rails against Tarkovsky, the persecuted genius.

"I nearly acted in one of Max's films . . . ," Eva says softly, glancing out of the window.

"Oh dear, not his *Red-Blooded Tsarina!*" exclaims Oleg, feigning prudish alarm.

"No. It was much later. Already after the Wall came down. A scenario based on my father's life. I told you about his past as a soldier: aerial reconnaissance over Leningrad . . . Pfister struggled hard to find a producer . . . But they thought the subject was out of date . . ."

Oleg suddenly grasps what it was the previous evening that had surprised him about Pfister. Yes, this out-of-date aspect of him. A West

German, Max really belongs to the period of the war, of the Wall, a generation ultimately very close to Eva . . .

He no longer seeks to be ironic.

"And since then have you done more acting? I imagine a lot of walls have come down in the world of film as well . . ."

Eva lays the table—he has not noticed that lunchtime has arrived. Pasta, peppers, olives, and a bottle of Italian wine.

"Yes . . . As a good, disciplined German, I've made every effort to become integrated into the cinema now proclaiming its victory over totalitarianism. After reunification they offered us well-defined roles: those of poor idiots from the East who, on arrival in the paradise of the West, commit all kinds of blunders because, for example, they've never eaten pasta like this, or drunk Chianti. Poor relations, at whom Germans from the other side of the Wall laugh heartily . . . I had to earn my crust so I acted in three or four of those turkeys. And then . . ."

She gets up, switches on a lamp above the table. The afternoon is gray, it is raining, the snow is melting and leaving patches of earth that swallow up the light.

"And then this cinema, liberated from the totalitarian fetters, began to get interested in the last war and we've seen films in which Hitler seemed almost lovable, especially around the time when the Third Reich was collapsing. As a result, it was the Russians who became more and more appalling. They bombed, killed, pillaged. It was so cunningly devised that audiences began to ask themselves: 'But what on earth did these barbarians come to Berlin for?' I was offered a part: a woman of Berlin raped by a Russian soldier. Rapes have been committed by all the armies in the world. But the USSR had just collapsed and the filmmakers, like good whores, saw which way the wind was blowing and started to rewrite history. Now this was all they were showing: the Russians coming, crushing the German army's heroic resistance, violating everything that moved . . . I turned down that part and then another in the same vein. They pigeonholed me as one of the people nostalgic for the Wall and forgot about me . . ."

She falls silent, her gaze fixed on the shadows parading past in her mind, hinted at only by the trembling of her eyelashes. Oleg attempts a soothing platitude: "It's the price you have to pay for freedom, Eva. People say whatever comes into their heads. Sometimes it's totally crazy: all those Russians obsessed with fornication instead of fighting. It makes you wonder how they ever got from Stalingrad to Berlin. But it's better to have this craziness than Soviet censorship. I know a bit about that."

He sips his wine, adopting the air of a veteran of film in the days of dictatorship. Eva gives him a weary, mocking glance.

"The problem, my dear Oleg, is that, despite your terrifying Soviet censorship, you managed to make a short film about your father's life. I've seen it, your *Return in a Dream.* A very fine film! Whereas we, Pfister and I, despite the freedom of the West, were not able to make ours. About my father. It's a paradox, isn't it? As for Tarkovsky, he wouldn't have been given a single mark to produce his early films in the West. About that, Max is absolutely right."

The meal is over, they are drinking their coffee, gazing at the window, already dark, streaked by damp snow. Oleg realizes he cannot possibly leave on this note. He adopts a cheerful tone, as if to evoke a memory, a shared passion.

"You know, I haven't abandoned that idea of writing something about Catherine and Lanskoy. I've often talked to a historian, an old specialist on the Catherine century, Luria. He's put his finger on a very little known fact: under cover of making a coin collection, Lanskoy was accumulating foreign currency for their traveling expenses . . ."

Eva has risen to her feet and is now standing with her back against the shelves of a bookcase. The shadow enlarges her eyes, and once again Oleg tells himself that a trace of youth lights up her slightly angular face. She speaks without hiding her bitterness.

"Your historian ought to talk to you about Lanskoy's death . . . Yes, I know, there are two possible versions: poison administered by Potemkin's agents or else an excessive consumption of aphrodisiacs. But what's even more tragic is what happens after his burial. Catherine is shattered, very close to suicide—for the first time in her life. A woman of fifty-five, incredibly youthful and energetic for her years, she sinks into premature old age. And at this moment they find Lanskoy's tomb, desecrated. His body dragged out onto the ground, stripped naked. Butchery: his face slashed, his stomach open, his genitalia ripped off . . . Historians say 'Macabre' and hold their noses. And yet here we are touching on the very essence of society. It keeps a vigilant watch on those who try to step aside from the game. Even if we're talking about a tsarina in love, who no longer wants to play. Such imprudent people are hounded right into their graves . . . A trip to Italy, you say? It was a dream. Like our wanderings in Leningrad. We believed that the world was going to change, thanks to our films and the way they outwitted the censorship, thanks to the fall of the Wall. But the world is a film set, the parts are allocated, the script is always the same, and the director loathes anyone walking off the set without permission . . ."

She smiles, puts down her cup, switches on a computer that stands on a long table piled high with books.

"Don't hold that metaphysical digression against me. It's our German specialty, as you well know. For me, it's time to get back to the role that keeps me alive. I'm a translator. The Russian that Catherine used to speak is very useful to me, too. She and Lanskoy used to translate from one language into another. Sometimes from Swedish, Swedenborg's *Journal of Dreams*. 'I was walking through a town that seemed so familiar to me. Suddenly I grasped that this was an unknown town . . .' That must have been how they pictured the towns on their future journey. Now then. Safe home. I'm so sorry I'm no longer the Catherine of the old days . . ."

In the night Oleg understands why Eva seems to have grown younger. Playing Catherine in her mature years, she was made up as a woman of fifty, sixty, then seventy. His last memory of her relates to the journey to the Crimea in 1787, when Catherine was fifty-eight: a figure in a long dress between two lines of poplar trees on a road leading to the sea . . . There is an even more obvious logic: he was then twenty-eight, Eva ten years older. In the eyes of a young man, that made her a woman on the threshold of old age. Now that he is forty-two, a woman in her fifties seems to him almost of the same generation as himself . . .

He toys with these calculations, half mathematical, half romantic. From time to time he switches on the light, leafs through the notebook in which, before setting off, he had made a note of the trips he planned and the matters he was hoping to discuss with Pfister . . . Here, for example, are notes on what Luria had told him: Catherine learned that Peter the Great invented a mobile scaffold so as to be able to execute rebellious subjects throughout the whole of Russia—in no time at all the scaffold was set up and heads rolled. The tsarina condemns this itinerant barbarism. Before discovering, toward the end of her life, that in the land of her dear Voltaire the guillotine itself goes on the move. A much more efficient machine than the heavy, chipped execution block of the Russians . . .

This note, too: after Kiel, he would like to go to Kassel. Some of his ancestors came from that town.

And then, a note in red crayon: not to forget to send a card to Zhurbin's child in Lugano. He will do it tomorrow.

It is already past ten o'clock when he wakes. He leaps out of bed, calling himself a fool, realizes he has missed breakfast and probably his train to Kiel as well. At all events, the morning train. He draws back the curtains and all at once his haste calms down. Snow is falling heavily, slowly, a city disappearing beneath the whiteness, and even the appalling motorbike he had spotted beneath his window now looks like a handsome, downy animal . . . That was the reason for his lethargic sleep: the thick layer of snowflakes deadening all sound, calming all speeds . . .

Outside, he is dazzled by the snow. He pictures Eva walking along in these white streets, in this hypnotic swirling. With an ease that surprises him, he changes his plans, walks into a florist's shop looking for a bunch of flowers that might . . . He's not quite sure what he'd like to give. The saleswoman in the store shows him a dry, gray woody plant. "Quite soon, in two or three weeks' time, it'll be covered in blooms," she says. He emerges carrying a pot with what would, at a distance, look like a dead shrub protruding from it . . .

"If she's not at home," he says to himself, "I'll leave it outside her door."

And at that moment he sees Eva. She is waiting at the streetcar stop in a little crowd of people white with snow. He notices what he had not observed the previous day: the old overcoat she wears and her way of stooping a little, of shielding her face—not from the snowflakes, but from passing stares. Tucked under her arm she is carrying several files in a transparent plastic bag . . .

"I wanted to give you this before leaving . . . It's not much to look at but it's a shrub that will flower for a long time . . ." He holds out the plant to her.

The streetcar arrives. Eva hesitates, stammering out thanks, words of farewell, moves to get in, then steps back. Her voice is both firm and offhand. "After all, I can go later . . . Or even not go at all!"

The streetcar disappears, they remain facing one another, study one another intently, as if recognizing one another at last. Then, without conferring, they walk away from the stop.

"You're covered in snow . . . ," says Oleg when they are back at the entrance to the apartment building.

And he sets about brushing the layer of snowflakes off Eva's shoulders. She does the same for him, knocking away the white crust.

"Well, I'll leave you now, Eva. I have to go to Kiel . . ."

"I can take you, if you like. I have a car . . ."

They sense that a threshold has been crossed—not in their relationship but in their freedom to do what they choose with their lives. Lives that, for all these years, had been concealed beneath a flood of nonsense, pointless waiting, greed, fears. Everything could go either way now. As it could have done one winter's evening long ago, beside the little Swan Canal . . .

"Kiel's really the other end of the world, Eva. Four or five hours in the car . . ."

"The hardest bit will be digging my old jalopy out of the snow . . ."

In the apartment she puts the plant in the middle of the room, like a Christmas tree, waters it and begins packing a traveling bag. Then breaks off: "No, if I start making preparations we'll never get away. Let's go. We'll find what we need on the way . . ."

They set off, conscious that the life they are abandoning is still very close, with a slyly powerful gravitational pull.

They do not so much have to dig the car out as actually locate it again under a white burial mound. Its contours appear, Oleg recognizes the old station wagon he saw long ago at Peterhof . . . They manage to open it, settle into it, feeling as if they were in an igloo, waiting for the ice on the windows to melt.

"I forget the name of that French actor who always wore eccentric hats," Eva says. "When they asked him where he found them, he used to reply: 'I don't find them, I hold on to them' . . . Rather like this antique of mine."

The deiced windows reveal a city that seems very different from the one they were looking at an hour ago.

This feeling will increase the farther they travel toward the Baltic. In fact, they will be thinking less and less about the world they have left behind.

"In accordance with some statute or other, it was Louis the Fifteenth of France who could authorize Catherine to adopt the title of empress. He was slow to grant her this right. She was a parvenu who irritated him. He did what his mistresses told him and complained of having less power than a colonel. Catherine governed alone and promoted her lovers to the rank of colonel, general, and even king! Louis and the tsarina loathed one another from afar. Catherine egging on the belligerence of the French philosophers: the French king longing to 'drive Russia back into its cold wastes.' At Lanskoy's death Catherine, already devastated, learns of the outrage: her lover's remains have been desecrated. But Louis suffered a similar tragedy. While he was mourning Madame de Vintimille, the people got hold of her body, tortured it and profaned it . . ."

As they travel along Oleg is recounting stories from this past he has never managed to tell. A sequence of discrete truths, in the margin of History's great epic tale. Sometimes Eva intervenes, without taking her eyes off the white lashing against the windshield.

"These byways of history always loop back on themselves. You remember in Kozin's film: Peter the Third is a good violinist but Catherine disparages his musical gift. Then, at the end of her life she has to endure her young lover Zubov scraping away with his bow—like the grating of badly oiled hinges . . ."

Oleg smiles, happy to be rediscovering the shared language they spoke in the old days. "When he lost the throne Peter asked to be allowed to leave for Germany with his violin under his arm. They killed him. You know, it could well have been the same violin that Zubov later tormented . . ."

That evening they reach the Baltic, drive along the eastern shore of the Bay of Kiel, pass through Laboe, and stop away from the street lighting. The snow continues falling into the silvery depths of the sea, in great, slow flakes.

"They probably stood over there," Oleg says softly. "Two children who knew nothing beyond that moment. The future tsar and tsarina. Twenty years later the little boy who watched the snow falling would be the man beaten to death, strangled and disfigured by the lovers of the woman who was the little girl he held hands with . . . It's a scene that haunts me. The beauty of that moment and then a tidal wave of absurdities—plots, conquests, rebellions, massacres, in a word, History. Everyone understands the madness of this mode of existence and yet in every generation it starts all over again. Just imagine: at this very moment, over there, across the bay, stand two children thrilled by this swirling whiteness. In ten years' time they'll be recruited to join in the games this world plays, its greed, its lies, its ugliness . . ."

Eva takes his arm and shakes it gently.

"And yet you've already written two films without ever talking about the beauty those children experienced. You've told what happened after that moment—the alcoves, the wars, people's rapacious desires . . . History . . . How can you expect all that not to be repeated if no one dares to say that another life is possible?"

Again they have a sense of a frontier crossed, a time unfolding differently. Sitting there in the car, they remain still, conscious that returning to Berlin, going back to life as it was before, is now impossible. Eva talks in apologetic tones.

"Don't think I'm reproaching you for lacking courage. I once told

you about my Italian friend, Aldo Ranieri, who wrote a screenplay based
on Catherine's life. We began filming but Aldo was very weak from his
illness, the producer abandoned us and . . . At all events we didn't manage to tell anything other than the well-known story of her reign: coup
d'état, conspiracies, favorites . . . One day Aldo had the idea of filming
the things that were not a part of that whole farce. Like that moment at
Kiel . . . And also Lanskoy's love . . . We shot the first few scenes and that
was when the producer cut off our supplies . . . Over the past few years
I've had a great longing to watch that unfinished film again. Aldo's sister
kept a copy of it at her house, near Ravenna . . ."

Oleg thinks of the scene he had never succeeded in working into
a film: the tsarina and Lanskoy planning their itinerary for a secret
journey . . .

"You know, Eva, I've brought the maps you gave me, yes, 'Lanskoy's
maps' . . . They cover northern Italy, maybe as far as Ravenna. I have a
visa that's valid for a month. We have time to go there . . ."

Eva laughs softly, closes her eyes, runs a hand across her brow.

"Before that I have to translate the complete works of Pushkin in
order to be able to pay for the gas and everything else . . ."

"Listen, I'm not trying to pass myself off as a Russian oligarch,
but Catherine has made me almost rich. That terrible series of Zhurbin's
has made me quite well off. I've even bought myself a very expensive
Italian suit that I've never really worn: Zhurbin says when I put it on
my sexual identity becomes uncertain. To cut a long story short, I've
brought the maximum amount of currency it's possible to take out of
Russia: ten thousand dollars. I've got at least eight left. That ought to
see us through . . ."

That evening at the hotel, they study the photocopies of the maps,
stuck together in a continuous sequence, so that there, at the heart of a
Europe that no longer exists, a sinuous line appears, a dream two centuries old.

In driving through Germany from north to south, they occasionally deviate from the itinerary on the maps, passing through towns Oleg has heard his parents speak of. Towns where his ancestors had roots and that they left, one day, at the invitation of a Russian tsarina. "All this on account of that little princess who decided to come to Russia . . ."

Often the facade of a palace, lit by a low sun, strikes him as grievously familiar. Yes, he has seen it before! Neither in a photograph nor in a film, but in the fanciful terraces of the model constructed by his father. He remembers that voice, all of whose inflections, touching bursts of enthusiasm and hidden sorrows he can now fathom: "I told you about that beautiful forest at Reinhardswald. Sababurg Castle is there. Look. I'm just building it . . ." His father begins humming: *"So hab ich dieses Schloss erbaut . . ."* He breaks off, studies his son with distraught compassion. "You know this castle without ever having been there. When you were little your mother used to tell you stories. And they all happened at Sababurg . . ."

At Kassel, in the window of an antique shop near their hotel, Oleg sees an old magic lantern, very similar to the relic preserved for generations by the Erdmann family. Characters in wigs revolving in a slow repetition of scenes for which there can be no development, no outcome . . . What strikes him is the madness of this haunting little ring of tiny figures within the narrow confines of the glass lantern: the world of human beings is no different! The same merry-go-round that conceals the preparations for wars, the coming to fruition of slaughter. The great park Eva takes him to was landscaped on top of the ruins of the town of Kassel, flattened by bombing. With a bewilderment that chokes him, Oleg tells himself that before that catastrophe the magic lantern's little figures used to revolve like this, and that, after it, once the mechanism was rewound, they would be ready to go through their paces all over again. And that what these snow-laden trees in their beauty are hiding is, in truth, ruins, broken lives, thousands of dead . . .

Their journey seems to him to be a mad undertaking, a ridiculous attempt to resist the earth's rotation. He senses the same doubt in Eva. Back in their room, before taking off their coats, they stand there facing one another, at a loss, waiting for an admission of failure to be made. Then, suddenly, they put their arms around one another in an awkward embrace, silent, as if seeking to shield one another from an explosion . . . And that night, their first night of intimacy, Oleg grasps that love can also be this protective tenderness, one that holds grief at bay, one whose very essence is the gleam of snow coming from the window, as well as the trembling fingers of this sleeping woman's hand. A very simple certainty: the goal of their journey was this somnolent city, this room looking out over the tall, white trees, the bluish resonance of the dark shadow on the woman's hand where his lips brush against it.

From Stuttgart Eva calls her translation agency, succeeds in negotiating more time. Oleg makes several vain attempts to reach Zhurbin. Finally he calls Tanya on her cell phone and she exclaims: "So that's it then. You've gone back to your Teutonic roots!" This observation is followed by a yell: "But this call is costing me a million! Your Zhurbin's been arrested. They're charging him with misappropriation of funds . . . Ciao!" A fairly run-of-the-mill charge, Oleg thinks, and one that will enable the "hunters" to carve up all the businesses Zhurbin has been running.

He tells Eva that Zhurbin has been jailed, talks about the child who lives in Lugano, the little girl to whom, when in Berlin, he forgot to send a postcard. "We could go and see her," suggests Eva. "It's almost on our route. Provided the Swiss don't block your entry. You don't have a visa . . ."

They cross the border early in the morning, with Oleg hiding under a pile of clothes on the backseat. "If they find you, pretend to be asleep," Eva advises. "After all, you don't have your pockets stuffed with watches . . ."

Once in Switzerland they decide to pass through the country without spending a night there, still on account of this lack of a visa. They drive on, relieving one another at the wheel and taking turns sleeping, and succeed in reaching Lugano around three o'clock in the afternoon. "We ought to buy the little girl a gift," suggests Eva. Oleg remembers Zhurbin telling him about the child communicating with fishes. They buy two fish, fairly ordinary, but swimming around quite energetically in a transparent plastic pouch, into which, apart from the water, the salesman has put a little pondweed.

The management of the boarding school where Nina lives have no objection in principle to their visit. "We're a couple," Oleg whispers in Eva's ear. "If I were on my own they'd never let me near the child." The director's assistant is consulting a large visitors' book. Suddenly her face tenses, she asks them to wait a minute, and disappears behind the heavy door of the neighboring office. "If worst comes to worst," they agree, "we could simply ask them to give the fish to the child . . ."

The assistant returns accompanied by a very plump man with very white skin whose look signals real embarrassment.

"We're very happy to be able to speak to Mr. Zhurbin's friends because . . . well, it's a rather delicate matter . . . his payments for the fees are already a month overdue. And for a week, now, we've not been able to reach him."

Oleg surprises himself with his own cool composure. ("My his-
trionic experience in films has not been wasted.") In the tones of one
who is completely solvent, he says: "Doctor, I'm telling you this in great
confidence. Mr. Zhurbin is preparing to take up a highly important post
in the Russian government, so this is not a matter of forgetfulness on his
part. There's been an unfortunate malfunction during the breaking in of
his new team. He knew I was planning to visit Nina and has asked me,
as I was coming, if I could settle this small financial matter. I suppose
you accept dollars . . ."

They leave the office, and guided by a nurse, follow a footpath
among fir trees. "I now have a thousand dollars left, and that's it," whispers Oleg, looking like a gambler who's just been cleaned out. Eva smiles:
"It doesn't matter. We'll eat pasta and sleep in the car . . ."

The footpath leads around a small pond fenced in by a wooden
trellis. Some ten children, accompanied by three teachers, are playing
around this patch of water. At a call from the nurse a little girl in a
woollen hat detaches herself from the group, runs up, and takes hold of
Eva's hand, as if she had always known her. "Come and see. My fishes
talk to me!"

They go up to a narrow gate fastened with a hook. Nina opens
it, under the vigilant eye of one of the teachers, goes up to the edge
and starts reciting a nursery rhyme. The water quivers, is streaked with
fins, flashes with golden scales. The child takes a piece of bread from
her pocket, throws crumbs to the fish, calling them by their names.
"Naughty things!" she murmurs suddenly, as a light lapping sound can
be heard—that of mouths snapping at the last crumbs, or at nothing.
"They say the bread was good but they prefer cookies . . ." The child
crouches down, watches the fish swimming away, seems to forget the
grown-ups. Her lips are moving in an inaudible conversation. Oleg realizes that these few moments leave him the time to see the sky upturned
in the dark transparency of the pond, to hear a bird, to breathe in a more
measured way. Yes, to feel he's alive. "Nina, we've brought two more for
you, but they don't know how to talk yet," says Eva. "You can teach them

Russian." The child opens the bag and whispers: "Take care, the water's chilly. Don't catch cold." With a glint of orange, two bodies vanish into the pond. She stands up, looks at Oleg and Eva, makes an effort to find words not known at her age: "I'll wait for you . . . I'll show you my turtles as well. Next time, Daddy will come with you, yes?"

They do not stop for the night, make themselves very strong coffee, drive on, as if in flight from the child's question. At the frontier Oleg no longer hides—everything seems trivial to them after Nina's last words. Her father will get eight years at least. When he comes out Nina will be in her teens and he a derelict, his health ruined by the camps.

Eva talks with a fury Oleg has never heard in her before. "She's not a maladjusted child at all! It's our world that's badly adjusted to beings like her. Can you picture her, she who only knows trusting and loving, can you picture her in St. Petersburg or Berlin?"

"Zhurbin knew he couldn't remake the world. He chose that little island at Lugano. A third-rate television series meant he could pay six thousand dollars a month for this paradise. And that's the snare: to create an island free from the filth of this world, we have to dirty our souls. Yes, we have to show Catherine copulating with guardsmen and then with a horse!"

"Your friend, Zhurbin, has an excuse: his child. You'd do better to think of all those men who make the same garbage and buy a 'Lugano island' just for themselves and their mistresses."

"You can count me among them, Eva. There was a time when I earned my living making documentaries commissioned by oligarchs. And with that money do you think I tried to make a film about Lanskoy

and Catherine? Not at all! I bought myself a great big car. I rented a big
three-room apartment near the Nevsky Prospekt and at one moment I
even had two girlfriends. I convinced them I was going to get them dream
parts in the movies . . ."

"And then?"

"And then Kozin died and I got the message: the real death was
this life I was leading . . . And so I decided I would outsmart the world. I
began making that television series but in every episode I hoped I could
add a touch that would transform everything. I remember there was a
scene of rape: one of Catherine's favorites has abandoned her and married
a lady-in-waiting. The tsarina lets loose her henchmen on them. Zhurbin
wanted a very raw, physical scene . . . In the young couple's bedroom I
managed to include a shot of a rag doll that was watching this rape,
though in reality it was an outrage that never took place. The episode was
a huge success. And, as for the doll, no one noticed it . . . The world is
much craftier than we are. It simply wipes out all our 'Lugano islands,' or
else it turns them into snares. Go ahead then, sell your soul in the hope
of saving that of a child . . ."

Around midnight they stop, parking beside a little bend in the
road up in the hills. The night is clear and the air coming off the mountains smells of ice, a hard, mineral texture, with no breath of life. The
stars have the same cutting hardness—indifferent to these two human
shadows lost in the darkness. To rid himself of drowsiness, Oleg walks
a few steps, fills his lungs, looks at the sky: a void with not the least
sign of compassion for what happens beneath its vault. "What's happening here is Eva's life," he says to himself. "A child conceived during the brief return to Germany of a soldier on leave in 1943 . . . That
soldier went back to the eastern front, back to his military service: in a
reconnaissance plane he used to fly over Leningrad when it was under
siege, where twenty thousand people were dying every day, and he took
pictures, so that the Luftwaffe could bomb the city's defenders and its
factories more effectively. One day he saw a railroad junction, children
and old people boarding a train to be evacuated. He didn't photograph

the place . . . His daughter, Eva, was born in April '44, the soldier had already been taken prisoner by the Russians. Around that time another soldier stopped on terrain churned up by artillery shells. It marked the frontier between Russia and Poland, they told him. He was so exhausted the event made little impression on him. He just gave a faint smile. 'So I, Sergei Erdmann, being of German descent, have liberated Russia . . .' Suddenly his face became tensed up by one of the spasms that had been tormenting him for three years, since that winter's day when, in the middle of a village torched by the Germans, he saw the bodies of four children burned by a flamethrower . . ."

Oleg closes his eyes to avoid the sight of this sky that has looked down indifferently on these births, these deaths, the cries of children overwhelmed by a burst of fire, as well as the childhood of that little Eva, who, before she had learned to talk, knew how to distinguish bombers just flying in from those that, having fulfilled their mission, were leaving the city where very few buildings remained intact. The sky saw all that without one of its stars being dimmed by compassion.

In the darkness they find one another and embrace, offering, as a challenge to the icy blackness that stares down at them, this brief moment—a frail bond that is the strongest human beings can hope for in their lifetime.

"I don't know what Nina will feel when she sees her father after an absence of eight years. Mine was liberated by the Soviets in '48. I was four when I saw him for the first time . . . Don't worry, Oleg. We'll find a solution for her. We'll go back . . ."

They resume their journey, feeling as if they were launching a rearguard action. The world is vast, impassive, confident of its right, the right to continue with its perpetual round of wars, departures, disappointed hopes, human lives wiped away, like this flurry of snow sweeping across the road and disappearing, to be replaced by a fresh swirl of snowflakes.

The morning is misty and the road now passes by vast, gray, damp slopes, hillsides where sleeping trees stand sentinel. The air that fills the car is quite different now—the mildness of a weary winter, one that no longer lacerates their lungs. Their thoughts grow lighter, become veiled, lose some of their cutting edge.

This region of Italy is covered by the old "Lanskoy maps": Lake Garda, the Valley of the Po, Mantua . . . They are doubtless driving along within a few miles of the route Catherine intended. She might have even stopped in this village, Grazie, where they decide to take a break . . .

They leave the car at the entrance to an empty square surrounded by little houses. On one side of the square is a colonnaded gallery and the modest, almost impoverished architecture of a church. They go into it, mainly to escape from the rain, the cafés are still closed.

Santa Maria delle Grazie. They smile—a proud name for such a simple building. A bare, flat facade and they open the door expecting the interior to be similarly austere . . .

The exuberance that spills out over them has nothing to do with richness or luxurious decoration. No, the nave is of average height, a lack of windows means the light does not come pouring in, the prettily painted vault is not vertiginous. A humble church. What is dazzling is the multitude of body parts—symbols of the most ordinary human frailty. The low columns, halfway up the walls, are covered with ex-voto offerings. Plaster casts of hands, hearts, women's breasts, and, not immediately identifiable, appalling buboes from the plague. Cures, fertility, lactation, wounds, and illnesses . . . And between these columns, covered with thousands of organs, are carved images of doomed people, saved by the grace of the Mother of God. One of them is preparing to be hanged, another has already laid his head on a block . . .

This primitive abstract of human hopes and fears carries through onto votive tablets of an even more disarming candor. A child whom, watched by the Virgin Mary, two men are raising from a well, a carpenter protected from a fall of beams by heavenly intercession, a narrow escape from a fire . . . This chronicle of misfortunes avoided moves forward in time—the Mother of God, floating on her cloud, rescues cyclists in danger from a locomotive, as well as passengers in car crashes . . .

Before leaving the church Oleg looks up. The irresistible and child-like appetite for life filling the church finds its ultimate expression there: suspended beneath the vault is a crocodile! A real reptile, stuffed and shackled—its jaws held fast by thick ropes. A gargoyle more real than all the stone monsters.

They pause in front of the church, under a sun still invisible but whose touch can already be felt. A dazzling headiness, the brief feeling of belonging nowhere, a lack of any trace of a past, of origins, of a life history . . . Beneath their feet, on the asphalt of the square, faded drawings can be made out—large, ephemeral images that go back to some festival when sidewalk artists left these copies of Leonardo, Raphael, and Titian there . . .

A little café on the corner of the square has just opened, they sit down there, order toast and coffee. They talk about Catherine and Lanskoy and their desire to escape, no doubt to find just this release: to be tsarina and favorite no longer, no longer to have the ages they had, nor their titles, nor everything that time and other people had made of them. To be nothing but that morning, on an empty square, a few steps away from a church that contains the quintessence of the lives of human beings, their suffering, fears, hopes. To go into it, immersing themselves one last time in that abstract of this world and then to emerge, reborn with a new identity, in a different life.

"Catherine and Lanskoy would not have been able to do that in Russia," says Oleg, when they return to the car and continue on their way. "In St. Petersburg too many constricting ties, too many bruised memories. Nor in Germany either—for the same reasons. We . . . well, the Germans, are too serious, their thought puts life in a straitjacket. No, the only place to be transfigured, as they dreamed of it, was that village, Grazie . . ."

Without noticing, he is slipping toward sleep and an hour later is woken by the neighing of a horse. Eva has parked the car on a dirt road and has fallen asleep herself. They shake themselves, see a man on horseback riding away at a vigorous, free pace. The sun is already high, the fields are shining, like lakes.

From Ferrara, Eva calls Aldo Ranieri's sister. The old woman says she will be back home in the evening.

"We have time to make a little tour . . . ," murmurs Eva in a somewhat mysterious manner.

They set off once more, amazed at the extreme clarity with which life presents itself to them.

"What has always struck me about Lanskoy's story," says Oleg, "is the hatred his relatives had for him. Generally the nearest and dearest were delighted to see one of their number sharing the tsarina's life: relations were showered with sinecures. His case is different. He becomes the black sheep of the family, a shame to his lineage. After his death the Lanskoys commission a fresco of the Last Judgment for their manorial chapel: in it their deserving ancestors bask in a green paradise, while Catherine's poor lover writhes in the flames of hell . . ."

Eva seems to hesitate as she speaks: "He loved her . . . A situation without precedent. And, for his relatives, an affront to common sense, an unnatural passion . . . Lanskoy asks for nothing, angles for nothing, and, as a result, brings no profit to his family. He's simply in love. It's intolerable, wouldn't you say?"

They laugh, the world seems to them so stupid. It was this stupidity that Catherine and Lanskoy wanted to get away from. To cross Russia, Poland, Germany, and Switzerland and find themselves here, on this road lit by winter sunshine, to melt into the light reflected from the bark of the trees, into the rippling of the tall reeds, as their stems rock back and forth beside a pool . . .

What Oleg feels is utterly new to him, he passionately wants to explain to Eva. Tell her how the sense he has carried with him since childhood of being torn between his Russian and German identities is slipping away and he is going to learn to live without thinking about it. He expresses this in a muddled way, gets confused. Eva smiles, softly recites a line Aldo often, she says, used to quote: "'Non son chi fui. Perì di noi gran parte' . . . Aldo imagined Catherine repeating something like this when preparing for her escape. *I am no longer the one I was. A great part of me is dead* . . . She hoped to come back to life. If only for the duration of a few days in February on a little road bathed in sunlight like this one . . ."

They also talk about their film. The story line for it has never seemed so clear to them. It must start off as Kozin's did: evoke History, the inevitable, with all its wars, the splendor of its reigns, its verbose solemnity. And then show how it repeats itself insanely, the way it comes around again, like a cartoon film. It is no coincidence that Catherine used the word *theater* so often . . . Finally, when this tragic vaudeville has revealed all its absurdity, it must be allowed to exhaust itself—all that will be left on the screen is the deposed emperor leaving St. Petersburg one night in June with his violin under his arm . . . And that other one, too, emerging from his cell, climbing up onto the fortress wall and seeing the sea that surrounds the keep on every side, where he has spent more than twenty years of his life . . . And a woman and a man walking through a park covered in hoarfrost, who, suddenly say to one another, without conferring, "Why don't we escape? Forever . . ."

At about two o'clock in the afternoon they leave the main road, drive through a village that seems to be fast asleep in the mildness of this winter's day. They get out of the car. Eva begins walking down an avenue of poplar trees whose upright branches gleam in the sun. Oleg, detecting a smell of roasted beans, follows the main street, looking for an open café . . .

When he returns, carrying two cups, full to the brim, Eva is already quite a long way down this road that seems almost white in the luminous air. He takes several steps and, suddenly, he sees!

A line of blue, deeper than that of the sky, cuts across the road at the end of the avenue. He would like to run, shout for joy, greet the sea, but he's afraid of spilling the coffee.

As he walks, having slowed his pace, he has time to grasp that he has seen this figure of a woman walking along between two lines of poplar trees once before. It was in the Crimea, in a vanished country, in a life where he hardly recognizes himself. In those days he was someone struggling between his two origins, suffering from his past, frantically ambitious to make a success of his future. A man who did not know how to define himself as he confronted the world, inventing complicated identities for himself, alibis, justifications for his existence . . .

Eva turns around, stops, waits for him. He tells himself that a very brief definition is all he needs now. A simple identity, free as this airy avenue that leads to the sea.

A man being watched by a woman he loves.

ANDREÏ MAKINE was born in Siberia in 1957 and has lived in France since 1987. His fourth novel, *Dreams of My Russian Summers (Le testament français)*, won both of France's top literary prizes, the Prix Goncourt and Prix Médicis. His work has been translated into more than forty languages. Makine's most recent novels, *The Life of an Unknown Man*, *Brief Loves That Live Forever*, and *A Woman Loved* are all available from Graywolf Press.

GEOFFREY STRACHAN was awarded the Scott Moncrieff Prize in 1998 for his translation of *Le testament français*. He has translated all of Andreï Makine's novels for publication in Britain and the United States.

The text of *A Woman Loved* is set in Centaur, a typeface originally designed by Bruce Rogers for the Metropolitan Museum of Art in 1914 and modeled on letters cut by the fifteenth-century printer Nicolas Jenson. Book design by Ann Sudmeier. Composition by Bookmobile Design & Digital Publisher Services, Minneapolis, Minnesota. Manufactured by Versa Press on acid-free 30 percent postconsumer wastepaper.